THE SECRETS
OF
MOONSHINE

ISBN:1466318627

ISBN-13:9781466318625

ACKNOWLEDGMENTS

This book is the culmination of a dream. I consider myself a story teller. I create characters; plan out their lives, and in the thick of the plot, I hope to inspire the reader. It is my desire to impact the reader in such a way, that their lives are forever changed, for having entered my story.

I am in love with the greatest story teller ever. He is writing the story of my life and is certainly making it exciting. He is tossing in a ton of suspense, a load of comedy, a bit of intrigue, a touch of romance, a pinch of tragedy and an enormous amount of thrills. I wish to thank Him first and foremost. Thank you God, my father, for you are brilliant at doing life.

Just as I invent characters to influence my stories, God has put some amazing people in my path to shape the story of my life. I would like to publicly thank them now.

To my amazing four daughters, Autumn, Brittany, Kendall and Journey, you make my life worth living. We have learned joy in the worst circumstances. We have laughed and cried and loved. My favorite times are when we had nothing but our dreams; they inspired us to believe in the invisible and do the impossible. God made us learn faith so we could see him; and isn't he beautiful?

To my former husband Paul, thank you for being a great man. Thank you for your sacrifices and for always loving me even when I was unlovely. I will always love you.

To my best friend Carleene, Thank you for your friendship, your belief in me and your encouragement. Thank you for that day at Santee Lakes when you looked at me and told me to write because it was what I loved to do. Thank you for always being there; whether we were building sets, dressing like angels and flying high, signing our love to the Father, creatively moving, anointing with oil, doing facials, drinking acai juice, or heading to a healing. You have always been there, and I love you for it.

To Mark Batterson who inspired me to chase my lions, thank you for your ministry and being obedient to the call. You changed my life.

To the Bradley Starbucks Baristas, Austin, Kari, Andrew, Ryan, Kyle, Ricky, Mark, Todd, and all the others who make the best caramel frapps, and greet me every day with a smile, I enjoyed using your dining room as my office. You guys are great!

To Jacob Robison who was the best Huck ever. Thank you for listening to the voice of God and being obedient to what he said. You are the reason this book is in print. I could never say thank you enough. You have impacted my life. I will never forget you.

To the special ones of "The Secrets Club," Christina Raynes, Shannon Wilson, Sandy StClair, Dottie Sandoval, Shelane Paraiso, Celina Hernandez, Grace Corning, Mish Mucho, Debbie Binsfield, Tashawni Crosby, Sandra Raynes, Carleene Parra, Chris Malone, Deborah Fischer, Kendall Plunk, Julia Myers, Alicia Stevers, Mendy Cady, Kim Rugama, Phyllis Montoya, Kevin Binsfield, Shannon Ortiz, Maranda Davis, Jamia Binsfield, Brittany Griffin, Nathalie Santiago. Rejoice, you know the secrets and you will always be on the nice list.

And... to the real life Travis, Scott Dazey, Thank you for little golden envelopes, birthday dinners, mountain hikes, picnic spots, late night tacos, dizzy juice, chess matches I never win, cuddling on the couch, and most of all for simply liking who I am. You make a great Travis. I love you.

In Loving memory of Ruby Nell Parton

My Big Granny

THE SECRETS

OF

MOONSHINE

CHAPTER ONE

THE ARRIVAL

Had Bronwyn been paying attention, she would've seen them moving through the forest, following her, lying in wait to attack. But, she didn't see them. Her mind was preoccupied; just as it always was, and for the life of her, no matter how hard she tried, she couldn't get him out of her head.

She despised herself for being weak and allowing him to consume her thoughts. She was grateful he had no way of knowing how many times a day he invaded her head; because if he had known, she was sure he would be quite pleased with himself. She wondered if he ever thought of her, but doubted he did, now that he was with Gabriella. The thought of them together caused her stomach to ache; so she shook her head, hoping to clear the image crowding into her mind.

She shifted in her seat again. Months of traveling on the old bus and you would think she would have grown accustomed to sleeping in the uncomfortable seats, but she hadn't. Listening to the snores and heaving breathing of her eight traveling companions, only made her wish she could join them in their peaceful slumber; but she knew it would only be an open door for him to enter her dreams as well.

Sighing, she wiped her hand across the window, clearing away the fog, and peered out into the darkness. The drama troupe did this same tour last summer; and even though it had been a year, she was certain she would have remembered this narrow two-lane highway, but she didn't. That only meant Walt must have taken a wrong turn somewhere, which also meant a delay in arriving at the hotel and getting off the cramped bus. She usually wasn't easily irritated, but tonight something had her on edge. Maybe it was the stifling heat in the bus, or the lack of peaceful sleep over the past few months, but whatever the cause, she could not shake the premonition of impending doom. Slipping from her seat, she crept to the front of the bus.

"Are we lost?"

Walt startled. "Dang it Bronwyn! Why did you sneak up on me like that?"

"I didn't sneak, you're just nervous because you're lost aren't you?"

He ignored the question and pressed on the gas; pushing the bus to its limit, then nodded his head toward the thermostat.

"I'm afraid we're 'bout to overheat. I think this steep mountain road may be a little too much for our engine."

Bronwyn looked through the windshield; struggling to see into the bitter darkness, hoping he was mistaken.

"You better figure something out. It looks pretty desolate out there."

He sighed in relief when the bus reached the top of the incline, but as it began taking the curvy descent on the other side, a strong vibration accompanied by a loud hissing exploded from underneath the massive vehicle. The headlights dimmed, flickered, and then darkness.

"Damn it." He cursed. "I've lost power!"

The veins in Walt's scrawny arms bulged beneath his skin, as he grasped the wheel, turning it with all the strength he could muster. Bronwyn clutched the seat in front of her; holding her breath, aware of the deep ravines that lined the sides of the mountainous highway. She feared an unavoidable plunge into the deep canyon below.

"For God's sake Walt, just stop where you are!"

"I'm trying damn it!" He cursed again which was a shock to her; in all the years she knew him he seldom used profanity.

Standing from the driver's seat, he stomped on the brakes, pumping them in his desperate attempt to stop the bus. Bronwyn dug her nails deep into the upholstery; as if the force of her grip could somehow help him bring them to a stop.

Lightning struck within inches, provoking more profanity from Walt. The sudden flash of light illuminated the dark highway long enough for Bronwyn to see a man standing in the road ahead. Her grip intensified and she gasped, figuring the bus was sure to plow into him. The flash lasted a fraction of a second before casting them back into darkness. However, a sphere of golden light created an orb around the man, allowing her a better look. His clothing resembled that of an ancient warrior. His saffron eyes penetrated through the windshield of the bus; searing into her soul, invading her body with a sudden rush of heat.

"Bronwyn...." A voice spoke her name. She looked around unnerved by the beckoning call. Everyone was still asleep. Walt was still cursing; besides, his voice was too high pitched to be a match. The voice summoned her again, much louder this time, and seemed to be accompanied by the sound of rushing wind. Covering her ears, she looked at Walt. He didn't seem to hear it. A deafening silence followed her eerie encounter, so she never heard the gravel and debris racing into the wheel well, spraying the sides of the bus, as it skidded toward the deep ravine.

Walt clenched the steering wheel; his arms trembling in his attempt to regain control. Then, without warning, the wheel turned in the opposite direction, nearly snapping his wrist. The bus continued skidding sideways before coming to an abrupt stop; launching Bronwyn into the stairwell. Bracing herself, she struggled to grasp the handrail, all the while praying the door would remain closed.

Letting out a long sigh, Walt quickly shifted the bus into "Park." He sat still for a few seconds, attempting to calm his nerves, before turning to face her.

"You okay?"

She nodded, trying to find her voice.

He pulled out his hanky and mopped the sweat from the back of his neck.

"If it hadn't been for that flash of lightning, I'd have driven this bus right off the highway. I had no idea how close to the edge we were."

He didn't mention seeing the man; and that disturbed her. She felt a bit of uneasiness crawl upon her. She knew what she had seen, and was certain that whoever it was had seen her too. Besides, she still felt the intense heat that penetrated her when the eyes of the man somehow looked inside of her.

Glancing out the window she searched for the strange apparition but the road was too dark. Thunderclouds hung ominously in the night sky, obscuring any light the moon had to offer. Another flash of lightning ripped through the darkness of the night. A slight shiver invaded her. The road was empty, the man gone. Only ghostly trees stood vigil, barring entrance to the dense forest that lined both sides of the forgotten highway.

Walt turned to his other eight passengers, now awake, jarred by the sudden stop. The touring bus was home to the traveling drama troupe. Each member claimed a section of seats as their own personal apartment. Myriad complaints and questions began rising out of the darkness from their concerned voices.

"Is everyone okay?" The sound of his voice seemed muffled to Bronwyn; her hearing coming back slowly.

Marcus, the director of the troupe, made his way forward.

"What the hell happened?"

Karley joined him spilling her complaints in the blinding darkness. "Did you fall asleep at the wheel again?"

"No, I didn't fall asleep at the wheel, Karley, nor have I ever." Walt expected the accusations from the troupes most opinionated and over-confident technical engineer. "I just saved your lousy ass. A little respect would be nice."

Marcus jumped in quickly in an attempt to derail another blame-game argument between the two.

"So what happened?"

Walt collapsed in the driver's seat, defeated. "We lost the engine."

Simultaneous groans sounded throughout the bus.

"Everyone just sit tight and stay calm," Marcus sighed, not at all pleased with the situation. "You sure it won't start at all?"

Walt attempted to re-start the engine to prove his point.

"Dead as a doornail."

"Did you try calling for assistance?"

"Haven't had cell reception for the past fifty miles."

"Karley?" Marcus looked hopeful.

"There ain't nothin' I can do. I've been warnin' Wilbur this would happen. He knows this bus is a pile of crap; but he's so dang cheap, he thinks duct tape and a coat hanger can fix everything. Now look at us. It's damn near midnight and we're broke down, stuck out in the middle of nowhere." She looked out of the windshield, "Where are we anyway?"

Walt cleared his throat nervously, "I'm not sure of our exact location. I think the map I was using was an old one."

"We're lost." Bronwyn admitted to Marcus.

"Not entirely," Walt refused defeat. "I saw a sign a ways back that said, 'Moonshine eight miles.' If there is a town ahead, there should be something on the outskirts. I guess we could do some hiking."

Karley crossed her arms in front of her and cocked her eyebrows.

"We? Don't be lookin' at me and sayin' we. I'm keepin' my ass right here on this piece of shit while you, Mr. Wrong Way Walt, go get us some help."

Walt continued to look out his window. Bronwyn could tell by the way he was rubbing the back of his neck; he was somewhat skittish about venturing outside. Keeping his eyes closed, he pinched the bridge of his nose as if embarrassed by his next statement.

"I hear there are a lot of eerie legends and folklore told about the Appalachian's. They say these mountain people can call down curses on you and you'd never know it."

Just as expected, Karley mocked his jittery behavior.

"You tryin' to blame some poor mountain folk asleep in their beds for disabling our bus. The only people you need to blame for this mess is you for takin' a wrong turn and Wilbur Hogg for not puttin' the money in this bus and fixin' it when I told him too."

Walt shoved aside the accusations again.

"All I'm saying, is something kept us from plunging over the side to our death. I was definitely not in control. Believe me when I say it wasn't me that stopped the bus."

The same feeling of impending doom that invaded Bronwyn earlier swept over her again. Walt still had not mentioned seeing the man in the road, and now, his declaration made her believe that maybe she did actually see their guardian angel. But if that was true, then why did she feel such unrest?

Walt continued his morbid warning. "All I am saying, is a person could bring a hex down upon themselves, venturing out alone, accidentally stumbling upon some kind of ancient, sacred ground."

Marcus sighed and Karley laughed. Bronwyn felt for Walt, sensing the anxiety rising inside him due to Marcus's frustration. In spite of her premonition, she came to his rescue.

"I'll go with you Walt."

He blushed. Everyone knew he adored her. She was his favorite among the troupe; so lovely, his definition of true natural beauty. Her dark brunette hair contrasted her ivory skin as it fell past her shoulders, sweeping across her forehead, framing her deep emerald eyes. Her eyes usually occupied a multitude of mischief, however; everyone noticed she seemed to have drawn into herself lately.

"You wouldn't mind coming along?"

She smiled. "Not at all."

Marcus stepped forward needing a bit of reassurance before allowing a female member of the troupe to venture out into the forbidding darkness.

"Are you sure?"

She wasn't sure and had no idea why she volunteered to go; except for the disturbing feeling, that something beyond her control was luring her away from the bus. In any case, she would give Marcus the excuse he needed.

"Actually, I'm grateful for the chance to escape the stale air in here and stretch my legs. Walt's right, there should be something up ahead. I'll be fine."

Realizing it would be a futile effort to argue with the headstrong Bronwyn, Marcus relented. It was no secret that once Bronwyn made up her mind, it was hard to persuade her otherwise.

Grabbing his flashlight from the small utility box, Walt opened the door and lit the path outside.

The thick humid air wrapped around them like a damp blanket as they stepped from the bus and into the dark night. A slight glow of moonlight escaped its lunar entrapment, as a gust of wind blew, scattering the hovering clouds. The low rumble of thunder in the distance gave a subtle warning not to leave the protection of the bus. Despite the hot muggy air, a cold chill made its way up Bronwyn's back. The eeriness of the night caused her to wonder if accompanying Walt had been a wise decision.

CHAPTER TWO

The cloaked figure pulled at the hood covering his head, and peered out from behind the trees. There was too many of them and that presented a problem. He never expected a bus load. How was he to know who was the *one*?

He sniffed into the air, the brewing storm was proof they had re-opened the portal. The scent of rain hanging heavy in the air did not erase the stench of the shadows. They were infiltrating the woods in full force, and he sensed their presence. Foul smelling spies that they were, had no doubt alerted the enemy, and soon the forest would become a battleground.

Revenge occupied his mind for years, and now the opportunity for setting things right presented itself. He had spilled blood before with no remorse. Tonight, the rivers would run with blood if need be.

He glanced across the highway and saw his men moving through the trees. He'd given orders to guard the bus. The enemy disabled it nearly sending it over the ravine; had Barak not intervened, the travelers would have plunged to their death. Since the enemy's plan had been thwarted, he knew they were sure to attack again. They would not rest until the *one* was dead and since no one knew who it was, they would surely kill them all. Two of the passengers disembarked, and were on foot heading toward Moonshine. He'd stay with them, they were the most vulnerable, neither one having any clue of the danger surrounding them. Besides, he recognized one of them. Dread filled his heart. Even though it had been years, he was sure she was the one they were searching for.

CHAPTER THREE

Bronwyn walked alongside Walt down the center of the narrow road; her fear of oncoming traffic dissipating, realizing no one was traveling on this forgotten highway. Walt mentioned he had not passed a single car the entire time he had been driving; this confirmed her suspicion, that he had indeed taken a wrong turn many miles back. There was no way of telling where they were, or how far off course they traveled.

A sudden gust of wind blew from behind, giving her another intense chill, a warning that the impending storm was creeping closer. Walt shook the fading light in his hand. During the course of their walk, the beam gradually changed from a bright white, to a fading yellow glow.

"I swear I replaced these batteries just last week."

He switched the light off and on a few more times, shaking it violently, before it lost all light completely.

Bronwyn sighed. "Now you broke it."

"It's not me." His voice quivered as he defended himself. "I swear these are new batteries. Like I said before, it's a force beyond our control."

Up until now, Walt's extreme superstition would have completely annoyed her; but after her own somewhat supernatural encounter with the man in the road, she thought Walt could be right after all.

They continued their walk in darkness. In the distance, streaks of lightning danced their eerie ritual, while the thick boughs swayed to the mournful ballad of the wind. The rolling thunder applauded their woeful performance. Another flash of lightning exploded in the sky, briefly illuminating the road, allowing Bronwyn to catch a glimpse of a dark hooded figure darting between the trees directly ahead.

She grabbed Walt and gasped, choking on her words.

"Did you see that?"

She hoped he had. She didn't want to think she was beginning to see things, and for some reason she thought if Walt had seen it too, it would somehow bring a feeling of comfort.

"See what?" His voice squeaked a bit.

Her heart fell.

"I saw someone moving in the woods up ahead. Don't tell me you didn't see them?"

He scratched the back of his head nervously.

"Probably just a deer."

"No, it looked like someone wearing a black hooded robe."

Despite the darkness of the night, Bronwyn saw the color drain from Walt's face. She knew he was hiding his fear for her sake.

"It was more than likely just the branches of the trees blowing in the wind," he offered, trying to convince her as well as himself. She stepped in closer grabbing his arm, and shivered, sensing a sinister spirit hanging in the air. They were uninvited guest, trespassing in a forbidden land, while all of nature shrieked out its ominous warning.

The lightning was crackling across the sky more frequently now, its intense flashing made it difficult to see. Still, she was certain she saw the hooded figure following them from the trees, stalking. Her anxiety grew as the wind increased from a gentle gust to a forceful push, howling as it drifted through the trees. A cool burst of air swept past, encircling her, blowing her hair in front of her face, impairing her vision all the more.

She stopped walking and glanced around. A faint whisper floated along with the wind, falling slightly upon her ear, calling her by name. Shivering, she pulled her untamed hair together, holding it down with her hand. It was the second time tonight she heard a strange voice call her name. She looked at Walt to see if he'd heard it too, but apparently he hadn't, since he was still groping along in the darkness; the same expression of uneasiness still on his face.

The breeze scattered more leaves and debris onto the road. Again she paused to listen; certain she heard a woman singing a mournful song. The faint melody called her from deep within the woods.

"What now?" Walt's anxiety was increasing with every passing moment. "Why are you stopping?"

Bronwyn tilted her head to the wind. "Can't you hear that?"

Fear plastered itself across his face. "Hear what?"

"I hear someone singing." Her words chilled him. Again, he paled.

She glanced into the woods sensing something menacing inside; a threatening evil manifesting just beyond the trees. A deep longing beckoned her, a longing she could not comprehend, and she wondered what force was emptying her of her fears and drawing her inside. The summons was not asking her to embrace the malevolent, but rather to vanquish it. The woman's voice gave her courage. She released Walt's arm and moved toward the woods. He reached for her hand, but she slipped past him.

"Where are you going?"

"There's something in there."

He didn't hear her words for the howling wind overcame them, tossing them away.

"Are you crazy? There's nothing in there but a death trap!"

She stepped off the highway into the tall overgrown grass.

He grabbed at her arm, catching it this time.

"I can't let you go in there alone. It's suicide!"

"Come with me then."

Bronwyn's emerald eyes appeared more intense than he had ever seen. He swallowed hard. Any other time, he would revel in the opportunity to hold her hand and take a moonlit walk in the woods, but not under these circumstances. He ran his hand through his overly curly hair.

As if God had answered his prayers, heavy rains began showering down, drenching them, drowning out the woman's call. Bronwyn's courage suddenly gave way to anxiousness, her peace shattered by sudden panic. Just as she decided to do an about-face and make the long run back to the bus, a bolt of lightning hit nearby, revealing an old-fashioned covered bridge on the road ahead. She sprinted for the shelter with Walt at her heels, running against the wind and pouring rain, while dodging the lightning striking painfully close. They arrived at the wooden structure just as hailstones began plummeting down, bouncing off the rooftop, and collecting at the edge of the road.

She collapsed in the center of the narrow highway; her clothes soaked, clinging to her skin. Walt fell in the road beside her.

Wiping the water from her face she glanced around. The wooden roof sheltered them from the falling rain, but unfortunately blocked out any visible light the moon offered; leaving the bridge in almost total darkness. She scooted closer to Walt, as another chill traced its bony finger up her spine. Her body tensed, sensing a presence in the dark recesses. Her heart leaped into her throat; fear engulfing the courage she experienced only minutes before. Someone was on the bridge with them, and the thought of the hooded creature caused her pulse to race. She guessed the cloaked figure was watching her and Walt, their eyes more than likely accustomed to the darkness. Despite the howling wind, she heard a scuffle, and saw the blade of a knife, reflecting a bit of moonlight, making its way through a small hole in the roof. Desperate to escape whoever was wielding the dagger, she grabbed Walt's arm and sprung to her feet, ready to bolt out into the storm.

"Let's go!"

"No." He protested, never moving from his sitting position. "The lightening is striking too close."

She was ready to leave him to fend for himself. She was perturbed with him anyway. If he hadn't taken a wrong turn or broken the flashlight, she wouldn't be in this predicament. She was half tempted to leave him sitting there, but couldn't bear the thought of him being stabbed to death, or sacrificed to some cult god of the mountains.

"Someone is under here with us." She yelled above the pounding rain. "I'm heading back to the bus. You can come with me, or wait here by yourself."

He began to argue with her and she wondered where he suddenly got his courage. Only minutes ago he was superstitious, afraid to venture out alone, now he was just being lazy and more afraid of the storm than anything the mountains had to offer. She knew she was only wasting her time pleading with him, but if she dashed out into the severe weather, he was sure to follow.

Her body tensed again sensing a presence close behind her; sending another chill up her spine. Despite the scent of rain and wet earth, she smelled the strong aroma of cigarettes. She was ready to bolt, when the headlights from an oncoming truck motivated a change of plans. Instead, she leaped in front of the vehicle as it approached the bridge, causing the truck to come to a skidding stop.

Walt jumped to his feet; yanking her away.

"Are you crazy?"

The headlights dispelled the darkness enough for her to see the figure jump from the side railing into the raging river below. The fabric of the cloak billowed in the wind, as whoever was wearing the masquerade, made their escape.

The door of the vehicle swung open, bringing her attention back to the truck and the man stepping out of the cab. Any fear that manifest in Bronwyn earlier, suddenly dissipated, as she looked into the dark eyes, peering through the long brown hair, hanging in wet pieces over the man's face. Moving away from Walt, she stepped into the glow of the headlights, oddly lured into this stranger's presence. She couldn't help but notice his expression as he caught sight of her. Astonishment spread across his face, as if he were looking at a ghostly apparition. Steadying himself, he grabbed hold of the truck door, and swallowed hard, clenching his jaw.

He closed his eyes for a moment and then opened them again, as if he half expected her to disappear. The same heat sensation she felt earlier, on the bus, gathered in the soles of her feet and permeated upward through her body, tightening her throat. She felt dizzy and her thoughts began scrambling. The feelings enveloping her were euphoric, yet mingled with intense sorrow. Her eyes locked helplessly on the man with no strength to pull away; and somewhere, in the recesses of her mind, she had witnessed this event before. She attempted to recall a suppressed memory of standing in falling water, staring into the eyes of this stranger. Perhaps she had dreamt of it once. Whatever the reason, her heart ached for something she couldn't explain.

Walt offered his hand in an attempt to break the long awkward stare between the man and Bronwyn.

"The name's Walt Kellogg. Our bus broke down a couple of miles from here. We're looking for some help."

The man shook Walt's' extended hand, yet never removed his eyes from Bronwyn.

"Name's Travis. Get in the truck."

CHAPTER FOUR

Bethany stood at the front of the bus shielding her eyes from the intense lightning; frustrated that Bronwyn had not told her she was going for help. She would have gladly ventured out into the storm with her had she asked. Granted, the past six months had been extremely painful for her, yet this pulling away so to speak, and distancing herself from everyone, was beginning to be somewhat annoying.

The two had become best friends in fifth grade and while everyone clamored around Bronwyn, Bethany was the one she chose. Her choice instantly gave Bethany elevated status in the social circles. She cherished their friendship; just knowing Bronwyn made her mundane existence much more thrilling. Bronwyn's overly active imagination seemed to always land them into a world of adventure. The distractions of such mischief helped Bethany make it through many tough times, including several break ups, rejection by the college of her choice, and her parents painful divorce. Her own imagination and knack for finding adventure didn't quite compare to Bronwyn's, but still she wanted to return the favor and help her friend through her tough times as well. But how could she when Bronwyn continually pushed her away?

The storm was raging now, vigorous winds pushed hard against their vehicle, rocking it back and forth, taunting her while she waited in the darkness along with the rest of the troupe. Looking out of the window was pointless; she could see nothing but the torrential downpour, coming in sheets, veiling her from what was transpiring right outside the bus. Had she known what lurked about, she would have spent less time worrying about Bronwyn and more time on her knees praying for her own deliverance. However, she was not aware of the sinister plans being plotted right outside the bus so she sighed, switched on her flashlight, and made her way to the back. She joined her friends, anxiously awaiting the return of their two comrades; while amusing themselves with mundane tasks to pass the time.

Marcus attempted to comfort Lillian, their distraught leading lady, by massaging her shoulders. Bethany thought it to be a chivalrous effort indeed, but an impossible task of trying to calm the pampered prima donnas' nerves. She walked on passed, daring not to take a seat, and subject herself to Lillian's constant whimpering.

Across the aisle Daniel and Anna were discussing a recent piece of political news. Anna, an elegant and proper woman in her early sixties, argued her perspective with grace. Daniel, who provided the comic relief in every role he played, could only attempt to win the argument with Anna by dismissing the discussion as serious, and making sport of the entire topic. He wasn't really interested, but was only participating to be polite to Anna and pass the time. Bethany thought it best not to try and join in their conversation; besides the topic did not interest her in the least.

Karley and Wilbur both had fallen back asleep. How they could possibly rest in the stifling heat and constant roar of explosive thunder was beyond her. Karley rested with her head leaned back, eyes closed, and her ear buds in. Her iPod drowned out the falling rain.

Wilbur, their portly and tight-fisted bookkeeper, sat slumped in his seat, dozing. A bag of sunflower seeds lay upon his ample stomach. Bethany wanted to give him a swift kick. Everyone knew the bus was in poor shape because of his tight hold on the money. It was his fault Bronwyn was out in the storm.

Trent, their handsome leading man, sat alone in the back of the bus. Now, far away from his audience and swooning fans, he blindly plucked unwanted eyebrow hairs while reciting his lines softly. Everyone had a crush on Trent and although she would never admit it, she was somewhat infatuated herself, and thought his British accent was quite charming. Making her way to the back, she sat down beside him.

"Any sign of them love?"

A deafening thunderclap erupted before she could respond.

"God!" He held his eyebrow in pain. "It sounds like a bloody nuclear explosion."

Lillian peered out of her window.

"The lightning strikes are so close I can sense the electricity permeating through my body."

"That's not a good sign," Daniel warned, though thankful the thunder had ended the long discourse coming from Anna. "They say it's the sensation you feel right before you're struck."

Lillian leaped from her seat as a wave of hysteria came over her.

"Do you think we'll be hit?"

"If by chance we do receive a direct hit," Marcus said, "we're well ground."

"That would be true," Daniel contradicted, "if these tires weren't worn down to bare metal. If we get hit sitting on these babies, I'd say we're toast."

Marcus shot Daniel a disapproving glance while Lillian collapsed into her seat.

"This is ridiculous. I just want to be safe in our hotel."

"Don't we all?" Bethany said, "But at least we have shelter. I'm worried about Bronwyn and Walt. They're out in all of this."

"Yes, I agree. The poor dears." Anna said. "It's a shame we don't have cell reception or we could call and check on their status. I can only pray they have found shelter."

Anna was right. Bethany already checked her phone and there were no bars, no signal, and no missed calls. She sighed again. They were stuck out in the middle of nowhere and where was that? No one knew. All they did know was they were on their way to their biggest venue of the summer and should have arrived at the hotel hours ago. Walt had obviously taken a wrong turn somewhere.

She'd caught Marcus looking at a map scanning the paper with his flashlight. He told her he was searching for a town called Moonshine, because Walt had mentioned seeing a sign. She helped Marcus look, neither one of them found such a place. Seeing that they were in the Appalachians, she was convinced the sign must have been advertising the location of a still; and the way she was feeling, she could use a swig of the potent drink.

A sudden gust of wind pushed up against the bus rocking it violently. Lillian screamed along with the rest of the troupe, troubled by the forcefulness of it. It would take an incredibly strong wind to rock such a heavy vehicle. Daniel's suggestion of the possibility of tornadoes only unnerved Lillian all the more. Marcus mocked Daniels ignorance, stating he'd never heard of tornadoes hitting in the mountains. He attempted to calm the group once more by saying they were just in the eye of a severe thunderstorm, and being at such high elevation caused it to seem more intense than any other storm they had experienced. His argument did sound convincing but Bethany could tell he was just as concerned as everyone else; and when the sides of the bus began popping like someone squeezing an aluminum can, she watched his face grow somber as well.

Outside, a cloaked figure soared through the air, slamming his two victims against the side of the bus. The force of the blow pushed in the metal, denting the vehicle, the sound would surely draw attention so he worked fast.

A quick slicing of his knife and the trespassers slumped to the ground. Their blood mixed with the rain, evidence of his kill washing away and rushing like a river down the side of the highway.

The cloaked man pulled the bodies off the ground, tossing them from view. He would dispose of them later tonight, but right now, he must get rid of the rest of them. Asa was coming and it would be a catastrophe if any of them caught a glimpse of his face. None of them knew this was where he'd been hiding all this time; and it was his duty to keep it that way.

CHAPTER FIVE

The bus shook hard. The obvious guess was a tree must have blown over denting the sides. Marcus grabbed his flashlight and asked Trent if he'd accompany him outside to take a look, to which Trent laughed and said not a chance. If trees were being uprooted and slamming into the bus, then he had no intention of sticking his head outside the door. Whatever the damage, the surveying could wait until morning or at least until the storm passed. Marcus agreed and was just beginning to sit back down, when another loud thud was heard near the front. The bus door swung open letting in the blowing rain. Marcus aimed his light.

"Get your damn light out of my eyes!" Walt cursed.

Everyone in the bus breathed a collected sigh of relief. Walt and Bronwyn forced their way through the gawking troupe. Their wet clothes hung heavy on their body and water poured off their faces; dripping from their noses and onto the bus floor.

Marcus apologized and lowered his light.

"What's the word? Did you find anything?"

Walt grabbed a towel from his duffel bag.

"There's an inn about four miles from here. We can stay there tonight and deal with the bus in the morning."

"Four miles!" Lillian protested. "Please tell me they are sending a shuttle."

Walt mopped the water from his face and tossed the towel to Bronwyn.

"The man who owns the inn is waiting outside in his pickup."

Lillian wasn't satisfied.

"A pickup? In this weather? I'm expecting it has a covered bed?"

"It's either a quick ride in the back of an uncovered pickup, or a four-mile hike in the storm," Bronwyn said. "Take your pick Princess."

"Neither of those will do."

"There's always staying put." She snapped back.

Walt interrupted their banter.

"I suggest we all grab a small bag for tonight. Just what you need. There won't be room in the pickup for everyone to take their luggage."

Bronwyn returned to her seat. Into her bag, she tossed a book she had been attempting to read. She hoped that reading a good novel would somehow inspire a thought that would force its way through a blockage of revelation that had kept her writing at bay for some time now. The book was not proving to be that inspiring. Still, she placed it in her bag. She didn't intend to read it. The book would be her defense, a barrier she could retreat behind, to sit alone with her thoughts. People were less likely to drum up a conversation with someone who appeared to be engrossed in a book.

The opening of the bus door diverted her attention from packing. Once again, she was taken aback with Travis as he entered.

Walt made the introductions.

"This is Travis; He's giving us a ride to his inn."

Bronwyn observed him scan the interior of the bus. Their eyes locked again, causing the peculiar heat sensation to re-engage her body, re-creating the inexplicable emotion. She removed her eyes from his gaze; the intensity of his stare unnerved her. She looked to see if the others had noticed their unusual encounter. No one seemed to pay any attention. Everyone was immersed in packing his or her belongings. Bronwyn glanced at Bethany, surely she had noticed. Not much escaped her; however, she remained completely aloof.

Bronwyn cautiously returned her eyes back to Travis. He was still watching her; their eyes locked again. She found it difficult to pull away.

"We need to move quickly and get you out of here while there's a lull," his eyes never left hers when he spoke. "More storms are headed this way. Believe me when I say it's only going to get worse."

He descended the steps, giving her one final glance, and disappeared into the night.

The sky remained black as massive storm clouds formed obscuring the moon. The utter darkness cast pure eeriness into the night. The headlights from Travis's truck offered the only light to assist the troupe in finding a way to their ride. Bronwyn held her bag close to her side as she made her way to the pickup. Travis stood at the uncovered bed of the truck, holding a tarp.

Bethany shook her head in disbelief.

"A tarp?"

"Why is he holding a tarp?" Lillian asked. "Surely it's not the cover to the bed!"

"No, I think it's what he uses to bury his victims in," Bronwyn offered an attempt at evil humor.

Lillian wasn't amused. "Stop it! Do not bring those dark thoughts to my mind. You know how it affects me!"

Bethany gave Bronwyn a sly grin. It always gave her perverted pleasure to torment Lillian anyway she could. Bronwyn returned the smile, despite the fear gnawing inside her that her statement might be right.

Travis and Trent offered the girls their hands helping them into the bed of the truck. Bronwyn waited to board last; graciously allowing Karley, Anna, and an extremely fearful Lillian to enter before her. After they were all safe on board Travis turned to Bronwyn and extended his hand; with his strong grip, he pulled her upward. At the touch of his skin, the heat sensation began again, this time with a bit more intensity and she wondered if he could feel the warmth as well.

Handing the tarp to the group, Travis yelled over the rain, instructing everyone to place it over their heads. Hail was coming; the tarp would offer some protection from the falling balls of ice. Bronwyn grasped her end lifting it high above her head to create a canopy.

Slamming the door to the cab, Travis sped towards the Inn. The sudden movement of the truck combined with the gale force winds yanked the tarp, ripping it from their hands, sweeping it away into the black night. At the very same moment hail began falling, pelting the truck as well as the unprotected passengers. Bronwyn raised her duffle bag, placing it over her head, shielding herself from the plummeting hailstones. Had it not hurt so much, the situation would have been one of the most comical she had ever experienced with the troupe; but for some reason she couldn't seem to find her laughter.

The truck pulled off the road and onto a narrow driveway, rolling to a stop a hundred yards later in front of a three-story Victorian inn. The inn stood in total darkness, save for a few flickering candles in the windows. A bolt of lightning struck just behind the inn adding to its ominous appearance.

Bronwyn read the uneasiness on the faces of her friends. Anna, who usually put on airs and offered positive outlooks, was surveying the inn as if it would be her final resting place.

Bronwyn thought about making a run for it but where would she go? It was pitch black and there was nothing for miles. She envisioned herself running through the drenching rain, into the woods, only to meet her demise by encountering the hooded figure and disappearing off the face of the earth forever. A second bolt of lightning interrupted her thoughts, striking only thirty yards from the truck. The crackling sound of splitting wood, accompanied by a burning aroma was enough incentive for her and the rest of the troupe to bolt for shelter.

She entered through the doorway into the gloomy atmosphere of the inn. The scarce lighting made it difficult for her to make an accurate assessment of the place. She seemed to be standing in an entrance hall of some sort, evidently it doubled as a living room. It felt comfortable enough, furnished with soft leather couches in addition to several overstuffed armchairs. The colors and fabrics remained hidden in the darkness. A mammoth stone fireplace took over an entire wall, and a sizable picture window without covering gobbled up another. The floor was a well-polished hard-wood, covered in places by soft throw rugs that cut the chill off a bare floor. An elevated antique desk stood at the far side of the lobby matching a colossal banister that came to rest at the end of a spiraling wooden staircase.

"Welcome, weary travelers," the cheery southern voice rang out from behind the lofty desk.

Bronwyn stepped further inside the room to view the person who offered the greeting. The light of a small glowing lantern revealed a woman who appeared to be in her early forties. Her loosely braided hair hung to the side of her head. Her welcoming smile covered most of her face, revealing a missing tooth on the left. A noticeable scar traveled from the corner of her left eye halfway down her jawbone. Despite the flaws, Bronwyn could see the beauty hidden deep within her face, and was certain that in times past, this woman had been quite lovely. Nevertheless, an obvious accident had taken its toll on her.

"Sorry 'bout the darkness. Our power got knocked out by the storm. Should have light some time tomorrow. Just step right up and sign my register here and I'll be gettin' y'all into your rooms."

Wilbur forced his way to the front demanding a private room on the first floor. His chubby fingers curled tightly around the pen as he scribbled his name in the book.

The woman glanced at the written name on her register. "Sorry, Mr. Hogg, we only got four rooms here at Sandalwood Inn and every one of 'em's on the second floor. They all have king sized beds in 'em. You're gonna have to double up for the night. Y'all can decide amungst yourselves how…makes me no never mind."

Trent listened in awe to the words that poured from the woman's mouth. "Makes me no never mind? What the hell does that mean?"

Bronwyn stepped forward and signed the book. She took the key from the woman who flashed a perplexing smile and then quickly exchanged glances with Travis. Their knowing glances made Bronwyn feel all the more uncomfortable. The strange bit of heat once again rushed through her body. Maybe it was the premonition of danger; after all, she had heard stories of people who had a sixth sense, enabling them to foretell impending doom. Like people who bolted from a flight at the last minute, only to hear that the plane crashed moments after takeoff. She prided herself on her intuition and discerning abilities, but she had never felt something this strange before. Perhaps, it was because she had never been in extreme danger until now. Her heart raced as the heat wrapped around her neck.

"The names Mavis." She said, interrupting Bronwyn's thoughts of doom. "Travis and I own this here Inn. If you be needin' anything, you give us a holler!"

Bronwyn nodded and noticed the plaque embedded in the wood of the desk.

"Sandalwood Inn. Travis Colton and Mavis Colton proprietors."

The three girls ascended the winding staircase and located room number two. Bronwyn inserted the key and pushed open the door. The room was dark, except for the glow of a flickering candle, burning on a nightstand, sitting beside a rather inviting feather bed. An heirloom dresser and mirror also occupied the room, along with a desk and an overstuffed chair. There was an adjoining bathroom, complete with a quaint old-fashioned tub on legs. Clean towels and washcloths lay folded on the vanity top, along with a basket of sweet smelling ointments and homemade soaps.

Lillian quickly tossed aside her wet clothing and dashed for the bed, throwing her overstressed body across the feather mattress. Bethany followed Lillian's lead. As much as Bronwyn wanted to do the same, she decided on a bath instead. The old-fashioned tub seemed rather inviting and despite the heat and mugginess of the night, she shivered in her wet clothes. After lighting a candle and placing it on the small table near the tub, she filled her bath with warm water, adding the sweet milky potions from the basket. Delightful scents of lavender and jasmine quickly permeated the room. Removing her soaked clothes, she stepped into the inviting tub. Her body melted into the balmy water. She closed her eyes and leaned her head against a soft foam pillow attached to the tub. Outside, the fierce winds and rain continued to wreak havoc, causing the inn to creak and the door to shake. Even though she was uncertain of her surroundings, she was content to finally be in the shelter of the inn.

She sank deeper into the tub and found herself dozing off and on as the candle cast hypnotic images on the dark wall.

Her sporadic dreams were nightmarish. She could see the stranger standing behind sheets of falling water; his black eyes revealing much distress. In her vision, she longed to reach for him, to be where he was, yet he was pushing her away. Then, without warning, the ground disappeared from underneath her and she felt herself falling, plummeting into darkness…

The fall jolted her awake so she kicked her leg violently, splashing water over the side of the tub. She shivered, the water having turned cold during the duration of her dream. She climbed from her bath deciding it would be best to continue sleeping in the bed rather than a tub filled with water. She toweled off and dressed quickly. Tiptoeing into the room, she tried not to wake Lillian who was sleeping soundly in the middle of the bed or Bethany who staked her claim on the left side, furthest away from the door. After checking to see that the door was indeed locked, she blew out the remaining candle and climbed into the soft comfort of the bed. The rain had backed off to a gentle patter and the winds diminished from a deafening roar to a steady whistle.

"You know what's weird?" Bethany whispered.

Bronwyn flinched; surprised she was still awake.

"Besides everything?"

"You saw Travis, the man that picked us up?"

"Uh huh," Bronwyn wondered if Bethany had experienced the same peculiar heat sensation that she had when he looked at her, or if she had noticed the long stare between them on the bus.

"Did you see his wife? I mean how do those two go together at all? Is she lucky or what?"

Bronwyn smiled in the darkness. "Beth, I think you've reached an all-time low in shallowness."

Bethany sighed into the blackness of the room. "You were pretty quiet all day. Must have been a good book you were reading."

"Uh hum."

"When are you going to snap out of this funk? When do I get my partner in crime back? I miss you."

Bronwyn remained silent. Although she agreed with Bethany that she hadn't been herself lately, she had no answer as to when she would snap out of it, as Bethany had so simply put it. She hopelessly tried to move forward and continue with life; however, it wasn't that easy, especially when she felt no energy or motivation to do so.

"I wish I could," she sighed. "Believe me, I wish I could. I don't know what's wrong with me. Everything's just blah. There's no color, no joy, no excitement, no intrigue, no motivation, no cause, nothing worth existing for."

"All this because of Ryan?"

"Don't give him so much credit."

Despite the denial, Bronwyn knew her low spirit stemmed from exactly that.

"Good night, Beth." She refused to enter into any conversation about Ryan. She knew this was the reason Bethany had been waiting up. She was her dearest friend and usually she enjoyed her company tremendously. However, Bethany's persistent questions and concern over her personal affairs, combined with her endless advice, had begun to grow wearying.

A final rumble of thunder sounded in the distance. The last bit of rain tapped gently on the window. Bronwyn's eyes grew heavy as she faded off to sleep.

Just outside the inn, a shadowy, cloaked figure cleaned the blood from his knife and placed it back inside the folds of his robe. Camouflaged by the massive fir trees, he stood his vigil, watching the inn, and waiting.

CHAPTER SIX

DAY ONE

The morning sun streamed through the picture window, piercing through the linen curtains and filling the room with light. It wasn't the gleaming rays of sunlight however, that stirred Bronwyn back to consciousness; but rather the delicious scents traveling from the kitchen, up the winding staircase, and directly into room number two.

She opened her eyes squinting from the brightness, raised her head from its cushioned cradle, and looked over the bed. The middle was empty, and Bethany still lay in the exact position as the night before. She was glad to see they were still in one piece and that no one had crept into the room while they slept. Lillian was missing but Bronwyn figured she was downstairs having breakfast since she was known to be an early riser; besides, there was no sign of a struggle anywhere. Considering the uneasiness she felt right before bed, Bronwyn was surprised at how soundly she had slept. She yawned and looked over at Bethany.

"You awake?"

Bethany stirred groggily. "My body's still asleep but my nose woke up some time ago. Have you ever smelled anything so amazing?"

"Not since I was a little girl."

The two sat up and looked around the room. Bronwyn admitted that the morning light gave it a more inviting appearance. Pale Yellow walls, trimmed with white crown molding and adorned with beautiful oil paintings, hugged the room with warmth. White lace curtains hung over a sizable picture window; the fabric complimenting the snowy comforter covering the enormous four-post bed. Everything about the room felt friendly, cheerful and inviting. It was so different from the feelings of the night before.

Bethany was the first to climb from the feather mattress. She gave a loud yawn and then crossed over to the window.

"Whatcha say we follow our noses?"

"Sounds good." Bronwyn reluctantly climbed from the bed, pulled a pair of cotton shorts and a tank out of her overnight bag, then headed into the bathroom.

Bethany pushed back the curtains as she opened the window. Lovely floral scents immediately rushed into the room along with the morning air. The new day's sun not only gave a different feel to the inside of their room, but unmasked a world of beauty outdoors as well.

"Wow, this is amazing!"

She announced her discovery so that Bronwyn could hear her from the adjoining bathroom. Surrounding the inn, as far as the eyes could see, were the most exquisite gardens. Plants, flowers and trees of every species bloomed in the fertile soil below. An ornate fountain stood in the center of the circle drive bubbling over with fresh water. Numerous flowering plants and crawling vines found their way up the fountain all drinking from the water in its basin. To her far right, a river lazily trickled over droves of natural rock.

"This is amazing," she repeated.

Movement to the right, near the stream, caught her attention, bringing her eyes to Travis. He was busy, clearing away broken branches and debris that fell during the storm. The morning heat had obviously caused him discomfort, which to Bethany's delight, had resulted in him removing his shirt. She watched eagerly as he grabbed a hefty branch with his gloved hand and tossed it effortlessly into a pile of collected rubble. With a jerk of his head, he swept his wet hair away from his forehead and continued his clearing.

"Bronwyn, come here! Quick!"

Still brushing her teeth, Bronwyn emerged from the bathroom.

"What?"

"Look." Bethany pulled back the curtain. "See what I mean about him and Mavis not going together? My God he is in great shape! Look at those muscles!"

Bronwyn rolled her eyes as she walked away from the window and returned to the bathroom. She feared if she took a small peek he might see and lock eyes with her again. She made sure to avoid any more disturbing encounters with the man. She spit the toothpaste from her mouth, rinsed and then realized her hands were trembling. She splashed the cold water on her neck, hoping to cool off the heat sensation and stop the trembling, before Bethany noticed and begin asking questions. She took a deep breath and walked back into the room.

"Pull yourself away from the window, Beth. He's a married man, and more than likely has an inn full of kids."

"You're probably right." Bethany sighed and removed herself from the window; allowing the curtain to fall back slowly, while she took in every glimpse she could possibly manage.

CHAPTER SEVEN

Larry Earp eagerly surveyed the bus engine. His excitement went unnoticed by Karley and Walt who were hovering over him. Walt, eager for anyone who would listen, relentlessly spouted off his signature story about the time he had fallen ten floors from a building during firefighting school. Larry only half listened as he pulled and prodded at the complicated engine, offering only a grunt every now and then just to keep Walt satisfied. A soft spoken country fellow, Larry was the only mechanic in the small town. He kept busy repairing anything from car engines to lawn mowers. Much to Larry's delight, a challenge worthy of his expertise presented itself. He stood from his squatting position and slammed the door to the engine compartment.

Karley interrupted Walt's story. "Can you fix it?"

Larry spit out the tobacco juice that had been pooling under his bottom lip for some time.

"I can fix it. It'll be a full day's work."

"That's great." Karley starred at the black gooey substance hiding under Larry's bottom lip. "That shouldn't put us too far behind."

"Full day's work if I had the parts. I'm gonna have to order 'em. You're lookin' at seven to eight business days."

"Oh." That was all a stunned Karley could muster. "You're serious?"

Wilbur, who had been resting on the bus steps during Larry's diagnostics, suddenly jumped to his portly feet.

"That will not do! We have an extremely important engagement three days from now, and we cannot afford to miss it!"

Larry shrugged.

"Lookin' like you'll have to go without your bus. Cause it ain't movin'."

"Just rig something up to get us on the road! We'll make the needed repairs when we get to where we're going."

Karley was exasperated.

"Now that's what got us stranded here in the first place, Mister Procrastinate! We've done all the riggin' we can do. Now it's time for some fixin'! Walt and I warned you this was going to happen!"

"You should've listened to 'em." Larry spat once again, this time barely missing Wilbur's swollen feet with the brown juice. "Prevention is a heck of a lot cheaper than replacing. 'Fraid this one's gonna cost you a pretty penny."

Wilbur's brow furrowed deeper at the threat of losing money.

"Are you even sure you know what you're talking about? I bet a country hick like you has never seen an engine this big. I for one would like a second opinion!"

Larry removed the rolled-up ball cap from his back pocket and placed it on his head as he climbed into the cab of his truck.

"Good luck with that, seeing I'm the only mechanic in town." He spat once more before starting his engine.

Karley ran to the truck and peered into the window.

"Just go ahead and order whatever you need to fix it."

Larry put his truck into drive.

"Alright, but first thing we need to do is get your bus to my garage."

"How the hell we gonna do that?" Her inquiry remained unanswered, as Larry's truck disappeared around the corner.

CHAPTER EIGHT

Downstairs in the kitchen Mavis was busily pouring more batter into the waffle iron as she hummed a happy tune. A bowl of brown eggs sat next to a sizzling cast iron skillet, along with a platter of diced potatoes waiting to be cooked. Fresh strawberries and various types of melons lay on a tray, peeled and sliced. Glass pitchers full of orange juice and iced water sat on the massive wooden table near an open kitchen window. The morning air wafted into the window and swirled about the room with the aid of a large ceiling fan. A massive stone fireplace, doubling as an oven for baking fresh bread, completed the other side of the room.

Mavis closed the waffle iron, grabbed a pot of fresh brewed coffee and headed to the table to replenish the empty mugs; it was then Bronwyn noticed Mavis used a walking stick for assistance.

Bethany refilled her glass with orange juice, marveling that it was indeed the best juice she had ever tasted. She asked Mavis an onslaught of questions from what brand of juice she was drinking, to why the eggs were brown instead of white, and was delighted to learn everything was homegrown, including the orange juice in her glass along with the organic eggs in the bowl. Mavis even claimed that the two children who had stormed into the kitchen with their own barrage of questions were homegrown as well.

Carla Jo, the eldest of the two, zeroed in on Trent as she bit into her fluffy waffle.

"Are you all really famous actors from California?"

Mavis eyed her daughter as she stirred the cooking potatoes. The girl was only twelve and already boy crazy.

"Carla Jo, you know the rules about bothering the guest."

"Momma!" Carla Jo was quick to defend her actions. "Actors are used to this. It comes with being famous. They actually love it!"

"You're beautiful!" Molly's small voice rang out as she stared in awe at Lillian. Lillian smiled, pleased with the adoration.

"And so are you dear. Come sit here, next to me."

"Is it alright momma?" Molly asked, wide-eyed. Mavis smiled as she cracked another egg, sending the yolk into the sizzling hot skillet.

"I reckon so dear, but mind your manners."

Molly eagerly climbed up into her chair and took her seat beside the famous guest.

Bronwyn stared out of the open window, sipping her coffee while ignoring the idle chatter at the table. She preferred the sound of birds chirping, the low honk of the geese out on the water and the wooden wind chimes playing their lazy tune as they hung on the porch. The cool morning breeze floated through the window touching her tenderly on the face while bringing in the many scents of the outdoor gardens. She welcomed the aromas; they were much different from the musty stale air of the touring bus.

She wasn't certain, but she thought she sensed a bit of inspiration…a feeling foreign of late. The sudden stimulation made her want to venture outdoors, fall into the soft green grass, inhale all the scents and sounds and lay there for hours and dream. She predicted her dreams in the inn's gardens would be peaceful and untroubled not like the nightmarish haunts that accompanied her nights. She hoped she would get the chance to tour the inn's grounds before the bus was ready for departure. It would be a shame to miss such an opportunity.

"Bronwyn!" Bethany annoyingly nudged her in the ribs, bringing her attention from the outdoors and back into the busy room. Travis was in the kitchen, washing his hands at the sink. Bethany shoved her hip into Bronwyn's with the intention to have her move down the table to make room for Travis. Bronwyn fumed inside and suddenly found the food on her plate interesting.

"Thank you." Travis took the offered seat. Mavis hobbled over to the table handing him a plate. She patted him lovingly on the cheek before limping back to the stove. He poured himself a glass of water and then dished only fruit and eggs onto his plate.

"You know Ryan Reese?" Carla Jo fairly screamed with delight.

The name brought Bronwyn's attention away from her eggs and to the trivial banter. It was as if someone had tossed the pitcher of ice water right into her face.

"Ryan is my absolute favorite actor in the world!" Carla Jo gushed on about her crush. "I've seen his movie so many times! Tell me everything you know about him!"

Bronwyn searched the faces of her comrades, wondering who had betrayed her secrecy.

"Sorry, Bronwyn." Daniel offered his lame excuse. "The kid wanted to know if any of us knew Ryan."

Carla Jo sat wide-eyed. "So you really know him?"

Bronwyn tried to hide a grimace. She wanted to say no; and if she did, she didn't think it would be a total lie because his actions of late made her feel like she really didn't know him.

She met Ryan six years ago when they were cast in the same show. He loved reading all of her stories and his genuine interest in her writing was one of the things that drew her to him. One evening, after attending a movie, the two sat in a coffee shop critiquing the shallowness of the story and the predictability of its characters. It was then and there they decided to write their own screenplay, the beginnings of which were formed on napkins. After all if Keats could write the immortal "Ode to a Nightingale" on a napkin, well then, they could start their masterpiece on one too.

The months that followed were thrilling. Together they created the story, developed the characters, and fabricated amazing twist and plots. Bronwyn thoroughly enjoyed their late-night writing capers. Whenever the two experienced writer's block, they would venture out into the night, and find a run-down donut shop that stayed open until the wee hours of morning. They would feast on sugary donuts and black coffee until an idea broke though. The night they completed the script, Ryan suggested they celebrate by dressing up in their most elegant attire and treat themselves to a nice dinner at an overly expensive restaurant. It was at the end of that dinner that Ryan got on his knees, presented Bronwyn with a beautiful ring, and proposed. They set the date that night and she immediately began making wedding arrangements.

It so happened that on the day she found her perfect wedding gown, Ryan's agent called with the phenomenal news that one of his auditions had paid off. He landed a substantial role in a feature film. Thrilled for his good fortune, they agreed to move the wedding date back to accommodate his shooting schedule. The movie was a remarkable success, skyrocketing him to instant fame. He was immediately signed to do the sequel. This time, the shooting took place in Australia. Again, Bronwyn changed the wedding date.

He was gone for months and his calls became scarce. She was faced daily with pictures of Ryan and his alluring co-star Gabriella Mendez, plastered on the cover of every magazine. Each one full of articles accompanied with scandalous pictures, all insinuating a brewing relationship. None of the articles mentioned a fiancé back home. She refused to read anymore. Besides, Ryan was never quoted in any of them. The reports were merely speculation. She loved him and was certain of his love for her, so she continued on with the wedding plans.

With Ryan's birthday approaching, she decided to fly to Australia to surprise him. The visit was different than she had envisioned. His schedule allowed them no time together and as much as she hated to admit it, she sensed a noticeable distance from him. Her heart ached when he introduced her as his good friend instead of his fiancé. She forced a smile and good humor throughout the remainder of the week and was actually relieved when it was time to board the plane and return home. It was only a few days after her return when she received an email from Ryan. The letter broke off their relationship… along with her heart and optimistic spirit.

She sighed. When would the memory stop being so fresh?

"Sore subject, hon."

Mavis immediately came to Bronwyn's rescue. "That's enough kids; your breakfast is more than done. Y'all got chores to do."

"Awe momma."

"You heard me. Now scoot!"

Carla Jo gave a pleading look at Travis, who flashed a sympathetic smile. "You heard your mother."

Carla Jo removed herself from the table along with her sibling; with slumped shoulders, she left the room to do her chores.

"I'm sorry," Bronwyn apologized to Mavis. "She didn't know...."

"It's all right honey. That Carla Jo could worry the horns off a Mulley cow."

"What the hell is a Mulley cow?" Once again Mavis left Trent mesmerized by her strange choice of words.

Daniel didn't hear Trent's comments.

"What the...."

His words fell flat as he gazed out of the window. Bronwyn turned to see what could have possibly stunned Daniel into speechlessness. Simultaneous gasps erupted around the table as the troupe saw their beloved tour bus towed by a small green tractor. A man in a straw hat and overalls drove while Karley sat perched on the back.

"Bloody hell!" Trent burst into laughter. "Where's my camera when I need it?"

The tractor continued towing the enormous bus past the inn and down the highway. Anna stood. "Marcus, I think it's time we hook up with Karley and see what's going on."

Marcus pushed away from the table and wiped his mouth with a linen napkin. "I couldn't agree more."

"Looks like Larry's towing you to his garage," Mavis said.

"And where might we find Larry's garage?" Anna asked.

"In town."

"And where would town be?"

"A mile down the highway. Just follow the road; it'll take you right to it."

Anna tried one more time for a definite location. "Could I please have a business address for the garage?"

"Don't need one. You'll see it when you get there and iffin' by chance you miss it, ask anyone they'll point it out to you."

Unsure, Anna took in a deep breath. There was no other choice than to follow Mavis' simplistic advice. Bronwyn could see that Anna was irritated, befuddled by Mavis' nonchalant nature. As always, though, Anna kept her very professional and agreeable disposition, thanking Mavis for the information as she and Marcus left the kitchen.

Trent and Daniel agreed it would be an experience of a lifetime to venture into this mysterious and yet unseen town of Moonshine. After eating more than they should, they left to scout out the town. Lillian also left the table to shower, and Mavis exited to retrieve fresh laundered towels for her use.

The once populated kitchen cleared instantly, leaving only Bethany, Bronwyn and Travis at the table. Much to Bronwyn's dismay, Bethany, who thrived on chatting, quickly tried to drum up a conversation with him.

"So, lived here all your life?"

"Pretty much," He responded.

Bethany's upper lip curled at the thought of it.

"Why?"

Bethany irritated Bronwyn. Why did she feel the need to talk to Travis? Why couldn't she just leave things alone? Bronwyn purposely avoided looking at him the entire time he had been sitting at the table, not wanting another uneasy gaze from his direction. Her frustration with Bethany turned into a quick reprimand.

"Bethany! Don't be rude."

"I'm not being rude. I'm just curious as to why someone would want to spend their entire life in such a small, secluded place when there is a whole world out there to enjoy. It's an honest question."

"Well, it sounds rude." Bronwyn's voice was scolding.

Bethany tried sounding innocent.

"Did you think I was being rude?"

Travis shrugged his shoulders.

"I just figured that's how you big city folk are, or maybe it's just the theater types. I've heard they're strange like that. On the other hand, it could be that you didn't have proper raisin' and are lackin' in manners. But no, I didn't think you were being rude, a bit ignorant maybe but not rude."

Bronwyn suppressed her laugh; it was rare to see Bethany embarrassed. Travis remained stoic, cutting his eyes over to Bronwyn. Bethany didn't give up.

"Okay. I'll try re-wording my question." She spoke slowly, as if there were a language barrier. "Have you ever considered that there might be a better, more fulfilling life for you someplace else? And how would you know if this is all you want, if you have nothing to compare it to?"

Satisfied with her question, Bethany sat back in her chair, awaiting his reply.

Travis took the last bite of his fruit and finished off his water before answering her.

"I'm not sure you can define a fulfilled life by a location. I think the best life you can have is contentment, no matter what your circumstances. You can live in paradise and not be at peace. You make your happiness."

Standing, he took his and Bronwyn's empty plates to the sink.

"As far as missing something," he said, looking directly into Bronwyn's eyes, "who knows? You might find what you've been searching for right here."

The heat sensation began again in the soles of her feet; rising upward thru the rest of her body, making her dizzy. She knew this was not the reaction of a giddy infatuation, or the result of nervousness. This sensation was something she was certain she had never experienced before and it frightened her. She desired to look away; fearful he would notice her discomfort. He gave her a slight nod and left the room.

"Now there's someone to write about," Bethany gushed. "If that man doesn't inspire torrid thoughts inside of you then your brain dead. You see what I mean about him and Mavis not going together?"

Bronwyn had enough.

"Be quiet, Beth! She might hear you!"

Bethany pouted. "You're beginning to sound like Anna, proper, diplomatic, and boring! I want the old Bronwyn back. I miss her so much. I have no one to have fun with." She sighed melodramatically, "I guess I'll have to train up Lillian."

Bronwyn smiled at the thought. Pampered Princess Lillian; her partner in crime? Bethany's threat went undaunted.

"Tell you what," Bronwyn suggested. "Why don't we venture into this metropolis of a town and see what we can find."

"Will you be fun?"

Bronwyn smiled at her friend.

"I'll be a blast."

Soon, the girls were headed across the Inn's lawn to the main highway, accompanied by Lillian, who eagerly invited herself on their quest. The scents from the garden filled their lungs as the girls followed the cobblestone path that wound its way to the main road. Bronwyn was amazed at the variety of plants. Foliage literally covered every inch of ground.

"Sandalwood Inn." Bethany enlightened them by reading aloud the words on the beautifully hand-painted sign near the property's edge. The girls came to a stop when they reached the narrow highway. It was unnecessary, for there was not a single car traveling this forgotten winding road.

CHAPTER NINE

Larry's garage was easy to find. It was one of the first businesses when entering Moonshine. The place resembled an old time service station. Soda and vending machines stood out front, offering refreshment to anyone with pocket change. A large garage housed several vehicles awaiting repairs; along with a very large tour bus that Larry proudly displayed out front.

Larry thumbed through a parts catalogue at his rustic desk that doubled as a workbench. During the past hour, he had placed several calls. All responses were the same. There was no other way of looking at it. The troupe would have to remain in Moonshine for at least a week.

Anna sipped the cold drink she purchased from the machine and sat the bottle down hard on the table.

"I can't believe this. I can't believe we're actually stranded. How could this have happened?"

Finishing off her second bottle of soda, Karley placed it on the table in front of them. She gave it a spin. The bottle whirled around a few times and finally came to a stop, pointing at Wilbur.

She laughed. "Could I have said it any better?" The guilty party has been identified by the all-knowing bottle."

Wilbur grunted and waddled over to Larry's makeshift desk.

"I need to call a rental service and get my hands on a truck and a couple of vans."

"We don't have truck rentals here," Larry said, never looking up from his catalogue.

"You don't rent any vehicles of any kind?"

"Just bikes and canoes down at the dock."

"What do you think, Hogg?" Karley's voice was a jeer.

"Maybe we could load up a couple of canoes and paddle there Indian style? If we get a good current, maybe we could make opening by Friday."

Anna gave Karley a disapproving look. It was no secret that Anna didn't particularly like Wilbur, and his bossy, overindulgent ways; but she liked unnecessary confrontations even less. It seemed to Anna that Karley delighted in saying or doing anything to annoy Wilbur, and if things weren't stressful enough, the last thing she desired was to be a captive audience to their verbal assaults.

"I'm sorry," She said, attempting to detour Karley's provoking comments. "I don't see we have any other choice than to cancel."

"How far is the nearest town?" Wilbur barked his question again.

"You're lookin' at hundred miles and it's smaller than Moonshine," Larry said.

Wilbur's chair groaned as he sat back down defeated.

"Call and cancel," Marcus said softly.

Larry left his desk to tend to the ailing engines he had neglected all morning.

"Phones all yours."

Karley watched Larry feed change into the soda machine and retrieve his cola, popping off the cap and taking a swallow before heading into his garage. She watched him until he disappeared under the hood of a truck. Then she turned her attention back to the group, only to find Walt giving her a curious grin.

"What are you looking at?"

"I could ask you the same question."

She rolled her eyes as she tossed her empty soda bottle into the recycle bin.

"I'm starved. Let's go find some food."

CHAPTER TEN

Bronwyn was only half listening to Bethany and Lillian's conversation as the three continued their trek into Moonshine. It was nearly one in the afternoon and the midday heat was taking its toll. However, the heat wasn't the reason she was disengaged. It was the image she could see following them, masking itself in the gargantuan trees that provided a shaded tunnel over the winding road. She figured it to be the same person she saw last night, and whoever that may be, was hiding underneath the hood of the black robe, hot on her trail again. With every curve, she desperately hoped to see some hint of a town ahead but every turn proved more of the same endless highway.

She didn't want to alarm Bethany and Lillian by telling them of their stalker; certain that one word of impending danger would result in a wave of hysteria from Lillian and a barrage of questions from Bethany. Her best defense was to be aware of the person without them knowing. She continued walking silently, blocking out the conversation and lending her ear to the woods on her right.

Casually glancing over her shoulder, she watched the cloaked figure move alongside, in rhythm to their steps, like a long shadow. Her mind traveled back to the bridge and the knife she saw gleaming in the moonlight, followed by the figure jumping into the river. A cold chill tickled her spine.

"Bronwyn!" Bethany's exclamation interrupted her thoughts, startling her, so that her response seemed somewhat biting.

"What?"

Bethany's expression soured.

"You promised you'd be fun, but you haven't said a word since we left. Are you certain we're going in the right direction? We've been walking forever and there's no sign of a town anywhere."

Bronwyn shrugged.

"How should I know? Mavis said it was this way. I'm wondering if there is a town. I mean think about it. We trusted a couple of strangers we know nothing about. And, for that matter, why are there no other guests at the inn? In the height of summer? Only us, and do you realize, no one knows where we are right now? No one. Not even us. We can't call anyone because there is no cell reception and the phones at the inn are supposedly out because of last night's storm. We've all heard of people who just disappear never to be seen or heard from again. I wonder if this is how it starts. We all saw our bus being towed away, but to where? They could have been removing evidence that we were ever here."

Bronwyn's words were taking their toll on Lillian, whose facial expressions of impending heatstroke changed to full fright.

"Stop it! I refuse to be the victim of your outrageous stories."

Bethany grinned at Bronwyn thinking she was playing around just to frighten Lillian, so any warning of impending danger was dismissed. Bronwyn decided to let it go for now.

The three continued walking without conversation while Bronwyn was left to think of the direst circumstance that could possibly befall them.

A rustling from the woods shattered their silence.

"What was that?" Lillian gasped.

Bronwyn decided that maybe she should say something.

"I didn't want to scare you, but I'm pretty sure we're being followed."

Bethany smiled smugly, believing Bronwyn was continuing her attempt to spook Lillian.

"We are?" Lillian nearly yelled. "How do you know?"

Bronwyn hushed her. "Don't make a scene Lillian, but something or someone has been following us the entire way."

"How can you tell?"

"If you look over to your right, you can see it moving along with us, over in the trees."

Lillian glanced over her shoulder.

"I don't see anything."

Bronwyn kept her eyes fixed on the road ahead.

"Just keep walking. Don't try to look."

Lillian picked up her pace, turning the girls' casual stroll into a brisk power walk.

"Could be a bear or a mountain lion." Bethany suggested, trying to evoke more fear. "I've heard about mountain lion attacks they're horrible. My god, I don't want to be mauled! What should we do?"

Bronwyn knew it was not an animal following them. However, she decided to keep that bit of information to herself, to avoid frightening Lillian any more than she already was but it was too late.

Lillian had broken into a full-on run. Bronwyn and Bethany began jogging just to keep pace with her.

"Slow down Lil," Bethany said laughing. "Dang, I've never seen you move so fast! Don't get too far ahead. There's safety in numbers."

Bronwyn turned her head just in time to see the hooded figure move between two trees. Just as she was about to suggest they make a run for it, the loud blast of a horn sounded behind them. The girls screamed at the unexpectedness of it.

A familiar truck drove up, the only vehicle traveling on the highway since they began their journey. Bronwyn breathed a sigh of relief when she saw Travis in the cab, and the two children standing in the back, waving wildly at the girls. Glancing towards the woods, she witnessed the dark shadow retreat and disappear deeper into the forest.

"Would you like a ride?" Travis asked through his open window.

"Oh my God yes!" Lillian responded, her relief overflowing. Travis stopped the truck in the middle of the road and climbed from the cab to lower the tailgate.

Carla Jo eyed Bronwyn, her enthusiasm brimming over. "Get in and tell me all about Ryan!"

The last thing Bronwyn desired was a conversation with a twelve-year old about Ryan Reese. At this point, though, she realized she would do anything for a ride.

Bethany nudged Bronwyn with her elbow. "I'll take care of this one. You sit up front."

"I owe you one," she whispered, climbing into the cab and wondering why her anxiety continued to rise, even though she was safely in a vehicle, and no longer vulnerable to the stalking figure in the woods. The truth be known, the thought of a few minutes alone with Travis frightened her almost as much as the cloaked predator. She decided to take the opportunity to investigate what she could about the strange person lurking in the woods, without giving away the fact that she was actually aware of anything. She still wasn't sure how much to trust Travis, or if she could at all. She looked out the window.

"Are you sure it's only a mile into town? It seemed longer?"

"It's a country mile. If you stretch it out, it'd probably be three."

"That figures." She wished Mavis had explained that simple fact before they had ventured out on foot.

"What kind of wildlife do you have around here?"

"Just opossums, raccoons, deer and grizzlies. Why? Did something spook you?"

She turned away from the window to look at him. Something had spooked her, and by his nonchalant answer, she had a sneaking suspicion he knew exactly what she was talking about. The premonition of danger began to overwhelm her all over again.

"You could say that. I thought I saw something following us in the woods…"

He said nothing as he steered the truck around a few sharp curves.

"…Except animals would run away, not follow…" She waited for a response from him, but to her dismay; he offered none so she tried once more.

"...Actually I'm pretty sure it wasn't an animal at all..."

Again, he gave nothing away, not even in profile, so she went for broke.

"I think it was a person."

Again, nothing but silence from the driver's side of the cab.

"That doesn't surprise you?"

"Why should it? It was more than likely some kids gawking at the actors from California. A thing like that's a big deal around here."

"But how could anyone know we're here? We arrived late last night; the phones have been out...how could anyone know?"

"Word travels faster than you can dial a phone around here. Besides, I'd say that bus of yours being towed into town early this mornin' might have announced your arrival."

She felt a bit silly. Maybe he didn't know. His explanation seemed so obvious. However, she knew what she had encountered, first on the bridge last night, and now on the road in broad daylight. Gawking teenagers wouldn't have been out in a storm of such magnitude, and certainly wouldn't have been wielding a knife.

She decided to leave the matter alone. Either Travis knew of the person in the woods, or he didn't. Either way, she would play innocent, feeling it was her best defense. After all, they would probably be leaving soon. Once gone, she would alert authorities to the suspicious activity.

"I guess you're right." She turned her face back to the open window, unaware that Travis had taken his eyes off the road, and was watching her intently.

Within minutes, he rounded the final curve, unveiling the elusive town of Moonshine. Any fears or anxieties she may have experienced dismissed themselves promptly as she gazed upon this storybook town. It was as if the heavy curtains on a stage swung open to reveal breathtaking scenery behind them. Hidden within the bosom of the mountains was the most charming town Bronwyn had ever seen. Quaint old-fashioned storefronts lined the main road.

Each business was unique unto itself, untouched by corporate franchises and chains that littered most of the country. Cottages and cabins of various sizes dotted the rolling hillsides, each residence surrounded by beautiful gardens like that at the inn. Lush green grass blanketed the town for miles, interrupted occasionally by glistening brooks of clear water. The fragrant bouquet of pine, spruce, and balsam fir, along with various floral aromas, wafted through her open window. The man-made scents of fresh bread and sweet pastries drifted from the local bakery, accompanying nature's delicious smells.

The citizens of Moonshine were about, walking the streets. Travis drove much slower now as the happy residents waved, calling out his name. He nodded slightly each time, acknowledging the greetings. Bronwyn noticed their tour bus sitting outside of what she figured to be Larry's garage. She felt ashamed; their bus was an eyesore that spoiled the beauty of this lovely place. Adults and kids gathered around the bus, pointing and talking, excitement in their faces. Some people were taking pictures of the broken down vehicle. She felt somewhat embarrassed. Maybe Travis had been right. Possibly, she had let her imagination overwhelm all reasoning. She glanced his way, catching his eye and gave him a slight smile.

"It's alright," he said as if he had read her thoughts. "Story tellers are meant to have large imaginations."

Without warning the heat sensation began passing through her body once more. Her heart raced stealing her breath. How did he know she was a writer? She'd never told him.

Her mind was reeling, racing through the conversation at the breakfast table. No, it had never come up. How could he have known?

A sharp rap on the back window grabbed her attention. Bethany was pointing to a cozy café on the side of the road where the rest of the troupe sat outside on the patio, enjoying lunch.

"You can drop us here," Bronwyn said to Travis, still suspicious as to how he knew her vocation.

He brought the truck to a stop, and as chivalrous as ever, he opened her door and the tailgate for the girls.

"I'll be in town most of the day. Let me know if you want a ride back."

She watched him climb into his truck and drive away.

The girls pulled up three extra chairs and joined the troupe at the table. The café was busy, every seat occupied. A single waitress scurried busily from one table to the next. The moment she noticed the girls join the group; she immediately left the party she was assisting and eagerly headed their way. Her hair was dyed a bright red, except for some blond near her temples that had only managed to turn a pale orange. She pulled it high on her head in a sloppy bun. She used a brick red pencil to color her eyebrows in hope of matching them with her hair. The line crooked and strayed from the natural brow line, as if she had applied her cosmetics hurriedly or in the dark. Green shimmer shadow painted both eyelids and bubblegum pink gloss covered her thin lips. She wore a badge onto which her name was handwritten.

"Can I get you girls something to wet your whistle?" Nell asked cheerfully.

"I don't have a whistle," Lillian answered confused.

Trent took the opportunity to enlighten Lillian on the culture of Moonshine that he was able to attain in the short time he'd been in town.

"She's asking if you want something to drink." He leaned across the table as if he just revealed a profound secret. "It's amazing really. It's as if there is a whole lost dialect in these mountains we've never heard."

Nell waited patiently while Trent leaned into the table, speaking only loud enough for the troupe to hear.

Realizing she did not need a whistle to place an order, Lillian happily requested strawberry lemonade. Bethany and Bronwyn decided to try the sweet iced tea. Nell swiftly disappeared into the small café to retrieve the refreshing beverages. Bronwyn glanced around the patio. Tables of many different sizes were adorned in non-matching linen table-cloths. Small vases with fresh cut flowers crowned the top of each. Strings of miniature white lights hung in the trellis overhead, offering a starry ambiance effect for the evening diners. A counter top table was fastened to the outside wall just below a large window from which you could peer into the café's kitchen. Whenever the chef would retrieve fresh baked goods from the oven, Nell immediately placed them on the counter top to cool. Mouth-watering aromas drifted from the hot cuisine and directly onto the patio, increasing everyone's appetite. As Bronwyn surveyed the place, she noticed the diners pretending to be engaged in their own private conversations, despite the fact that all eyes were constantly upon their table.

Lillian also picked up on this scenario right away. "I feel like a celebrity," she gushed. "Everyone's looking at us."

"Trent's already had his picture snapped twice, by a couple of desperate women interrupting our lunch." Karley said, rolling her eyes.

"I wonder if this is how celebrities feel." Lillian was delighted.

"It's not for me," Wilbur lied, attempting to sound humble.

Karley rolled her eyes again. "Now I know you're lying. You call in song dedications to yourself all the time just so you can hear your name announced over the radio."

Wilbur's fat face turned a bright shade of red. "You only caught me doing that once. Only once!"

Nell returned to the table, placing the cold drinks in front of the girls.

"You havin' lunch?" She laid the straws on the table. "We're serving tuna and cucumber sandwiches today with a side of strawberries and mango."

"Oh," Lillian said, realizing there were no other choices.

The girls agreed on lunch, the long walk had stirred their appetites. Nell scurried off to collect three tuna sandwiches, returning in record time and placing the healthy lunch on the table.

"I'm glad you girls joined us," Marcus said as Nell refilled his empty tea glass. "We need to discuss our present situation."

"So it's a situation now?" Bronwyn asked.

"I'm afraid so." Marcus breathed deeply folding his hands in front of him on the table.

"Looks like it's going to take some time to get the bus running again. The mechanic in town says he can fix it but he doesn't have the necessary parts in stock. He will have to order them, so we're looking at an eight to ten day stay."

Simultaneous protest rose up from the group. "We're opening on Friday," Lillian said, her shock apparent.

"Isn't it our biggest venue of the summer?" Daniel asked.

"What the hell are we going to do for ten days?" Trent demanded.

Marcus tried to regain control at the table. "I know, I know."

"Can't we rent a couple of vans or something?" Bronwyn suggested.

Marcus sighed. "Already looked into it. The only rentals in this town are bikes and canoes."

"How close is the nearest town?" She asked, "Maybe we could…"

"One hundred thirty three miles," Marcus said, cutting her off. "And it's not any bigger than this one."

"I guess it's ridiculous to ask if Moonshine has an airport," Trent said sarcastically.

"Let's face it, troupe. We're stranded."

"More like screwed," Daniel said.

Bronwyn pushed her plate away from her.

"I for one have no desire in staying here for more than one night, let alone ten days! I want out of here. I find this place a little disturbing!"

"Bronwyn lower your voice!" Bethany said. "People can hear you!"

"I don't care!" she shouted louder than before.

"Well, you bloody well better!" Trent shot back. "They're going to be your neighbors for a while."

She turned to Marcus deciding it might be best to inform him of her suspicions.

"Something's not right about this place! I don't think we're safe here!"

Her words surprised him.

"And why don't you feel safe? Everyone I've met so far has been quite accommodating and friendly."

She leaned toward him lowering her voice.

"Someone was stalking Walt and me last night while we were looking for help, and then I saw them again, while we were walking here."

Marcus turned to Lillian.

"Did you see someone following you?"

Lillian shook her head.

"I looked but I didn't see anyone."

"I think it was some kind of wild animal." Bethany told Marcus. Her supposed authority on the subject dismissed the issue and annoyed Bronwyn.

"Just because you didn't see anything Bethany, doesn't mean someone wasn't there. I know what I saw last night. Someone in a hooded robe wielding a knife followed us last night and was stalking us on the way into town a few minutes ago."

She could tell by everyone's expression that they thought she might be losing her grasp on reality.

She sighed frustrated.

"Call it premonition whatever, I don't feel safe here. I think we are being detained here for some reason and I think we should do what we can to leave."

Karley broke the humiliating silence.

"We're stuck here because the bus engine has been neglected and couldn't take these mountain roads. And that my dear is Hogg's fault, not the work of a crazy serial killer hiding on the side of an untraveled highway wielding a knife or a sawed off shotgun."

"I wish I did have a gun!" Wilbur barked. "I'd aim it right at you!"

"You damn near wouldn't!" Karley yelled back "Unless you wanted it rammed up somewhere the sun don't shine!"

"Guys!" Marcus' usually calm countenance was disintegrating into agitation. "Let's try and keep our cool. As Bethany pointed out, people are watching us."

Bronwyn looked around the patio, and although she knew none of her group agreed with her, she sensed there was something odd about the place, however picturesque it may appear. Marcus was right in the fact that the inhabitants of the town did seem friendly enough; a large group of Southern people lost deep in the mountains, living in their own small world, seemingly untouched by the latest technologies and modern conveniences. So what if they didn't have cell phones or internet? The world had managed to survive for years before their invention. Most of the people looked youthful, happy, healthy, and stress free. She had heard somewhere that the higher the elevation, the slower the aging process. Still despite their Norman Rockwell appearance, something wasn't right.

She continued to scan the patio, glancing at the many smiling faces, intrigued by the goings on at her table, when her eyes stopped abruptly upon a face of a man, sitting alone in the far corner. He leaned back in his chair with one leg thrown across his table, a cigarette hung from his lower lip. He appeared unshaven, with long black hair that hung in his face. His eyes hid behind a pair of dark sunglasses. He seemed to be looking her way; however, it was hard to tell for sure until he flashed an impish grin. Terror gripped her, and another disturbing feeling came upon her at the sight of his wicked smile. Now she was convinced all the more that something sinister was at play here in Moonshine. She looked away, not wanting the man to see the fear in her face, and returned her attention back to the table.

"I think," Marcus was saying diplomatically, "we should look at the positive side of our situation. We can be thankful that the bus decided to give out within a few miles of a nice comfortable inn." "The Bates Motel," she mumbled under her breath.

"With a nice family eager to take care of our needs," he continued, ignoring her sarcastic remark.

"We have every comfort right here. We could have had the misfortune of breaking down a hundred miles from Moonshine. Now that, my friends, would have been a disaster! Since there is nothing we can do about our situation, my advice to all of you would be to make the most of it."

"I, for one, do not think any of you should use this little detour in the schedule as vacation time," Wilbur grumbled. "Since we're all still on the payroll, I suggest every one of you use this time for self-improvement!"

"Every one of us?" Karley shouted her words. "What about you, Hogg? I think you should include yourself in that statement."

Marcus nodded. "It wouldn't hurt to set aside a few rehearsals. Our past few performances haven't been our best."

Wilbur jumped on the opportunity to criticize. "You're not kidding about that, the audience keeps laughing and the funny thing is, we're not performing a comedy."

Bronwyn decided to ignore Wilbur's barrage of insults and look across the patio, curious to see if the roguish man was still looking her way. She casually glanced around; her eyes fell on two girls who were openly flirting with Trent and Daniel. The guys, who were also ignoring Wilbur, were engaged and returning the flirtatious antics. However, the man's table was empty and cleared as if he had never been there. She searched the patio and the sidewalk out front. There was no sign of him. Another shiver tickled her skin.

She sighed and unwillingly turned her attention back to the table and Wilbur's bombardment of insults.

"Trent, you need to hone up on your acting skills. Your performances of late have been extremely shallow. Good looks will get you only so far."

Anna immediately intervened before Trent could toss a glass of cold water on Wilbur.

"As Marcus said before, a few extra rehearsals could do us all a world of good. Don't you agree, Marcus?" Anna made sure that Wilbur heard her emphasis.

"Have my performances been that horrid?" Trent asked.

Marcus took a swallow of his tea and wiped his mouth with a napkin.

"Horrid? No. They have however, been somewhat empty of the charisma that I know exudes from you. Tell me, Trent, what do you think is causing your performances to fall flat?"

The troupe eyed Trent awaiting his response. They all knew most of the fault sat within the poor writing of the last script. This meant Bronwyn. The group adored her. She had produced stellar scripts in times past, yet because of her recent heartbreak, her stories lost some of their passion and depth. No one wanted to hurt her any further by bashing her latest work.

Trent caught Lillian's eye and through her facial expression, she encouraged him to speak the truth.

"No offense to Bronwyn, but it's extremely hard to portray a three-dimensional character when the material we have to work with is one-dimensional, boring and quite predictable."

The remark brought Bronwyn's full attention back to the table. Before she could offer a word of defense, Wilbur jumped upon the insult.

"I couldn't agree more! My eight-year-old niece could have written a better script than that."

She pushed herself away from the table to leave.

"Bronwyn please," Bethany begged. "Don't take this personally. Sit down and let's plod through this."

"I don't want to plod through anything!" She bit back walking away. She stomped across the patio; angry, feeling the stares of everyone as they watched her leave. She avoided their glares keeping her eyes fixed ahead, and left the café, venturing on down the street.

Marcus sighed, "Bethany, do you think you should go after her?"

"No, I think its best we just give her some time. She's been through a lot, and I know for a fact, she still hurts over Ryan."

"Good God! It's been six months. How long is she going to brood?"

"I know this is hard for you to understand, Hogg," Karley said sarcastically. "Considering most people get over you in six seconds flat."

"Ah, the progression of a shattered heart." Trent felt the desire to wax eloquently. "Stage one, extreme sadness, mingled with torrents of tears, and the consuming desire to please and convince the person who dumped you, that you can change and be who they want you to be. When those sincere efforts go unrewarded, stage two begins. The bitter and angry stage. The person who you once loved, you now hate vigorously. You burn all tokens of affection you once treasured and held dear. You long for a casual encounter of the person just so you can act out your revenge, proving how intently you despise them. Soon stage two gives way to stage three, the rebellious stage, which in my opinion, is the most dangerous of all."

"Why is it dangerous?" Lillian asked; her eyes wide, absorbing all Trent was saying.

"Because my love, when a person rebels, they will do anything. They display desperate attempts for attention, go against all they have ever believed in, justify an affair... the list goes on. It's a dark world then."

Trent leaned back in his chair, balancing on the back legs, as he winked at the girls flirting with him from across the patio. He smiled smugly believing he had enlightened everyone at the table with his profound thoughts.

Bethany rolled her eyes and shook her head.

"Bronwyn's a smart girl. She's not desperate or dangerous. She simply has a broken heart and needs time. She was planning her wedding, for crying out loud. This wasn't a high school crush."

"Denying it doesn't make it any less true," Trent said with extreme confidence. "As I see it she's in the second stage. Hate and bitterness. If you care for her Beth, don't let her get to stage three."

Bethany's anger toward Trent grew.

"You're the one who started this by blaming her for your poor acting."

Trent chewed on the straw hanging from his lips.

"I'll ignore that remark love but I think you have noticed quite a bit of hatred and bitterness growing in Bronwyn whether you admit it or not."

"Maybe I have," she answered him, "but I don't appreciate you pointing it out to everyone and making predictions about her life. She's my best friend and I think I know her much better than anyone else at the table. I'm certain that time is all she needs and soon she will be her old self again, laughing, teasing, and ready for our next adventure. Who knows? Maybe she'll fall in love all over again."

"I hope your right Beth," Trent said. "But right now she seems like she might need a bit of intervention. All I'm saying, is since you are the closest to her, you need to look out for her. Sugar coating things doesn't help. Tell her the truth about herself so she can deal with her issues and get passed them. We all love her and I for one will help you with this if you trust me. After all I do have my degree in counseling you know."

Bethany ran her finger across the condensation on her tea glass. Trent could be right; she had noticed an unpleasant change in Bronwyn's personality, not to mention the sheer shock of her latest disclosure, believing they were in some kind of danger.

The troupe finished lunch and decided to take a relaxing tour of Moonshine. Nell informed them of an enormous lake and scenic waterfalls. She recommended the many nature trails that wound deep into the woods and mentioned several stables where they could go horseback riding. She also informed them of the bakery and sweet shop, and an old-fashioned soda fountain that made the most amazing malts and shakes. She told them about the library and a small museum of Appalachian history. With all this information, the troupe decided to kill a few hours in town before heading back to the inn. Marcus' plan was to meet back at Larry's garage at six. They would retrieve more of their belongings from the bus before heading back to the inn.

With the agenda decided, the troupe headed into town. Trent and Daniel were escorted, by two giggling girls.

CHAPTER ELEVEN

"Canoe Rental."

Bronwyn read the sign posted in the window of the general store. It seemed to offer the perfect tranquil escape, just what she needed.

It had been months since she experienced solitude. Just two weeks after she and Ryan split, she rejoined the troupe on their tour. Although she hated going back to her humble beginnings, she'd do anything to get away and take her mind off Ryan's betrayal. It had been extremely close quarters, the past six months, traveling from venue to venue. Whenever they stopped at hotels, they were always doubling up. Even now, at the inn; there were three to a room. She was in desperate need for some alone time, even if only for a couple of hours.

The tiny silver bells above the door jingled as she entered the store. The cool breeze from the much-overworked air conditioner pushed against her face. She hadn't noticed the intense heat and humidity of the day until now. Walking through the market, she glanced around looking for what could be a rental station for the canoes. The market was quite large. A produce section filled with fresh fruit and vegetables took up over half of the store; appearing much like the farmers markets she would frequent back home. A very small meat counter stood on the other side of the store. The selection was quite limited, consisting mostly of fresh fish, obviously caught in the local lake.

She noticed Carla Jo, accompanied by a couple of young girls, ogling over the latest movie magazine. Not wanting the girls to see her, she chose an alternate aisle. She was in no mood to make small talk with Carla Jo, or anyone else. She'd already power-walked the entire way from the café to the market, while dishing out forced smiles to all the people extending her a greeting. She felt somewhat guilty for her rudeness; however, she justified her behavior today as self-preservation. It was not her intent to make new friendships right now. Her stay here in Moonshine would be brief. What life-long friendships could she possibly develop in eight short days?

Successfully eluding Carla Jo and her clan, Bronwyn approached the deli counter. A man wearing a white apron and a huge grin greeted her. He offered no hello, and no how are you? His only greeting was an amusing antidote, not particularly humorous to Bronwyn. She feigned a slight courteous laugh.

"I saw a sign that said you rent canoes?"

"Sure do!" Gil responded enthusiastically. "You sure picked a great day to go out on the lake. Tell you what," he tore a yellow ticket from a pad. "No charge today. This canoe ride is on the house as a welcome to Moonshine."

Bronwyn's stone stature melted a bit.

"That's not necessary, I can pay."

"I won't hear of it." His cheery voice rang out. "Save all your money for the festival."

He pointed to a large sign hanging on the back wall. Her eyes shifted to the beautifully painted banner.

Midsummer's Night Cream

Moonshines Annual Ice Cream Festival

Saturday August 16th

"Best ice cream in the whole world. All of it made right here by the amazing people of Moonshine. It's a fun night of dancing, games, and prizes. You and your friends will have the time of your lives."

Bronwyn took the yellow ticket from Gil.

"Thank you I'm sure we will." She offered a half smile, realizing they would still be in town for the event.

"You head on down to the lake hon," Gil said. "And I'll send Kevin on ahead to pull you out a canoe."

Bronwyn placed the ticket in her back pocket and turned to leave; nearly tripping over Carla Jo and her friends. All three were bouncing up and down, as if the whole floor were a trampoline.

"This is the lady who knows him!" Carla Jo squealed.

Bronwyn looked down at the magazine in Carla Jo's hand. Ryan's face spread across the cover. She grabbed the magazine and the headline,

"RYAN REESE... The Hero the World's been Waiting For!"

She groaned. How stupid and naïve can people be? Did anyone realize he is not the hero he portrays in movies? Anyone could be a hero, if they quoted amazing lines that were written for them, had a stunt double to jump in and do all the dangerous work, and whose enemies were very nice people playing a role. Had the whole world gone mad?

"Tell us all about him, please!" one of the girls pleaded.

"For starters," Bronwyn said, "He's nothing like the characters he portrays in the movies. He's a coward and a big pompous jerk. Besides, I wouldn't get your hopes up girls. He's actually gay."

Handing the magazine back to the sad eyed girls, she left the store.

The lake proved much more delightful than she had imagined. Just as Gil had said, she met Kevin, a shy young store clerk, who blushed the entire time he spoke with her, down by the water's edge. He'd already floated her canoe into the water. He pointed out a small peninsula of trees jutting out across the water, telling her to paddle that way and make the turn. "You'll be delighted with what you see." He said.

He was right. The lake opened up before her like a vast mirror reflecting the cloudless sky. Lofty trees and colossal mountains stood vigil, protecting this serene setting. Cedars, spruce and fir trees of all kinds grew on the hillsides, releasing their sacred smell. Two hawks flew overhead, flapping their enormous wings before diving into effortless glides and skimming across the waters. Both hawks seized protesting but defenseless fish and climbed back into the sky, disappearing across the hillside. She closed her eyes and took in a deep breath, once again inhaling the invigorating aroma of the mountain and the warmth of the midday sun. She reveled in the quiet peacefulness of the place. There was no noise, save for the chatter of insects in the trees, an occasional splash from a jumping fish, and the chirping of birds. There was no traffic, no loud roar of the bus engine, no car alarms sounding off without an intruder, no annoying cell phone ring tones, and no loud obnoxious conversations. Bronwyn realized she had not received a call in over twenty-four hours. She usually felt a strong irritation when she could not get a signal for her phone. Now, in this setting, she was quite thrilled that no one would be able to interrupt her solitude...especially Ryan and his annoying, blood thirsty attorneys. Positioning her paddle in the canoe, she lay back into the boat, enjoying the tranquility of the moment.

CHAPTER TWELVE

The man casually approached the hidden cabin, raised his fist, and rapped softly on the door.

It opened immediately; the owner of the cabin stepped aside, allowing him to enter. Knowing the owner would never allow smoking within the confines of his cabin; he took the last draw from his cigarette and crushed the butt underneath his bare foot before he entered. The others were already there. He didn't take a seat as they had. In fact, he hardly ever sat; it was his conviction to never allow himself to get too comfortable. Instead he leaned against the wall keeping one eye outside the window.

"Okay I've seen them all," he addressed the men inside. "Damn odd group, if you ask me."

"Do you know which one of them is the one we've been expecting?" The soft spoken man asked from his cushioned chair.

There was an extended pause before the owner of the cabin offered the answer.

"She is called by the name Bronwyn."

Smoking man was shocked. "Are you certain?"

"Very," The owner responded, his answer brimming with conviction.

"That's just great," Smoking man said sarcastically. "More work for me."

He gave the owner a roguish grin accompanied by a slight laugh before his face grew somber.

"I'm sorry," he said. "I never expected."

"Neither did I," the owner replied. All the men remained silent for quite some time; each one understanding the severity of the situation.

"She doesn't know anything?" Smoking man asked breaking the hush in the room.

"No. Nothing at all."

"And you have no idea where she has been all this time?"

"No."

"Do you think she is trustworthy?"

"I have no reason to believe her not to be."

"Should you approach her?" The soft spoken man asked.

"No." This time the owner's answer carried ultimate authority.

"The situation is much too delicate. We've waited so long; a bit longer will not hurt."

"He's right," smoking man agreed. "Approaching her might set us way back, if not destroy everything."

"My advice is to wait," the owner suggested. "I will find a way to take her to the waterfalls; after she feels the pull I am sure she will begin to approach us. In any case, the prophesy is now fulfilled. After all, she is here; isn't she?"

CHAPTER THIRTEEN

Moonshine proved to be a delightful experience for everyone. Marcus and Anna had taken in the museum, learning some interesting trivia along with ancient Appalachian history. Walt found his way back to Larry's garage; spending the better part of the afternoon shadowing him in an attempt to learn a few things about engines. Larry hadn't minded. He actually enjoyed the company, and Walt was content having a chance to finish his hospital story. Wilbur found his way to the soda shop. He spent his afternoon in the air-conditioned store, treating himself to thick creamy shakes while reading a paperback novel he borrowed from the bookrack.

Meanwhile, the two girls' escorted Trent and Daniel through town while enjoying the prestige and envy of everyone. The guys signed several autographs outside the soda shop, surrounded by giddy teenage girls to whom they could exaggerate stories of their fame.

Karley, Lillian and Bethany checked out the local shopping. Karley suggested the nature trails, but Lillian quickly vetoed the idea after remembering their harrowing walk into town and the thought of receiving a mauling by wild animals.

It was now six o'clock and in keeping with Marcus' plan, the entire troupe re-grouped at Larry's garage. Anna shared her opinions regarding what they should retrieve from the bus and what they should leave behind.

"So how are we getting all this back to the inn?" Lillian asked, struggling with her suitcase as she pulled it behind her. "I'm quite certain I will not be able to roll this piece of luggage all the way back."

Bethany agreed it would prove to be quite cumbersome to roll their suitcases three miles down the narrow crooked highway. Remembering Travis' offer of a ride home, she suggested they look for him in town in the hopes of hitching a ride back to the inn. Karley volunteered to look and left in search of Travis. Larry offered to help, noting it would take more than Travis' truck to transport ten people and all their baggage.

"All the bags are out except for Bronwyn's," Walt announced closing the luggage compartment.

"Why isn't she here?" Wilbur barked.

Bethany quickly came to her defense. "She left before the plan was made to meet. She has no way of knowing."

"Didn't anyone run into her this afternoon?" Marcus asked. "It's a small place; surely one of you saw her."

The troupe remained silent. No one had seen her since she stormed out of the café. Anna suggested she might have walked back to the inn.

Travis' truck pulled into Larry's garage. Carla Jo and Molly were sitting in the back, just as before. Karley began yelling as she jumped from the cab.

"We gotta get out of here! He says there's another storm headed this way."

Looking across the rolling hills, Bethany noticed the boiling clouds.

"She's not kidding."

Marcus picked up the pace. "Let's get moving guys; I for one do not want to get pelted by rain and hail again tonight."

Scrambling, the troupe began dividing themselves up between the two trucks. Soon Larry was heading down the road, his pickup full of passengers. The wind began to increase as Travis slammed the tailgate shut, instructing the kids to sit tight. He climbed in the cab looking at Lillian and Bethany, who were patiently waiting inside.

"Where's Bronwyn?"

"Back at the inn, I hope." Bethany said.

"What do you mean, hope? You don't know?"

"She got upset at lunch and left the café. No one's seen her since."

Heavy raindrops began plopping on the windshield just as Travis pulled the pickup onto the road. The town had emptied out considerably, everyone taking cover from the impending storm. Travis searched the streets and Bethany noticed. His deep concern aroused her curiosity and she wondered why he would search so intently for Bronwyn. With the town now in their rear view mirror, the truck picked up speed racing toward Sandalwood Inn. The dark trees lining the road swayed with the wind, giving everyone an ominous feeling of doom.

Bronwyn sat up from her reclining position. Her canoe drifted lazily across the water. She wasn't sure how long she had been asleep... or when she had actually dozed off, for that matter. The peaceful quietness of the lake, the warm sun on her body, and the gentle rocking of the canoe provided the hypnotic elements to induce her to sleep. Retrieving the oar from the bottom of the vessel, she dipped it into the still, cool waters, and then gracefully and effortlessly guided the canoe to the dock.

Approaching the shore, she saw a lone figure standing on the banks, waving to her. She strained her eyes to see who had discovered her private escape. As she paddled closer to shore, a face came into focus...no, it couldn't be...no way...

Her heart leaped inside her chest. *Ryan?* What was he doing here in Moonshine?

She paddled closer, still not believing what she was seeing. No matter how much her mind wanted to disagree, her eyes didn't lie.

There he was, Ryan Reese, standing on the shore, as if he had just walked off the cover of the magazine from the store. Right down to the silly grin plastered across his face.

"Bronwyn!" he yelled out to her, waving. She paddled the canoe close enough to the dock for him to climb aboard.

"Take me out on the water." His smile grew; so without a thought, she paddled the canoe back out into the waters, all the while her mind reeling with questions.

"How did you find me?"

"You weren't answering my calls, so I did some investigating and found out where you were…and here I am." His arms stretched as wide as his grin.

The calmness of the afternoon suddenly shattered. Her anxiety level began rising within her.

"You came all this way because of our script?" Anger seared within her voice.

"No babe." Still, he smiled. "I came because I heard about the baby."

She gasped. Her mind searched for every possibility.

"How do you know about that? I never told anyone about the baby. Not Bethany, not even my mother."

He sat unmoved, the smile still plastered across his face. Feeling a bit of chill in the air, Bronwyn looked up and noticed the sky growing dark. Strong winds began to blow across the surface of the lake, making it difficult for her to maneuver the canoe.

"Ryan…" She struggled with her words, as well as with her paddling.

"There is no baby. I lost it."

His grin remained in place.

"Good. I came to ask you to abort it, anyway."

She wanted to scream at him or at least whack him upside his head with one of her oars, but the swirling waters around the canoe sucked in her attention. The wind had accelerated, stirring up large waves that washed over the canoe's rails, pushing it further onto the lake. She struggled with the oar, each wave tossing it back to the surface of the water.

"Can you please help me?"

He shrugged.

"You seem to be doing fine."

"No I am not!" She yelled above the wind. "I could really use your help."

He nodded.

"You don't need me. You're the strongest woman I know. You'll survive this." With those final words, he dove into the swirling waters, splashing her...

She gasped for air and sat up. Raindrops splashed on her face. She looked around. No one was there. Ryan was gone, lost in the mist of sleep from which he came. She breathed a sigh of relief, grateful it was only a dream but anger still gripped her, anger over how he'd once again invaded the peacefulness of her life, causing immediate turmoil in her soul. She shivered at the thought of his manic smile.

The sky had grown unusually dark. That part of her nightmare was real. A chill had fallen in the air, causing the wind to increase; bouncing the canoe about the water. She shivered at the sudden change of temperature. Only a few hours ago, the lake had been a peaceful paradise. The trees that before stood erect, pointing happily to the sapphire sky, now bent over, cowering in fear before the breath of the storm. The sky that had provided a playground for whippoorwill, warblers, larks, water thrush and an occasional hawk was now devoid of any fowl. The vexed howl of the wind replaced the delightful songs of the birds. It seemed to her as if all nature cowered in fear of the arrival of some hideous creature. She sensed an overpowering feeling of doom, as if there were some foreboding secret of which all of nature was aware. She shivered uncontrollably from the iciness of the wind and the eeriness that penetrated her soul. Thunder sounded in the distance as smoky black clouds rolled violently across the sky.

She attempted to maneuver the canoe to the dock. The muscles in her arms burned and her hands cramped from the tightness of her clutch on the oar. All her efforts to slice the water, met in futility. The tumultuous waves tossed the oar to the surface, as if it were nothing more than a wooden spoon. The rain smacked the lake in a downpour. The heavy wind blew the torrential rain into her face impairing her vision, making it impossible for her to see. Her heart raced within her chest. Her circumstances were not good. Considering her situation, she guessed she was near the shore, yet uncertain as to how close. With the increasing wind, she could feel her tiny canoe pushed further back into the lake, and the consuming waves. She contemplated abandoning the boat altogether, and possibly swimming to shore. She was a decent swimmer, and could perhaps move her body against the fierce waves, more easily than she could maneuver the canoe with a worthless paddle. However, as fatigued as she was, she feared running out of strength, and then having no place of rest. She decided to continue her paddling and get as close to shore as possible, before taking the eminent plunge into the angry waters.

A streak of lightning zigzagged across the lake directly in front of her. Realizing her situation was growing dimmer by every second, she placed her drenched arm across her forehead, shielding her eyes, in an attempt to get a visual assessment of her distance from shore.

Her heart leaped with excitement. She was closer than she realized! She eyed several trees growing out of the water; many of their branches extended farther out over the lake. Tossing her oar aside, she reached out to grab a branch. Her sudden movement, combined with the unevenness of the water and the overpowering waves, toppled her canoe, tossing her into the angry lake. The consuming waters rushed over her, the waves were much stronger than she had anticipated.

Disoriented, she tried to position herself toward the shore. However, the wind, waves and torrential downpour teamed up against her. She desperately needed a focal point. If only she could get a quick glimpse of the shoreline, she could swim there with all her might. She dare not waste her last bit of strength until she was certain of her bearings. Swimming in the wrong direction would cast her deeper into the lake, resulting in inevitable death. Her legs burned beneath her. Exhaustion was setting in. She feared she could not tread the water much longer, yet certain if she stopped, she would surely be overtaken by the monstrous waves.

The sky was almost dark now; there was little light left. Dismal gray surrounded her on every side. She strained her eyes for one small glimpse of shoreline. Just one glimmer of hope and she would exude every ounce of her strength to make it there.

Another bolt of lightning hit nearby. The flash provided just enough light to point her way to shore. Her heart beat with excitement. With the last bit of strength, she forced her way, fighting against the powerful waters. Yet each wave that rose high above her pushed her back, keeping her from the shore.

She swam hard, determined that this would not be how her life would end! Thoughts of her friends and family receiving the dismal news of her death invaded her mind. She pondered how the news would affect Ryan, and wondered if he would feel any remorse at all. More than likely, he would be delighted with her death then he would be free to use the screenplay he was so desperately trying to steal from her. Her simmering anger gave her an added bit of strength and new momentum. She tossed him from her mind. She would not allow him be her last thought.

Another wave washed over her, filling her mouth with water. She coughed, strangled by the sudden rush of fluid. The rain's intensity increased, pouring over her along with the continual crashing waves. She was losing her last bit of strength at an alarming rate. She lowered her legs, to see if she could touch bottom. Nothing.

Her heart ached. She wanted to cry. Her strength was completely gone. Her heart pounded so hard it seemed to be marching from her chest directly into her throat, choking her, suffocating her. Her heart pursed itself in desperate prayer; as she prayed to God for help.

Feeling a small tap on her back, she whirled around. The canoe! Although it had capsized, it was amazingly still afloat! If she could manage to hang on to it, she might have a chance to drift to safety. Just as she reached for the canoe, an enormous wave pushed it toward her causing it to violently crash into her head.

The sudden rush of pain choked the breath out of her. She gasped… all was growing dark and quiet. She felt her strength escape as her body went limp. With all her strength ebbing away, she attempted to grab the canoe. Her hand had no power to grip; it only slapped at the side of the boat before sliding down across the hull and into the water. All was dark, save for a bright piercing light that blinded her eyes, as the swirling waters took possession of her body.

There was no rain, no thunder, no howling wind and no final thoughts, only a bright light followed by a quiet cold darkness.

CHAPTER FOURTEEN

Mavis tossed dry, thirsty towels to every rain soaked member of the troupe who bolted for the door.

"Dinners ready in the kitchen when everyone's dry."

Bethany caught the towel Mavis hurled her way, and began to dry off.

"Mavis, is Bronwyn here?"

"Hadn't seen hide not hair of anyone all day."

Bethany dropped the towel from her face.

"You mean she's not here?"

"Lessin she snuck in while I was out in the gardens. But I don't think so; with the kids gone, it's been quieter than a mouse around here."

Bethany did not wait for Mavis to finish before bolting up the staircase and into their room. It was the same as they had left it earlier, except for Mavis' housekeeping. She pushed open the door to the adjoining bathroom. Empty!

"Bronwyn hasn't been back to the room," She announced returning to the foyer.

"I don't think she's here, hon." Mavis said. "Like I told you, I hadn't seen hide nor hair of anyone all day."

Travis said nothing as he headed for the door. Bethany followed him.

"If you're going after her, then I'm coming with you!"

"No, you'd do better staying put. This storm is deadly." The authority in his voice caused her to back down and not argue, even though she wanted to go with him.

"Take shelter if need be." Mavis' warning trailed him, as he left Bethany standing and headed out the door into the threatening storm.

He jumped into his truck and sped down the highway. He, if anyone, knew the dangers of this storm. It was angry, ready to take its vengeance. He also knew not taking immediate shelter was an invitation to death. However, the risk of taking shelter was too high. He had seen what the presence could do. He was powerless against the force. He could not stop it, but he would do all within his power to keep it from claiming another life; especially hers. The wind pushed hard against his truck, as if it sensed the confrontation. He grasped the wheel; the muscles in his forearms bulged as he attempted to hold it on the road. Though flicking back and forth at full speed, his windshield wipers were of no use. The rain swept over his truck in sheets, blanketing his windshield, making it almost impossible for him to see. Straining his eyes, he looked through the blinding downpour. The sky was dark; the only light came from the lightning that danced tauntingly around his truck.

He turned for the lake, hating to think she might be on it during this incredible storm. Nevertheless, deep in the recesses of his soul he knew that was exactly where she was. He drove through town at full speed, before connecting to the secondary roads surrounding the lake.

Storm clouds continued to boil over into the sky, blocking out any light from the waning sun or rising moon. Reaching into the floorboard of his truck, he retrieved a powerful flood light and then lowered his window. The rain blew in, soaking him instantly. Holding the light, he scanned the lake. *Nothing!* He reduced his speed and continued his search, the beam of light acting as a lighthouse tower on an angry sea, reflected off an object bouncing in the waters not far from shore. Leaning out his window, he aimed the light. It fell across the waters and landed on an abandoned, overturned canoe.

His heart sank. An overturned, drifting canoe was not good news. He practically jumped from his truck before placing it in park and ran down the bank to the lake, his feet slipping in the wet mud. Charging into the rushing waters, he made his way towards the bobbing canoe, all the while keeping his light aimed straight ahead.

Suddenly, his eyes caught sight of a hand, slowly sliding off the side of the boat, and disappearing into the dark lake. He hurled his light to shore and dove into the angry waters. Blindly, he searched for the sinking hand but saw nothing. He dove further down and could feel hair moving about his fingers. He wrapped his hand around the swirling tresses and yanked, pulling Bronwyn from her watery grave. With his other arm, he swiftly scooped up her listless body and carried her to shore. He tilted her head back, blowing a few short puffs of air into her mouth. Her body jerked, as a geyser of water spewed from her lips. Travis quickly turned her to her side as she continued to expel the lake water.

Travis straddled her as he knelt in the mud. He was soaked, rain poured from his hair and off his jaw line. Relief flooded his dark eyes as she raised her head and focused in on him.

"We have to get out of here!" he yelled above the howling wind and rain.

She nodded.

With every second, the storm seemed to increase its intensity. Lightning flashed through the sky almost continuously now.

"Can you make it to the truck?"

She looked over at the abandoned truck on the side of the road with the engine still running and the headlights floodlighting the falling rain. She took in a big breath of air and gave him an affirmative nod.

He helped her to her feet; however, her legs gave out almost instantly. With no time to waste, he scooped her up into his arms and ran up the slippery bank towards the truck. Kicking open the half-closed door, he fairly threw her into the cab. Stirring up mud and debris, the back tires squealed as he pulled back onto the road. He would head for the cabin. They needed to hide, fast.

CHAPTER FIFTEEN

Summoning all the strength she could, Bronwyn slid her body over, giving Travis enough room to drive. Unwillingly, she leaned against his strong frame. In any other circumstance, she would never sit so close to a stranger, let alone a married man. Still, she had no strength to move. Her body was exhausted and numb from the water that had long soaked through her clothes.

Lightning struck close by, splitting a tree. Travis jerked the steering wheel dodging the falling trunk. Bronwyn would have screamed if she had the air in her lungs to do so. She'd never witnessed a storm of this magnitude, let alone been caught in one. It was intense, yet for some strange reason, she felt no fear. Maybe she was too tired to panic, or maybe, it was being in the company of this mysterious mountain man, who plucked her body from the swirling waters of death and carried her to safety.

He turned onto a narrow gravel road that disappeared behind a line of thick trees. The storm denied any visibility, and the headlights barely offered any guidance. Travis drove off feel, off knowledge of the terrain, until reaching his destination.

He pulled into the driveway of a small rustic cabin. As the truck rolled to a stop, a warning siren blared, competing with exploding thunder. They ran for the cabin dodging flying debris.

Travis pushed open the door, the wind almost ripping it from its hinges. Wasting no time, he bolted across the room, slung aside a heavy rug, and opened a trap door lying flat into the floor. The opening gave way to a descending wooden staircase. Knowing her inability to maneuver the narrow stairs, he scooped her into his arms, and descended quickly. Reaching the bottom, he gently deposited her on a soft leather sofa. He climbed back up the stairs and secured the door before turning on a small lamp, revealing a warm, cozy room. With the glow of the light, she found she was able to focus and see clearly.

The well-furnished basement room seemed stocked for such an occasion. Besides the leather sofa, she was soaking with her drenched clothes, there was an overstuffed armchair and a couple of end tables. Thick, warm rugs covered a wooden floor. A fireplace took over one wall and a small kitchenette the other. A restroom complete with a shower lay at the far end of the basement. She shivered, wrapping her arms around herself to keep warm; as well as trying to stop her excessive trembling.

Travis noticed her shiver. "I can build a fire."

"It's okay." Her teeth chattered out the words. "I'm not sure if I'm cold, or just traumatized."

Opening a large cedar chest, Travis removed several pieces of clothing, along with several soft, warm blankets. He handed Bronwyn a t-shirt and a blanket and then pointed to the restroom.

"You should get out of your wet clothes."

She took the offered items and gratefully disappeared into the restroom. Closing the door behind her, she flipped on the light and gasped at her reflection in the mirror. Blood poured from a gash above her right eye; reminding her of the bouncing canoe ramming into her head. Seeing the wound caused her to feel an intense burning pain, making her feel weak and queasy. She continued to stare at her frightening reflection. Her hair hung in wet tatters, and any makeup she had been wearing was gone. Mascara pooled and lingered around her eyes, creating a smoky sensuous look she usually wore only for a night out on the town. Combined with her pale face, the blood, made her appear somewhat gothic and frightening.

She continued to tremble as she slowly peeled the wet, muddy clothes from her body. Grabbing a washcloth, she cleaned the mud from her skin then dried off with a towel she retrieved from a brass towel rack. Once dry, she pulled the t-shirt over her head, careful not to get blood on the white fabric. The borrowed shirt was soft, with a comforting, musky smell. Placing her wet clothes over the shower railing to dry, she wrapped the warm blanket around her and left the restroom.

Travis had also changed out of his wet clothes and removed the water from the sofa, giving Bronwyn a dry place to rest. With a fluffy pillow and more blankets he transformed the sofa into a nice, warm bed. A small fire burned in the fireplace. Travis sat on the large raised hearth with a small black leather case beside him.

The cabin creaked and moaned and even though they were several feet below the ground, she could still hear the storm raging outside.

Travis motioned for her to come join him at the fireplace. She approached the large stone hearth and sat down. He opened up the small leather case removing its contents of gauze, various ointments, and medical tape. Picking up a warm cloth, he dabbed at the blood on her face, gently cleaning around her wound. He leaned in to inspect her injury putting his face very close to hers. She was at a loss on where to focus her eyes. She desired to look at him, but feared an immediate attraction if she did. She had to admit that Bethany's observation of the man was quite accurate. He was extremely handsome, his body fit, hard, and muscular. He was the epitome of health and his silent demeanor added to his mysteriousness.

"You're trembling," he said quietly. "Are you sure you're alright?"

"Just a bit unnerved," she heard herself admit. "I thought I was dying."

"You were."

His words sunk deep into her soul. She realized the severity of the situation. She had nearly drowned. She remembered the blinding light seconds before she sank beneath the cold, black darkness, and the sudden sensation of rain pounding on her face once again. This stranger whom she had known less than twenty-four hours had risked the dangers of the storm to save her.

"Why?" Her thought became audible.

"Why, what?" He asked, as he opened a bottle of ointment.

"Why did you come looking for me?"

He dipped a q-tip in the ointment and dabbed it on the wound.

"You were born to live, not to die." He closed the ointment jar.

She smiled and inhaled the ointment. "That smells very nice."

He folded a piece of gauze and then tore off a couple of pieces of medical tape.

"It's lavadin. A hybrid plant developed by crossing true lavender with spike lavender."

He secured the gauze with one final piece of tape.

"It's used for sterilizing. It's also known for its relaxing and calming effects."

She smiled. Leave it to this mountain man to doctor her up with some Native American plant poultice.

He replaced the contents inside the leather case.

"You should lie down and rest," he said, motioning to the bed he made a-top the sofa.

She was thankful for the suggestion. Her entire body ached. She curled up on the smooth soft blankets and leaned against the comfortable pillows. As he walked past the sofa, to return the leather case to the cabinet, she spontaneously reached for his hand, stopping him.

"Thank you for saving me."

Travis looked at her hand lying across his wrist and then into her eyes.

"It was my pleasure."

CHAPTER SIXTEEN

Mavis hobbled down the halls of the inn, knocking on the bedroom doors and yelling over the warning sirens.

"That siren means we go underground! Everyone to the basement -- now!"

The doors to the rooms immediately burst open, each member of the troupe hurrying out, anxiously running down the staircase. Lillian bolted for the door, wide-eyed, but Bethany remained in the room. She pulled back the curtains from the window in a feeble attempt to peer outside. She hoped to see a returning Travis and Bronwyn. The sky was very dark and the window was fogged over and wet. The only thing visible was the outline of trees and the gardens that flashed into view each time the lightening zipped across the sky.

"Come on hon, let's get to movin." Mavis' voice carried across the room. Bethany knew she was right. She should be running for the safety of the basement along with everyone else. She felt so guilty taking shelter when her best friend was unaccounted for and possibly out in this horrific storm.

Mavis walked up behind her. "She's a smart girl. I'm sure she's found shelter somewhere, and you'd be best to do the same."

Hoping Mavis was right, Bethany let the curtain fall back in place and headed downstairs.

The inn's basement proved to be the most convenient place to ride out a storm. The room was designed for such an occasion. Barrack-style bunk beds lined the walls. There were enough beds for Travis, Mavis and the kids, plus eight guests. There were two fully equipped restrooms with showers and tubs and a good sized kitchen stocked with plenty of comfort food and drinks. Sofas and chairs provided rest, while bookcases filled with magazines, books and various board games offered entertainment. There was also a large cabinet filled with first aid supplies, lanterns, kerosene and matches.

Lillian was once again in tears, complaining terribly of the health and aging affects all the recent stress was taking on her body. Trent sat next to Bethany on the sofa and placed a sympathetic hand on her knee, patting it in reassurance. The wind howled overhead as the siren continued to blast. The inn creaked and moaned in protest to the abusive wind. Thunder resounded with a deafening crash.

"Are we going to be alright?" Lillian asked, her voice quivering.

"You're in the safest place you can be," Mavis said.

"I pray Bronwyn is someplace just as safe," Anna said hopefully. "And your dear Travis, God protect him as well!"

Mavis smiled gratefully.

"I feel so bloody guilty," Trent confessed. "If I had never criticized her writing, Bronwyn wouldn't have gone off alone. I fear it's all my fault."

"No, it's mine," Bethany took the blame. "I should have gone after her."
"Then you both would be out in this," Anna said.

"Or, we both would be here." Bethany's voice faded into her sadness.

A sudden explosion of thunder interrupted their conversation rocking the foundation of the inn. The electricity went out, casting the basement in total darkness. Even Karley reacted in a frightful scream.

"Shit!" She instantly apologized for her poor choice of words in front of the kids.

"No need for panic," Mavis's calm voice seemed to swallow the darkness. "We just lost the power is all. I'll light up a lantern."

The sound of a striking match penetrated the eeriness of the room as Mavis turned up the wick, giving light to the basement once again.

CHAPTER SEVENTEEN

Travis lit the lantern and turned up the wick. The kerosene lamp gave a bit more light to the basement than the small crackling fire could provide. The storm continued its relentless rampage outside, yet beneath ground level in the shelter of the cabin basement, and in the company and protective care of Travis, Bronwyn began to relax. He had given her a steaming cup of herbal tea and a bowl of piping hot soup. She only sipped at the both, still a bit nauseous, feeling full of lake water. Settling down on the floor, Travis leaned against the overstuffed armchair, facing the sofa. He took a swallow of his tea.

"What do you write about?"

His inquiry surprised her. That was the question of the century. This same question taunted her thoughts day after day. She knew the correct answer. In fact, there were actually two answers. The first was her default answer; the one that defined her "job" as a writer, the one that paid the bills and provided her a living. The other answer continually haunted her soul. She desired to write the story, she knew lay buried deep within her. It was a story that would make a difference, inspire and influence people for the good. Yet every attempt proved a disaster. Rejection after rejection of her work chipped away at her belief in herself as a writer. She rarely answered the question with the latter response.

"I haven't written much of anything lately," she sighed. "Just the sappy love stories the troupe performs."

"Writers block?"

"To the 'enth degree."

He set his mug of tea on the floor and gave her his full attention.

"What do you want to write about?"

Her heart skipped a few beats. No one had cared enough to ask that question. She'd desired to answer it for so long. Yet, this stranger, whom she had known less than twenty-four hours, this man who had just saved her from drowning was now asking.

She pulled the soft blanket closer around her.

"I want to write life-changing stories where everyday people survive and thrive in the most challenging of circumstances. I want to write of people who aren't controlled by their fear, but know that no matter how difficult or challenging their circumstances, no matter how impossible they may seem, the more amazing their victories will be. I want to write about people who overcome despite their oppression. You know, like legendary heroes that will inspire people, no matter their race, nationality, or social class. Inspiring stories that will cross the world and beyond. I want the words I write to be like the lyrics and melody of a much loved song evoking sentiment, allowing people to realize that there are better things to live for. I have no desire to write simply for entertainment anymore. I want my stories to be life changing and live on in the imaginations and hearts of people forever."

There, she had said it. The words had poured from her heart and through her lips, more easily than she'd thought. He hadn't laughed, either. He didn't whistle and say, "Big order;" he didn't even look amused.

"So what's stopping you?"

She sipped her tea and let his question settle.

"I don't want to be hypocritical. I have a hard time writing about something I am not sure is there. I'm not certain those kind of people really exist. Not in the real world, anyway. In the real world, Sam would have betrayed Frodo and taken the ring for himself. In the real world Jack would have hopped on the last life boat and let Rose drown."

As the words left her lips, she felt a tinge of regret for what she had said. How thoughtless could she be? He had just risked his life to save hers. He was a true hero and she had just ignored that fact.

"Anyway," she continued, hoping he had not taken offense. "I'm not even sure I can create amazing characters with these virtuous attributes if I am not sure I possess them myself."

"They are there. It's what gives your heart flight. It's those attributes that inspire you."

A loud roll of thunder followed his last words. She shivered and pulled the blanket even closer.

"You're trembling again."

He added another log to the fire. She shook from the inside out and no added log or raging fire could warm the chill she felt inside. She was not sure why she trembled so. The raging storm outside offered no threat to her, now that she was safe underground. She wasn't cold; the sofa and blankets offered a warm and comfortable cocoon of safety. Still, her body shivered. Travis certainly put her at ease. He was a kind and caring person, providing her with all the comforts she needed. Still she trembled. That in itself frightened her. She reasoned that perhaps it could be some sort of post traumatic reaction due to her near-death experience. However, deep inside, she was conscious of a growing fear, a premonition of something that must happen. She could not understand it. She could only sense it, but whatever the reason may be, she continued to shiver.

With each passing hour, the storm continued to build intensity. It was sometime past midnight, and she conceded to the fact that there would be no returning to the inn; at least not tonight.

She and Travis talked non-stop for the past several hours. She unfolded the entire saga of her and Ryan, from the moment they met, right up to the end and his heart breaking e-mail. Travis was an excellent listener, never moving his eyes or attention away from her as she spoke. Sometimes, she would be the one to look away, especially when she was confessing an intimate part of her story that left her feeling a bit vulnerable. She would glance at her hands, or find an interesting piece of lint on the blanket to pick, or stare into the flickering flame of the lantern. Whenever she returned her eyes back to Travis, she found him in rapt attention, his focus unwavering. He continued to look right into her eyes. Before realizing it, she'd poured out the entire story of her brief pregnancy and miscarriage, and the decision not to inform Ryan she was carrying his baby, after he had so coldly broke off their relationship. She told him of her fear in deciding to raise the child alone, and then the devastation of losing the baby after finally accepting the situation. The past several months had indeed, she said, been a roller coaster of emotion.

The fire in the fireplace burned down to a pile of glowing embers. The wick in the lantern now burning low, the light in the room was equivalent to the small flame of a lone candle.

"I've never told anyone that story. Not my mother, not Bethany, no one." Her confession was almost inaudible.

"Why do you choose to bear your burdens alone?"

"I choose to be strong." Her voice grew louder. "It's a hard place to be though; when you're strong you tend to be alone."

"Is it strength or is it pride?"

His accusing question took her off guard.

"Pride secludes itself because it won't ask for help." He explained. "Prideful people will not allow themselves to be vulnerable, nor will they let anyone know they're hurting. They're lonely because they refuse help. They want everyone to think they have it all under control."

"Sometimes you do have to have it all under control, if only to save yourself the pain and disappointment of depending on someone who will only let you down," Her words tinged with bitterness.

It had been a long day. With the light diminishing and the storm passing, her eyes grew heavy.

"So tell me about Travis," she asked sleepily.

He gave a slight smile.

"Not much to tell."

"I wouldn't say that. I think you're somewhat intriguing."

He offered another small smile. "Why is that?"

"Maybe because you're a man of few words, but when you do speak what you say is pretty profound. Maybe because you risked the storm and pulled me out of the water. Maybe because I can see things hidden behind your eyes."

Her last words roused his curiosity.

"What do you see?"

She took pride in her ability at reading people. She focused straight into his dark eyes, peering through his hair. It only took a few minutes before the words began spilling from her mouth.

"I see much wisdom, extreme integrity…" She smiled, choosing her words carefully…"mingled with a bit of mischief." Her voice grew soft. "I sense many deep secrets, and sorrow. There is an amazing amount of sorrow."

His demeanor changed; her words catching him off guard. His face grew serious; his dark eyes connected to hers looking deep into her soul. She felt hypnotized by his stare. Her head became dizzy as the strange heat sensation began again. Although resting and laying still, her heart began to beat as if she had just exuded extreme effort of some kind, and she wondered if he noticed, or if he himself was feeling the same rush of heat. Their eyes stayed locked for only a few seconds before a sudden clap of thunder startled her, breaking her gaze, though it seemed much longer to her. She was certain that they had not shared a romantic moment. True, she was growing very attracted to him, but there was so much more to the moment than romance. It was if their souls connected somewhere far from the dimly lit basement.

The cabin was dark now, save for a few glowing embers from the fire. Travis was fully reclining on his back; his head propped on his arms, his eyes fixed on the ceiling. Bronwyn lay on the couch and listened to the steady rain falling outside.

"Tell me about Mavis," she said quietly.

She had wanted to ask Travis that question for the past several hours, but for some reason could not drum up the courage. Now that they were in total darkness, it seemed easier to ask.

"What do you want to know?"

"How long have you two known each other?"

"Pretty much our whole lives."

"Really? Did you always like her?"

"No," He was matter of fact. "She was really quite a tease when she was younger."

Although she laughed, she remained somewhat cautious. "What happened to her?"

Travis took a minute before he spoke and as much as she wanted the answer, a part of her wished she had never asked the question.

"She was badly injured in a storm somewhat like this one. She didn't take cover soon enough."

"Do you love her?" She surprised herself by asking.

"Yes, I do."

There was silence, except for the popping and crackling of a few dying embers. She closed her eyes and began to doze off.

"You're a good man Asa," she said, yawning, drifting off to sleep.

Travis lay there a little while longer, his heart pounding with intensity while he stared at the ceiling. No one had called him by the name of Asa for quite some time.

CHAPTER EIGHTEEN

Smoking man tossed aside the drenched cloak and made his way to the sink. He pushed the lever on the bottle pumping out several squirts of creamy soap, and then scrubbed the blood from his hands. He grabbed a cloth from the cabinet and cleaned away the splatters that had sprayed onto his face. Leaning into the mirror, he examined the scar crudely cut beneath his left eye. It was his identity, his story, his proof of loyalty to those who might mistake his allegiance. He knew some of them doubted, but he didn't care. He knew where his faithfulness lie; he wouldn't waste time trying to prove it to those critiques that constantly made assumptions about his motives. Besides, who were they to pass judgment? He was angry at them for loosing track of her whereabouts earlier. How could she have slipped past them so easily? He had kept her in sight from the moment she stepped off her bus, following her as she walked into town, even watching the troupe at the restaurant until he was summoned to a secret council. He didn't think twice about leaving since the entire town was watching the group and would let him know if anything unexpected transpired. During the council meeting, the spies burst inside, notifying him of new trespassers. He summoned his men and headed back into the woods; all the while expecting her to be closely watched.

The executions didn't take long. The men Abaddon was sending over were predictable which made him believe he was training them himself. Knowing Abaddon as well as he did worked to his advantage, allowing him to calculate the men's moves with ease. After a quick kill he grouped the slain bodies together and wrote a single word across their foreheads before sending them back. A wicked grin spread across his face as he imagined the fury that would rise in Abaddon once he read the message.

He'd been warned not to live for revenge; nor, let the bitterness poison him, but for six-hundred years he had concentrated on nothing else but training for the day of promised retribution. He did consider his role in the matter vengeance and rightly so. He wasn't merely trying to get even with the one, who wronged him, but he considered himself a warrior, and the way he saw it, warriors always ran into battle, fighting for a worthy and noble cause. This he would do. He would fight to set things right again no matter how many he must kill in the process. Even if the quest demanded his own life, he was ready to give it. Some said he was obsessed, and that his obsession over the matter had driven him insane, making him quite dangerous. He agreed in a way, there was a madness inside of him, pushing him, driving him, and since he was at a loss as to how to control it, he allowed it to control him.

He moved away from the mirror, ran his hands through his hair and secured it back in a ponytail before changing out of his clothes. Once dry, he lit up a cigarette, took a seat against the far back wall, placed his dagger across his leg, and took a long draw off the cigarette. He looked into the dark room. He would stay here the remainder of the night, riding out the storm. It was exactly where he should be, seeing the lady scribe was below in the basement with Travis.

CHAPTER NINETEEN

DAY TWO

Bronwyn opened her eyes and looked around, confused as to her whereabouts. Within a few seconds her ordeal at the lake flooded her memory, leading to why she was alone in a dimly lit basement.

She raised her sore body to a sitting position and looked around the room. Travis was gone. With no windows or outdoor light of any kind, there was no way to tell what time it was, or if the weather had improved.

Pulling the blanket away, she climbed off the couch, her muscles protesting with every move. She decided to climb the cellar stairs and see what was waiting at the top. Realizing she was still wearing only a t-shirt, she entered the restroom to retrieve her clothes instead.

An audible groan escaped her mouth as she glanced at her reflection. Her bandage was still in place, but blood was visible on the outside of the gauze. There was quite a bit of swelling and discoloration around her eye. Her hair was a bushy mess with bits of leaves and grass tangled into the snarls. She laughed at the thought of what Lillian would say if she saw her, and for the first time, she wondered what her friends might be going through, not knowing where she was, or what had happened to her. For that matter, she wasn't sure how her friends had fared during the storm. Travis told her he dropped them all off safely at the inn, reassuring her that the inn had a protective shelter as well. He also told her Mavis would make sure they were all there and accounted for.

She reached for her clothes, only to discover they were still soaked. She shivered at the thought of putting them back on, so she left them in the bathroom and retrieved the soft blanket, wrapping it around her to hide her long naked legs. She climbed the stairs, opened the trap door, and climbed up into the main room.

She and Travis ran through the cabin so quickly last night, that she had not been able to see anything. With sunlight streaming through the windows, the rustic cabin came alive with personality. Deep brown leather furniture offered comfortable sitting. A massive stone fireplace covered an entire wall; oddly enough, there were no animal heads of any kind hanging over the mantle. Beautiful oil paintings of breathtaking scenery adorned every wall. She walked around the inviting room. An antique desk sat in the far corner, holding a computer along with several potted plants. Noticing that the front door was slightly ajar, she pushed it open and stepped onto the large porch that wrapped around the small cabin.

The fresh midmorning breeze swept across the lake and rushed upon the porch, gently kissing her on the face. She inhaled, taking in a deep breath of the invigorating air. Never before had she been more thankful for a new day. The birds sang their glorious songs as they flew across the cloudless powder blue sky. All the pleasing scents and smells perfumed the day, as if the storm had never hit. Yet, the storm had indeed left its calling card. Broken branches and limbs had been ripped from their trunks and tossed about, littering the grounds. Debris floated in the lake, yards from the front door.

Bronwyn spotted Travis clearing away the fallen timber and placing it into a large pile. She wondered if this was an every morning event for him. She watched him work, unnoticed. Again he was shirtless, his hair hanging in tatters over his face, already wet with perspiration. If only Bethany could see him now. A slight smile curled on her lips. Travis hurled another broken branch into a pile of debris. She found herself envying Mavis. She was fortunate to have him. He had risked his own life in a storm to save a stranger; then had been so kind and caring, providing for her every comfort. He had remained a gentleman and kept his distance, sitting across the floor from her patiently, listening to all the ramblings that poured from her mouth. Not once did he turn the conversation to himself. That was unusual in the company she kept. Her friends and acquaintances continually bragged about their income, their cars, their strengths and talents, or how many people they had slept with. Not Travis.

Bronwyn begin to feel a tinge of guilt. She knew he was married, yet she could not deny the feelings manifesting inside her. She remembered breakfast, just the day before, avoiding conversation with him at all cost. Now, part of her wished the storm was still raging so they would be forced to spend more time together. But that was not the case. The sun was out and burning with intensity. She watched him hurl another branch into his growing pile of debris.

"Need some help?"

Her words drew his attention from his task onto the porch.

"You're not dressed for it."

She shrugged and smiled. "My clothes are still wet."

He removed his work gloves and headed for the front porch; while looking at the bandage over her eye.

"I need to change that."

He entered the cabin.

She didn't follow. Instead, she sat on the porch swing, pushing off with her feet, gently swinging back and forth. The scenery was breathtaking. The cabin faced one of the lake's many hidden coves. A small wooden dock stretched out over the water. Tree-covered hills encircled the area, giving it a secluded privacy. The landscaping around the cabin was much like that of the inn, with varieties of flowering plants, vines and trees all emitting delightful aromas. Bronwyn thought that someone must take special care of these grounds and for the first time, she wondered about the owner of this small cabin. Who was it? She hadn't thought of that until now.

Travis returned to the porch with the black leather case. He sat on the swing next to her and carefully removed the bandage. His hands gently swept back the hair falling across her face as he tenderly removed some of the leaves entangling themselves in her messy locks. He caught her eye and smiled.

Her throat tightened. She wasn't sure where to fix her eyes. She gazed downward at his chest and noticed he wore a white stone pendant that hung from a silver chain around his neck. Deciding that staring at his chest was probably not the best place to fix her eyes, she shut them.

After removing the leaves, he began to gently clean the dried blood from around the wound.

"So," she said, trying to diffuse the awkwardness. "Whose cabin is this?"

"Mine," he reapplied the ointment.

She opened her eyes, surprised.

"Yours? I thought you lived at the inn."

"I do."

"Oh," she closed her eyes again before trying a little humor. "So is this your vacation spot?"

He un-wrapped a new bandage, and placed it on her wound.

"Thinking spot."

"Everyone needs one of those." She kept her eyes closed.

He surveyed his work for a minute, studying her face much more than the bandage.

"Beautiful," he said.

CHAPTER TWENTY

Mavis hummed a mellow tune as she cracked open an egg, allowing the gooey substance to drop into the cast iron frying pan. The egg bubbled and sizzled immediately. She had risen early, leaving the confines of the basement for the kitchen, figuring her guests would be extremely hungry since the rush to safety had cost them their dinner. They had spent the entire night riding out the storm underground, snacking on popcorn, peanuts, crackers and cookies.

The storm had been unusually severe; much like the one that hit the night before. It certainly wasn't one of those typical, relaxing thunderstorms that usually visited the mountains during mid-summer. Mavis was a bold spirited woman but she feared these storms, feeling they had a distinct disposition, taking personal vengeance on someone or something. They arrived angry, sweeping through Moonshine like ghostly soldiers, riding their stallions, trampling anything and everyone in their path, looking for someone to kill. She hated them.

Continuing her soft humming, she hobbled over to the table, carrying a pitcher of fresh squeezed juice. Her guests trickled into the area, much quieter. She knew why. One of theirs was unaccounted for.

Bethany awoke and sat up fast, nearly bumping her head on the bunk directly above her. Looking around the basement, she noticed everyone was gone. Bronwyn! Perhaps she had returned, and everyone was upstairs, listening to the story of her adventure. She jumped from bed and dashed upstairs. Bursting into the kitchen, she eyed everyone at the table... everyone but Bronwyn. Her heart sank. Lillian caught her eye and shook her head sadly. Mavis continued to hum as she removed a pan of hot biscuits from the oven.

"Did Travis come back last night?" Bethany asked.

"No honey, he didn't." Mavis dropped the hot biscuits in a cloth basket.

Bethany sighed, disappointed.

"Did he call?"

"Phones are down again hon." Mavis took the basket to the table.

"Would you like a plate, dear?"

"No! This is crazy. I can't eat...how can any of you? Bronwyn's been missing for almost twenty-four hours. She could be...."

Bethany stopped herself, not allowing the words to be spoken.

"Hon there's no need to get yourself all worked up." Mavis' words were soothing, consoling. "I'm sure she's fine, I'm sure they're both fine. The people in this town all look out for each other. If something had happened, there'd been someone on my porch early this morning to let me know." She said these things to comfort herself, as well as Bethany. "In my experience, no news is good news."

Bethany wanted to believe her, but for some reason, her distrust suddenly grew towards these curious mountain people. Travis' deep concern for Bronwyn's whereabouts unnerved her. He was more than eager to go searching for her and refused to allow her to accompany him. She had noticed Travis intently watching Bronwyn more than once since their arrival. She neglected to mention it, not wanting to alarm her friend, seeing Bronwyn had been going through enough lately. She remembered Bronwyn's paranoid outburst at lunch yesterday saying she saw someone following her. Maybe she was right; maybe they all overlooked it, believing Trent's diagnosis of the progressions of a broken heart. A sick feeling hit her stomach and she debated whether she should search for Bronwyn herself. She was certain Bronwyn would do the same for her. However, if Travis was some sort of serial killer, she would be walking right into her own death, let alone ever finding Bronwyn. In any case, the attempt would be futile. As soon as they were able to leave this place, she would alert the authorities, and if need be, drag the FBI up here herself and search every inch of this place with a fine-toothed comb.

The lazy squeak of the screen door interrupted her cascading thoughts.

Everyone in the kitchen let out collective gasps at the sight of Bronwyn and Travis. The quietness of the morning erupted into laughter, applause, a loud "Hallelujah!" from Mavis, and delighted screams from the kids as they ran to hug Travis.

An endless barrage of questions erupted from everyone's mouth at once. Trent's voice overpowered them all.

"My God, I'm glad you're alright. I don't think I could have lived with the guilt."

"What happened to you?" Lillian gasped. "You look absolutely horrid!"

"Are you okay, honey?" Anna asked.

Marcus hugged her lovingly. "You sure gave us all quite a scare."

"Girl, where were you all night? And where are your clothes?" Karley asked, rather loudly.

Bethany stood frozen across the room, arms folded in front of her, relieved, yet angry. At least there would be no need to call the FBI.

"I'm in desperate need of a nice, long shower," Bronwyn said, attempting to escape the onslaught of questions.

"Like hell you are!" Karley said. "You stay out all night long, come walking through the door without your clothes, wearing nothing but a man's t-shirt, trying to hide your nakedness with a blanket. You owe us an explanation and it better be good!"

"Karley!" Anna reprimanded out of concern for Mavis, who had returned to the stove and continued to cook, her humming much livelier now.

"I went canoeing on the lake after I left the café. I fell asleep and didn't make it back to shore before the storm hit. My canoe capsized hit me in the head and knocked me out." Bronwyn pointed to her bandage.

"Travis found me just in time and pulled me from the water. The sirens went off, so we rode out the storm in town."

Daniel shook his head. "Man that's intense."

"Head injuries aren't something to fool around with," Walt said. "When I fell head first ten floors of that building…"

Marcus turned to Travis, "On behalf of all of us, thank you for saving our Bronwyn."

"My pleasure," Travis said, his eyes smiling at her. He crossed over to the stove and gave Mavis a quick kiss on her cheek before leaving the kitchen. Bronwyn felt a bit of sadness as she watched him leave. Feeling such a strong connection to him, she found herself wondering when she would have another opportunity to be near him. Quickly she reprimanded herself. He was a married man, definitely off limits.

"Save you a plate hon?" Mavis asked. "Why don't you go take yourself a nice long bath. "I'll keep a plate hot for you."

She felt even guiltier. Mavis was so kind, offering her a warm breakfast, even after she'd been the cause of her husband risking his life in the terrible storm. Now she felt extremely selfish. Her stubbornness, anger and refusal to take constructive criticism nearly cost her and another innocent person their lives.

She looked into the faces of the people surrounding her. These were her friends, her family. Even Wilbur had left the table and his plate of food to greet her. She was thankful. She smiled and headed upstairs.

Nearly forty-five minutes later, Bronwyn reluctantly pulled herself out of the water. She had drawn herself a very hot bath, adding in several of the elixirs from the welcome basket. Whatever these potions were, they brought complete relaxing comfort to her tired, aching muscles.

She toweled off and dressed in a clean pair of comfortable sweats and a tank. She was grateful to Bethany and Lillian for bringing her luggage back from the bus. Hanging her towel on the rack, she looked back into the draining tub at all the dirt. She pitied the maid who would clean this mess. Realizing it would more than likely be Mavis, she made a mental note to retrieve some cleaning equipment and do it herself.

Opening the door to the bathroom, she was surprised to see Bethany sprawled across the bed.

"Spill it sister!"

"Spill what?" Bronwyn chose to be evasive. "I told everyone downstairs what happened."

"First of all, I am not everyone; I am your best friend. I get more than what you tell everyone. I get the uncut, uncensored version."

Bronwyn began combing the knots from her freshly washed hair.

"There is no uncensored version."

"Oh yes there is!" Bethany's tone was a bit harsh, accusing. "I can see loads behind that smile you're attempting to suppress."

This time, Bronwyn was actually pleased with Bethany's relentless prodding. She did feel a need to share her experience. It had been one of the most surreal, awkwardly romantic evenings of her life. She reasoned that if she talked things through, the feelings of a juvenile crush would subside.

She sat next to Bethany on the bed. "Alright, there is a bit more. But I'm a bit ashamed to admit it."

"I knew it the moment you came in the kitchen door! Did you have sex with him?"

"Sh-sh-sh!" Bronwyn glanced over her shoulder, making sure the door was closed.

"No, I didn't have sex with him! Good lord, Beth, he's a married man. We didn't even come close to that."

"Then why the guilt?"

Bronwyn sighed. "Because I do have a slight, and I mean ever so slight, attraction to him now."

"That's totally normal. It's some sort of damsel-in-distress syndrome. He gallantly rescued you, saved your life, and obviously doctored you up a bit. It's totally expected for you to feel a closeness to him. Plus, it doesn't help that he is extremely handsome with a killer body."

Bronwyn smiled. "It's not just his looks. We talked a lot last night, or at least I did. You know how I spill my guts when I get nervous..."

"Oh, no."

"Oh, yes. I was terrified of the storm, the sirens freaked me out, I was traumatized from nearly drowning, not to mention extremely tense because we were alone in a dimly lit basement."

"What basement? Where were you?"

"His place. He has a nice cabin on the lake. He said it was his thinking spot."

A cynical smirk crossed Bethany's mouth. "More like his cheating spot."

"I don't know, Beth. He seems to have plenty of integrity if you ask me."

"All men cheat Bronwyn." Bethany's proclamation sounded bulletproof, certain.

Bronwyn frowned at her assumptions and for a moment regretted confiding in her. This was how it had been lately, and why she had refused to divulge her feelings. Bethany couldn't listen without offering advice or her own perspective on the issue.

"Well, he kept his distance last night."

"Of course he didn't try anything. You guys just met. But given time and the right circumstances he'll make his move. I saw the way he looked at you this morning." Bethany leaned back against the head board, confident of her analysis.

"So, what did you two talk about?"

"Like I said, I was pretty nervous so I did most of the talking. I literally spilled my guts."

"No wonder he didn't try anything, you were pathetic."

Bronwyn rolled her eyes, and then thought a moment.

"He was a good listener. He seemed genuinely interested in what I was saying. I told him all about Ryan and our break up."

She stopped cold. She'd never confided to Bethany about her pregnancy and the lost child. If Bethany knew she had revealed this information to Travis and not her, she would be extremely hurt. Still, some things were easier to tell a stranger than a friend. She held the secret inside for almost six months, telling no one, not even Ryan. It had been quite therapeutic just to talk about it and get the emotion off her chest. She moved onward.

"I told him about the screenplay we wrote, and how Ryan and his attorneys are harassing me to sign my rights over, so he can make the movie with Gabriella. I told him about my severe writer's block. He asked me a few questions and then deduced that I was cynical and a bit prideful."

Bethany grinned.

"And you let him get away with that?"

"Well it was storming outside. I couldn't just march away angry again, seeing that's what got me in my situation in the first place." She felt a little sheepish in her admission. "I sort of had to stay and take it. I kind of liked it, though. When he was talking to me, it felt as if he were looking into my soul."

"I knew it! He got in!"

Bronwyn grinned slightly. "How so?"

Bethany sighed and grabbed Bronwyn's hand.

"Because my dear naïve friend, the eyes are the window to the soul. If he got the chance to stare into your eyes long enough to see into your soul, then that means you two were entranced with each other and that you connected on a whole different level. This means you also got into each other's heads and hearts, for that matter. Pretty dangerous, if you ask me. You're playing with fire there."

Bronwyn didn't want to admit it but Bethany's evaluation was somehow impressive.

"There was this one moment…"

Bethany leaned in closer, eager to hear.

"…when I was describing to him what kind of person I read him to be. It was like I nailed it. Like I knew him, even though I didn't know him. Make sense?"

Bethany nodded, wide-eyed.

"Our eyes just locked in on each other. I don't think either one of us could actually pull away."

"I knew it!" Bethany said, nearly jumping off the bed. "So what happened next?"

"It thundered really loud, I jumped, and the moment was lost."

"Be careful Bronwyn." Bethany warned. "It won't be long now before he makes his move."

Bronwyn shook her head. "You're wrong. He loves Mavis. He told me so."

"I'm sure he does," Bethany said dryly. "All men love their wives, but given the right situation, they all cheat. Be careful, my friend. I don't trust him."

Bronwyn shrugged.

"Well I do."

She made her way back into the bathroom and continued combing out her very tangled hair.

Bronwyn didn't realize how late she slept in that morning. By the time Travis drove her back to the inn, and she cleaned up and endured Bethany's interrogation, most of the morning had passed. Now it was well into the afternoon, clean and in fresh clothes, she decided to explore the grounds of the inn.

A beautiful stone driveway led up to the main entrance. A large porch surrounded the entire inn, offering cushioned rocking chairs, comfortable swings, and a breathtaking view on all sides. The front of the inn was well landscaped, with cottonwood, dogwoods, and magnolias lining the driveway, among others.

A peaceful river cut through the west side, with a wooden deck built over the waters. Large oak trees lined the banks; one offered a hefty branch with a thick rope to swing into the peaceful relaxing waters. Mammoth natural rocks lined the banks of the river, with a few covering the bottom, allowing the slow-moving river to wash gently over them.

The east side of the property was the site of a rather large garage that housed Travis' truck and Mavis' car. Sitting behind the garage were three similar sized buildings, each mimicking the Inn's outer décor.

Directly behind the inn, small cobblestone paths led to a variety of gardens each unique, each a particularly therapeutic destination unto itself. Bronwyn explored every one. A hedge or tall wooden fence surrounded all the gardens enclosing each one in privacy. She entered the first beneath an archway covered with hanging vines, and took in the sights and scents. Once again, the relaxing scent of lavender permeated the air. Numerous large trees offered ample shade and a comfortable hammock. She followed the path to the center, where an exquisite fountain stood. Water trickled from the top, flowing quietly into a pool-sized basin. A couple of bathing birds took flight. A small table and two rustic bamboo chairs sat nearby. A fresh linen table cloth covered the top, along with pitchers of iced water and lemonade. Empty glasses sat upside down on the table, awaiting their thirsty visitors. Mavis' many efforts to provide her guests as much comfort as possible really showed. Bronwyn desired to lay in one of the hammocks, sip icy lemonade, and wait for inspiration to strike. Nevertheless, she knew this was only the first garden; she desired to explore as many as possible before sundown.

All the paths she followed led to exquisite findings. Some gardens offered sweet floral scents; others offered earthy scents of pine spruce cedar, mint, and refreshing eucalyptus. Each carried some type of relaxing noise, whether the trickling sound of a waterfall or the melodious sounds of various wind chimes, playing their tune in the gentle breeze. A couple of gardens were home to beautiful natural ponds, complete with jumping fish, frogs sunning on lily pads, and an occasional lazy turtle sleeping on a rock.

She enjoyed every garden, not able to decide which her favorite was. Realizing she had walked at least three or four miles, she was surprised she didn't feel the least bit tired. Instead, she felt a renewed vigor with each garden she entered. Her tender muscles no longer ached; the warm sun caressed her like a gentle massage.

She approached the end of the cobblestone path and the last garden, surrounded by a towering wooden fence. It was also the only garden without a gate. Instead, a colossal wooden door barred the entrance. Into its center, the letters *BJC* were carved elaborately. There was a brass knob on the door with an old-fashioned key hole directly beneath it. She turned the brass knob. The door was locked, forbidding entrance to this secret garden. Stooping down she placed her eye over the small opening, and peaked inside. Rays from the setting sun broke through the many vines and ferns, shading a tiny moss path, disappearing into a grove of thick trees. Her sneak peek revealed nothing. Disappointed, she stood to leave but voices on the path motivated her to stay. Peering through the key-hole she noticed two figures come into view. Her throat tightened when she recognized one of them as the smoking man from the café. He was walking alongside Travis. The two were engaged in a conversation but she was too far away to hear anything they were saying. The men came closer then stopped on the path to finish their discussion before leaving the private garden. She strained her ear, trying to pick up a word or two. However, they spoke in hushed voices and in what seemed to be an unfamiliar language… perhaps a lost dialect used by the mountain people.

Her heart seized as the smoking man unexpectedly reached over and grabbed a black cloak clinging to a large rock. He put it on pulling the hood over his head. Her heart fell. Travis had lied to her. He did know of the cloaked figure! Her head began to swim. What was going on in this town? Why were they stalking her or better yet, what were they protecting? The smoking man swiftly disappeared into the trees and Travis walked toward the entrance.

Regaining her composure she quickly retreated, bolting down the path and entering into another garden so Travis would not catch her eavesdropping. She waited just inside the gate, her heart pounding. Hearing his footsteps, she held her breath until he passed, then, leaning her head outside the gate, she watched as he disappeared down the path towards the inn. She sighed but the anxiousness did not leave; and once again she feared for her safety as well as that of the entire troupe. Since Travis knew of the knife wielding cloaked man, was he an accomplice to his murderous intentions? She argued with her thoughts. She had an unexplainable trust for Travis. After all, he had risked his life to save hers, and had been more than a gentleman during the entire night. She had looked deep into his dark eyes and evil did not dwell there. Still, there was something secretive at play in this town and she thought it best to be on her guard.

The garden began to lose light as the sun sank lower in the evening sky. Mavis would be serving dinner soon; however, her appetite was gone. Realizing that Travis was more than likely at the inn by now, she ventured out of the garden, all the while unaware of the cloaked figure walking only a few feet behind her.

CHAPTER TWENTY-ONE

After a delicious evening meal, the troupe gathered in the inn's library for what Marcus considered a much needed rehearsal. As the largest room in the inn besides the kitchen, the library served as an ideal rehearsal area. Carla Jo and Molly had politely begged their way in, and were now sitting wide-eyed on the large leather sofa. The rest of the troupe grew comfortable on various pieces of furniture, waiting for their entrance to the makeshift stage in the center of the room. After their scenes, they exited back to their personal perches. The rehearsal found its audience with random giggles from the kids and an occasional sigh and burst of applause from a starry-eyed Carla Jo. Marcus occasionally stopped the rehearsal to suggest different blocking or to politely propose an alternative way to deliver a line.

Bronwyn sat on the edge of a small table, growing more bored as rehearsal continued. They had been performing this particular script most of the summer. Each time the production played out, she felt a sick feeling in the pit of her stomach. Trent was right; her story was shallow and hollow. This was not the kind of material she wanted to write. Other than the fact that the two children who sat on the sofa were totally enthralled by the whole of it, she felt ashamed and wished her name was not attached. However, she was relieved Travis had not come into the library to observe. Despite her new-found suspicious of him, he struck her as such a deep, insightful, man. She didn't want him thinking of her as shallow and trite because of the ridiculous story birthed from her pen. She hoped he would stay away from the library now that Lillian had taken the stage to unfold the worst part of the play.

Lillian gracefully stormed the stage, approaching Trent.

"Why me?" she demanded overdramatically. "You could have your choice of any woman. Why do you choose me? I need to know!"

"How can you ask me such a question? Look at you," Trent's stage voice rode on its gallantry.

Gently, he turned Lillian's face to an imaginary mirror.

"You see your reflection and still you ask?"

Lillian turned back to Trent.

"But one day, this reflection will be a small resemblance of what you see now. Time will take its vengeance and then what? Can you love what is left?"

Carla Jo moved to the edge of the sofa, eager to hear what the dashing Trent would say next.

"My love..."

Carla Jo's heart skipped a beat.

"Are you asking me if I love you only because of your beauty? I ask you, are you only beautiful to me because I love you?"

As Trent delivered his last line, he broke character by turning to Marcus with an exasperated expression. Raising his hand, Marcus stopped the rehearsal.

"Okay guys. That's where we lost our audience last performance."

"They bloody laughed!" Trent exploded. "Is it me? Am I saying it weird? Do I have a comical expression on my face?"

"No, you're wonderful!" The words exploded from Carla Jo's mouth, followed by an outburst of laughter from the troupe.

"Thank you, love."

Her face turned a crimson red.

"It's not you." Bronwyn said, diverting Carla Jo from her embarrassment.

"What are you trying to communicate here?" Marcus asked, approaching the subject delicately, not wanting to offend her again.

Bronwyn closed her eyes for a minute.

"I want to emphasize the point that beauty, true beauty is definitely in the eye of the beholder. She asks him if he would still love her if she wasn't beautiful, and he is attempting to let her know that no matter how she looks, she will always be beautiful to him *because* he loves her."

She paused a moment, her eyes still shut.

"His love for her only allows him to see her as beautiful."

She opened her eyes and turned to Marcus to see if there was a glimmer of understanding. Instead of seeing Marcus, her eyes fell on Travis, leaning on the back wall, arms folded across his chest. Her stomach churned, her pulse accelerated, and she felt her face burning possibly as red as Carla Jo's. How long had he been standing there? What had he heard?

Trent's next display of verbiage did not add comfort.

"It doesn't work Bronwyn, because Lillian is beautiful. Any man would love her. But if her character were flawed in some way, the dialogue would have more meaning."

Bronwyn desperately wanted to flaw Trent's appearance, yet she knew he was right.

"I'm sure make-up could take care of the problem." Karley's opinion sounded more like goading. "Maybe a prosthetic nose or chin, a fat suit or something."

"Or maybe instead of trying to make Lillian ugly, you could learn the lines and do the part yourself, Karley," Wilbur mumbled from one of the overstuffed chairs.

Marcus quickly jumped in derailing another onslaught of insults between the two.

"Can you fix it?"

Bronwyn wasn't sure she could fix it. Any other time, she would have answered with assurance. However, her inspiration for writing had abandoned her. She knew it would be difficult at best to fix the script. Nevertheless, she assured Marcus that she would work on a re-write.

Marcus promptly cancelled the remainder of rehearsal and Travis left the room.

She debated on whether or not to follow him. She was almost certain he could offer some profound insight on the subject. She gathered her script and headed for the door.

She had nearly reached the exit before Wilbur's gargling voice called her back.

"Before you go work on our much needed re-write, I'd like to have a word with you." His voice teemed with condescension.

She sighed, very loud, audible. The last thing she needed was a conversation with Wilbur Hogg.

"What's up Wilbur?"

"I'm glad to see you're doing better since the near-tragic events of last night. I trust Marcus asking for a re-write will not rekindle the anger from yesterday."

She wished Wilbur would cut the small talk and tell her what was on his mind.

"I'm over it."

Wilbur took a seat in a nearby chair. "The fact of the matter is you are a very gifted writer."

Her heart fell into the chair with Wilbur. If he was going to sit through this, it might take longer than she had anticipated. Longer than she wanted.

"I have always admired your work. We all are aware, however, that you are experiencing some sort of writers block, as well as a personal emotional struggle. I believe the best remedy for that is a little confidence booster and some friendly advice from the people who care about you."

She leaned her head against the wall, sighing. She was stuck with a lecture from a financial analyst who knew little about writing, let alone the subject of love. Wilbur removed a tube of Chap Stick from his pocket and smeared it over his plump lips.

"I'm referring to the screenplay you co-wrote with Ryan," he said.

"I don't want to talk about that."

"Now I am aware you do not wish to sign your rights over for personal reasons. But think of the notoriety if you did; the prestige it would offer our troupe. It would obviously be a blockbuster hit, with Ryan and Gabriella Mendez playing the leads."

At the mention of their names, Bronwyn bolted upright and headed for the door.

"I said I didn't want to discuss this!"

"There you go again, stomping off like a spoiled child, not willing to listen to any advice. Just like you did yesterday, when you nearly got yourself killed, not to mention someone else."

His harsh words stopped her in her tracks. Despite her anger at his interference, she had to admit he was right. She had developed a bad habit of walking away when she grew uncomfortable with a situation or conversation.

She turned back to Wilbur, who had hoisted his heavy body from the chair in an attempt to follow her.

"I'm listening." She said in a frosty voice.

"I care about you Bronwyn. And I certainly care about his troupe. The notoriety would be great for you, and us. Not to mention the money."

"So this is what this whole conversation is really about? Money? I should have known."

"Money is important. Not to mention necessary. Just think you could help us purchase a new bus, better equipment…in a sense you could own the troupe."

She sighed. "It's never been a dream of mine to own a traveling drama troupe, Hogg. There are just some things money can't buy. This whole thing is between Ryan and me. This isn't just a script. It's personal and represents our time together. That is something I cherish. I cannot and will not put a price tag on that."

"Well, he obviously isn't as sentimental about it as you are." His words stung. "I think you're jealous that he wants Gabriella Mendez to star in it instead of you. You're just being selfish in every way possible!"

Her heart ached at the mention of Ryan and Gabriella, a cruel combination of names that penetrated her heart like a knife.

She took a deep cleansing breath and glared at Wilbur.

"This is none of your business, Hogg. Never talk to me about it again."

She brushed past Wilbur and ascended the staircase to her room. Her heart was aching, her anger rising. She found Bethany and Lillian in the room dressed in shorts, t-shirts and tennis shoes.

"Hurry and change clothes," Bethany laced her shoe. "Travis is taking those of us who want to go on a moonlit hike to some waterfalls."

"He is?" Bronwyn's suspicion rose, remembering his private meeting with the smoking man. Perhaps they had been planning something devious that was soon to play out.

"I don't know. It's dark. Might be dangerous. Maybe we should stay here."

Bethany glanced up at Bronwyn, shocked.

"You're serious?"

"I'm just remembering the wild animals, you know, bears feed at night."

"Oh come on, please." Bethany gave a sarcastic laugh. "Travis wouldn't have asked us to come if he thought we would be bear food. Now hurry and put your swim suit on. It ought to be fun. He said the falls were breathtaking."

Bronwyn could not stop her heart from racing at the mention of his name. She scolded herself, reminding herself that he was married, not to mention the lack of trust she now held toward him.

The offer was inviting in spite of her suspicions. The thought of a night hike to the waterfalls seemed thrilling in itself. As a night owl, evening was her favorite, along with dusk. The heat of the day would lesson, the first star of the evening would appear, and the moon would enter the night sky in fullest brilliance. She loved the moon whether it was full or waning. There was always something peaceful about it, not to mention romantic... there she was again, obsessing on Travis.

Quickly changing her clothes, she joined Bethany and Lillian on the back porch, along with the others. Travis was leaning on the railing, an unwilling captive audience to Walt's legendary hospital story. Trent and Daniel were there, as well as an adventurous Karley, who said she was only going to scout out a secret place to dispose of Wilbur's body after she was done with him. Carla Jo also joined the group. Her presence eased Bronwyn's mind, dispelling any suspicion of malice. Surely Travis would not bring a child along on a night massacre. Anna, Marcus and Wilbur had decided to stay behind resting in the comforts of the inn, choosing to do their hiking in the light of day.

Travis turned his attention away from Walt's story, his eyes falling upon Bronwyn, a smile turning at the corner of his mouth.

"Let's go," he said.

"Shouldn't we take some flashlights?" Lillian asked concern in her voice.

"The moon is brilliant tonight," Travis said. "You won't need them."

He led the way, skirting past the west side of the inn towards the river, the others trailing him while laughing and talking. Carla Jo giggled thrilled to be coming along. They reached the river's edge, passing the small dock and grassy picnic area. Travis led them a bit further down the river bank then stepped onto a narrow path that disappeared into the thick woods bordering the property. The hikers were now forced to walk two by two down the dirt trail, with Bethany and Bronwyn bringing up the rear. Travis led. Carla Jo cozied up to Trent directly behind Travis, Walt and Karley paired up following Trent and Carla Jo. Daniel and Lillian fell in line next leaving Bethany and Bronwyn last. For some time, they wound in and out of the dense trees and down the sides of the river bank. The river snaked deep inside the forest. At times, the path would be blanketed in total darkness, as the light from the moon was unable to penetrate through the thick foliage of the trees. The darkness became so thick that at times, the hikers could actually feel it. Bronwyn placed her hand in front of her face. It was barely visible.

"This is why I wanted to bring a flashlight," Lillian said, her nervous voice ringing out. The pace slowed as each person's confidence diminished. Within seconds, the path wound into a partial clearing, moonlight flooding the area. Each time, the light appeared more splendid in contrast to the utter darkness that preceded it. Sighs and gleeful laughter often escaped the hiker's mouths, only to be silenced by the path, as it again wound into total darkness. This pattern continued for most of the hike.

The last part of the walk took place in darkness; it seemed to last much longer than usual. The chatter diminished altogether and Bronwyn could sense anxiousness within the group. There was a noticeable air of uncertainty as the path narrowed even more, splitting up hiking partners forcing everyone to walk single-file.

"Everyone grab a hand and stay close," Travis boomed from the front of the line. He took Carla Jo's hand who eagerly took Trent's, who grabbed Karley's, who reluctantly took Walt's, who happily took Lillian's, who gratefully took Daniel's, who casually took Bethany's, who took Bronwyn's. Bronwyn desperately wanted to reach back and take Ryan's, but again, there was nothing but emptiness behind her. She walked along in total darkness, clutching tightly to Bethany. The woods were alive with chirping crickets, croaking frogs, an occasional hooting owl and the lonesome howl of a coyote. The soothing sounds of nature being constantly interrupted by the whining cries of Lillian.

"You still with me?" Bethany whispered.

"Whose hand do you think you're holding?"

"Just making sure. I'm not sure what we've gotten ourselves into."

Bronwyn could hear the apprehension in her voice and admitted she did feel a little like a sheep being led to slaughter. Her thoughts traveled back to when she stumbled upon Travis and the cloaked man in the garden. What if they had met to plan out tonight's massacre? What if Travis was leading them to a hidden place, where a coven of knife-wielding hooded figures would come upon them and sacrifice the lot of them to some strange cult god of the mountains? But if that was the case, why bring along his little girl?

That offered small consolation, but not enough. Bronwyn's heart sped up as she reprimanded her vivid imagination. The cheerful chatter of the group had long since dissipated. She could sense everyone's uncertainty. The darkness was now almost unbearable.

She stiffened as she felt a presence behind her sending a shiver up her spine.

She glanced over her shoulder into the thick darkness. Her eyes could not focus on anything, yet she knew something was moving quietly along behind her. She took in a deep breath and smelled the familiar scent that clings to the clothes of smokers, the stale aroma of cigarettes overpowering the pine and spruce. The smoking man was nearby; she was sure of it. Uneasiness overpowered her. She half expected to feel the cold blade of a knife dig into her flesh at any moment. She glanced behind her once again. There was nothing but total darkness.

Lillian broke the silence, "How much further?"

"Almost there!" Carla Jo's cheerful voice answered from up front.

Something in Carla Jo's gleeful response put everyone at rest. She envisioned Travis taking Carla Jo and the kids on many a moonlight hike. There was something quite comforting in that thought that dispelled her imaginations of Travis leading the group on some psychotic slaughter.

Her ears picked up on the sound of rushing water.

"You hear that?"

"Hear what?' Bethany answered nervously.

"A waterfall."

No sooner had Bronwyn mentioned the word than the hikers reached a large clearing. The suppressed moonlight was released, illuminating the stunning view that lay before them. The hikers stood in silence, gasping and ahhing. Lying directly before them was a picturesque scene that appeared to be birthed from a wondrous fairy tale. A dark blue pool of water lay at the base of three impressive waterfalls, reflecting the silver glow of the moon. On both sides of the waterfalls were two of nature's magnificent staircases made of rock, which led up to the top of the fifty-five foot falls. The moss clinging to the rocks gave an iridescent green glow, giving the falls a fantastical look. Cobalt blue waters gently poured over them, emptying into the giant pool below. Steam and fog rose from the hot spring.

The watery paradise was enclosed by tall black mountains silhouetted against the dark cobalt expanse. Seemingly millions of stars dotted the night sky, surrounding the full moon.

Bronwyn stepped forward, speechless, her heart totally drawn to this magnificent place. A strange feeling invaded her as if she had been here before. She knew that was impossible for she would have remembered such a place yet there was a strange familiarity, as if she had recently run into a long lost friend. She felt like a child at home in her own backyard.

Carla Jo was the first to remove her outer clothing and jump into the balmy waters. Trent peeled off his shirt and dove in, much to her delight. The rest of the group followed.

Bronwyn had no desire to join. She'd had her fill of water in the lake. Totally oblivious to the others who were frolicking in the pool, she decided to climb the glowing rocky staircase to the top of the falls. The moon's reflection off the water spotlighted a perfect path for her to follow.

She walked the path eagerly. All the fears and apprehensions that had manifested during the hike were gone. The excitement of exploring, accompanied by the unparalleled beauty of the place, erased all suspicion from her mind. The stony staircase led in and out of the trees, spiraling away from the falls and then back into view. The closer she came to the falls, the louder the roar, until the sounds of laughter and frivolity of the troupe were totally overpowered by the rushing waters. A fine mist sprayed her face. She didn't mind, the brisk walk had caused her to work up quite a bit of perspiration. The blowing spray actually came as a welcome relief.

As she climbed higher and mounted each mammoth rock, she was forced to crouch down and grasp at sturdy rocks, as well as deeply rooted trees. She considered each step, continuing to climb with extreme caution. Her path wound into a view of the falls one last time.

Balancing herself, she turned and looked behind her. She'd climbed much higher than she thought. Below, her friends were dwarfed by the loftiness of the falls. She had a thought that maybe she should have told someone where she was going, but the roar of the falling water was so deafening that they would never be able to hear her, no matter how loud she yelled. She decided she could climb to the top and return before anyone noticed she was missing. Her overworked muscles burned. A few more feet, and Bronwyn found herself at the top of the gargantuan falls.

She stepped onto level ground. The scene before her was more spectacular than the one she'd witnessed below. It was surreal, like nothing she had ever experienced, and it seemed as if she could hear the instruments of an unseen orchestra, playing an anthem of majestic music, swelling to a crescendo as she reached the top. The feeling tore into her heart causing inexplicable emotion and for a reason she couldn't explain, she began to cry.

The moon faced her directly and seemingly took up the entire sky. She had never seen it so enormous. There was little room left for anything else. The water lay still before her as if she were standing on glass. There were no trees, no towering mountains, nothing blocking this midnight canvas...only moon, stars and still waters. She stood frozen, eyes locked on the grandeur of the moon. All was quiet, save for the gentle melody of a pan flute playing in the unseen orchestra. Its soulful tune called to her and she felt like she was literally standing in the heavens.

She stepped forward; the tears continued to flood her eyes as her heart ached. Her soul could hear a song, a tender voice of a woman singing a haunting melody. The language was unknown to her yet, strangely familiar. Each phrase, each note entranced her, calling to her as it did just two nights before. She felt as if her feet would leave the ground at any moment, allowing her to take flight, soaring past the moon, amongst the stars, flying with no regrets, no fear, no disappointments, only laughter and peace.

Her legs began to tremble uncontrollably. She found it impossible to remain standing. Giving into the weakness, she sat down where she was and allowed the water to gently wash over her. It seemed as if it was cleaning away her past and washing away her broken dreams, along with the ugly bitterness of disappointment. She felt as if she were being re-born in some way. She rested on her hands, leaning her head back, drinking in the euphoric feeling. For the first time in her life, she felt inspiration, as if her great story was climbing its way out of the rubble of her life where it lay buried. Her heart began to race, the heat sensation beginning again in the soles of her feet and rising upward through the rest of her body. The heat was much more intense than before. The feeling was so rapturous that it became frightening. There was an instinct to run as far away from this place as she could, yet an inner urge to remain close to this spot and never leave. The heat within her continued to rise, the two opposing feelings began to wage a war inside her.

"What is this?" She whispered softly as her mind began to scramble. Good thoughts gave way to darker thoughts, evil and disturbing thoughts....terrifying thoughts. Then, just as suddenly, they snapped back to good, pleasant and virtuous thoughts. Her pulse continued to race and the heat continued to rise as she trembled. She wanted to scream, yet there was no air, no voice. Never in her life had she felt such terror mingled with peace. Opposing forces seemed to be fighting over her. She could sense the fear and the darkness begin to overpower. It was so strong, convincing, enticing. She felt its presence overshadowing her to the point where she could almost see the invisible manifest itself before her. Terror and dread began to overwhelm her as she began to make out a horrific shadow approaching her.

"Enjoying the view?" Travis spoke from behind her. At the sound of his voice, the shadow dissipated and took with it the extreme distress.

Relieved, she desired to turn and face him; however, her weakened state would not allow it. She attempted to answer him, only to realize her voice was gone. All she could do was nod.

He studied her for a moment and then sat down in the water directly in front of her. His expression was serious and she wondered what he saw as he looked at her. Maybe her face had become paralyzed on one side, the exertion of the climb too much for her. This would explain why she could not open her mouth.

"Can you speak to me?"

She was able to open her mouth; however, her voice was gone. She was only able to communicate a small shrug of uncertainty. He moved in closer, positioning his body between her and the moon. He gently brushed her hair away from her face and as he did his hand fell slowly, stroking her face. She swallowed hard as she felt heat rush into her cheeks the intimacy of the moment catching her off guard. He let his hand fall slowly from her face, as he continued to stare into her eyes. He reached into the shallow water and tenderly lifted her trembling hands. He clasped his strong palms over hers and looked directly into her eyes as he placed her left hand over his heart. She could feel the steady rhythm of his pulse.

"Shut your eyes and keep them closed. You will want to open them but don't. Do not open them until I tell you."

She obeyed and closed her eyes; deciding it might be in her best interest to trust him. Her hand continued to feel the slow steady rhythm of his pulse beating against his chest. With every beat his skin warmed until it was almost too hot to touch. A bright light shone against her closed lids the warmth of it burning into her face. Her instinct was to pull her hand free and open her eyes to see what was transpiring in front of her. He must have anticipated her reaction for he held her hand tighter against his chest and whispered a quiet no.

Within a few moments, her pulse slowed to a natural rhythm, her hands calmed and she felt her voice enter her throat once more. Still, the heat sensation remained intense. This was becoming a normal experience with every encounter involving him.

"I am going to lift you to your feet and turn you around facing the other way. Do not open your eyes until I say."

She nodded

He removed her hand from his chest but continued to hold it as he took her other hand and lifted her to her feet. Her legs buckled as she struggled to stand. He instructed her to take her time, promising her strength would return."

She nodded, keeping her eyes shut, still feeling the warmth radiating around her. In her mind, she pictured the orb of light she first saw around the man in the road. She longed to open her eyes, yet feared what would happen if she did.

"I'm going to turn you around now. Are you ready?"

She nodded again clutching his hands, allowing him to gently turn her body in the opposite direction. Immediately she regained her strength standing on strong legs, his hands still clasped tightly in hers until the warmth dissipated. He waited a few moments before giving her permission to open her eyes. She opened them slowly. The night was much darker. Her view revealed a moonless sky covered in lofty pine trees, and mountainous terrain. The water rushed over the rocks and cascaded into the pool of water in which everyone else swam. Travis stood in front of her.

"What happened to me?" She asked, her voice quivering. "I heard music, and a song. I felt entranced."

He remained silent, offering no explanation. He only searched her face as she in turn searched his. There was so much behind his dark eyes, so many hidden secrets.

She longed to reach out and stroke his cheek as he had done to her. She found herself drawn to him yet she knew she must not give into her feelings. She must never allow herself to cross that line...though she knew he was indeed drawn to her in some way as well. She wondered how he knew she was at the top of the falls. Had he observed her leaving the rest of the group and followed her there?

He cut his eyes away before answering. "You must have climbed too fast. The intensity of the climb, combined with the increased altitude and the cool waters, more than likely caused your temporary paralysis."

She felt as if the wind had just been knocked from her lungs. His patronizing diagnosis irritated her. He was an innkeeper, not a doctor. She felt betrayed by him. After all, something out of the ordinary had just happened. Some sort of supernatural experience had just transpired. Even the treatment he had given was hardly standard treatment for paralysis. Bronwyn realized that he actually knew something, yet he continued to hide secrets.

She released his hands suddenly.

"You don't believe me?" He read her expression.

"Why do you insult me by expecting me to?" She brushed past him, heading for the stony path.

He suppressed a smile. "Going back down the long way?"

She stopped; dreading the thought of a long, slippery downhill hike in darkness besides she feared her legs might become wobbly once again, causing a tragic fall on her way down.

"Is there a better way?"

He nodded to the falls. "It's a big jump, but you get there in four seconds."

Her stomach dropped, as she looked over the edge of the falls. "You're kidding me," was all she could say.

"It's the best way down."

She peered over the edge again, her heart now in her throat.

"I don't think I could do it."

"Sure you can. It's easy; just let your feet leave the ground, and fly toward the water."

Again she sensed mystery in his words. Why was he encouraging her to jump 55 feet? It was if he was leading her, baiting her, yet every time she asked a question he was evasive. Why?

"I know you can do it." He was saying as he poised himself to jump. Then, gently, "I'll be waiting for you at the bottom."

Again, the heat began to rise with intensity. She felt that this event had happened before. A vision flashed into her mind so quickly, that she couldn't make sense of what it was. A dream perhaps and in it she could hear someone saying those same words…"*I'll be waiting for you.*"

He dove from the cliff, and into the water. She watched him as he flew, gliding majestically like an enormous hawk. He broke the waters, resurfacing almost immediately. He looked back up and motioned for her to join him.

Part of her screamed "No!" yet another part eagerly desired to fly off the cliff, soaring just as he did, breaking through the swirling waters below. Her soul longed to be near him, to be where he was. She could see his face, so inviting. So intriguing.

She felt her feet leave the ground. Her body soared through the night air, cutting through the spraying mist and as she descended toward the water, her spirit soared upward. The unseen orchestra began playing its rapturous song once again. Its melody rose to a crescendo just as her body broke through and she entered into the dark balmy, swirling waters.

The music was gone. Only silence. A strong hand clasped onto her, pulling her up.

She resurfaced to the pleasant sight of black, mystifying eyes.

CHAPTER TWENTY-TWO

DAY THREE

The early morning breeze gently pushed the linen curtains away from the window, allowing the warm sun rays their grand entrance. Bethany and Lillian were unmoved, sleeping in after returning from the night hike around two in the morning. However, Bronwyn had woken off and on all night with an anxiousness growing inside her; she wondered why she felt so agitated. Was she forgetting something? She lay in bed, staring at the spinning ceiling fan, trying to decipher the feelings inside. She dozed off and on. Ryan usually occupied her dreams, but now, Travis was the one she dreamt of. When she finally awoke for good, she felt somewhat guilty about her night-time fantasies.

Quietly, she climbed from the bed as a rooster crowed, then dressed and headed outside for an early morning jog. She ran in the soft dewy grass alongside the river bed, clicking off the miles. The brisk morning air filled her lungs with the perfume of mother earth. She did her best thinking early in the morning, when no one was around to distract her. She tried to concentrate and plan the re–writing of the dreaded scene. However, thoughts of Travis and the waterfall continued to invade her head.

Nearing the inn, she smelled the delicious aromas of breakfast. She decided against the heaviness of country waffles, eggs and biscuits, choosing instead a glass of juice and a small bowl of fresh fruit which she ate alone on the porch. Afterwards, she returned to her room showered, dressed, and hurried back outside with her computer just as a groggy Bethany and Lillian raised their waking heads.

"Hey, where are you going?" Bethany asked.

"Re-writes."

Lillian noticed Bronwyn's wet hair. "How long have you been up?"

"Woke with the rooster. I couldn't sleep."

"So, what's going on with you and Travis?" Lillian asked as she stretched and yawned.

"What?"

Bethany gave a sarcastic laugh. "Don't act so surprised, Bronwyn. It's so obvious."

"What is so obvious?"

Bethany and Lillian exchanged knowing glances, and then Bethany said,

"The obvious attraction between you two."

"I am not attracted to him." She lied.

"Maybe not, but he definitely is to you."

"Sh-sh!" Bronwyn closed the door and then poised herself on the edge of the bed.

"Why do you say that?"

Lillian's tired voice came alive with excitement. "Because, he kept his eye on you all night last night. And, he followed you when you took off rock climbing."

"You two sure were gone a long time." Bethany added sourly. "Just what was going on?"

"Nothing. I didn't know he had followed me. I thought I was alone until I reached the top. Then he showed up."

She paused, deciding not to try and explain what had actually happened on top of the falls. How could she possibly explain such a supernatural moment? They would never understand. So she told the girls Travis's explanation of the story.

"Did he have to give you more mouth to mouth?" Lillian teased.

"No" She said, trying not to smile. "You two are terrible."

"You better watch yourself," Bethany warned. "All kidding aside, I think he is attracted to you."

"I think so too," Lillian agreed.

Bronwyn shook her head.

"We've been alone twice now, and he's certainly kept his distance. He's been nothing but a gentleman."

"Give him time, Bronwyn," Bethany warned. "He'll find the opportunity. Then what will you do?"

She stood and smiled coyly. "I'll do nothing. He is a married man, and as beautiful and mysterious as he may be, if he would cheat on his poor crippled wife, then I would not want him. That would take all the beauty of him away and place him in the same good-for-nothing, cheating scoundrel category as Ryan and a hoard of other common men."

"Hear hear!" Bethany gave Bronwyn a high-five.

"I'm off to write," she said. "Wish me luck. I'll catch up with you guys later."

"Please don't write me ugly!" Lillian yelled after her.

Bethany leaned back against her pillow and stared at the door as Bronwyn left. Her stomach knotted. Her mind went back to the café and Trent's psychiatric analysis of Bronwyn's heart break. She hated to admit it, but his foreboding predictions of the progressions of a broken heart were playing out. She remembered stage two, the desperate attempts for attention. True, Bronwyn had stayed out of sight during a storm claiming to have nearly drowned, and then last night, walking off alone, professing to have experienced some sort of altitude sickness. Both times, she needed the aid of the dashing Travis.

The thought of stage three sickened Bethany.... the self-destructive stage. The one, as Trent said, will justify affairs with married men. Bethany sighed. Her concern lay with Bronwyn's well-being. She knew first-hand what it was like to be involved with a married man. She fell quickly for an amazing man once, only to make the gruesome discovery that, unfortunately, never surfaced during months of long walks, lunch dates, endless conversation, and random intimate nights. It so happened that she ran into him leaving a local theater, one arm around a tall, slender beautiful woman, his other occupied by holding the hand of a ten-year-old girl, whom he promptly introduced as his wife and daughter. Even though Bethany had appeared strong, it hurt more than she had ever revealed. She knew Bronwyn hurt badly from her broken engagement to Ryan. The last thing she needed was to give her heart away again, this time to a married man who would only betray her in the end. As Bronwyn's best friend, she would keep a careful watch on the situation, preventing any more alone time between the two, if necessary.

CHAPTER TWENTY-THREE

Bronwyn found a shady, secluded patch of thick green clover, far down the river, bordering the entrance to the woods along the edge of the property. The sun burned intensely, casting its warming rays upon her skin and glistening on the gently flowing waters. A line of large trees offered a nice canopy shading her from the beating sun.

Several large natural rocks lay scattered in the grassy area. She discovered that one of the smoother boulders made an ideal desk. Scooting next to it, she opened her computer and her script file. Whatever inspiration had fallen upon her at the waterfalls was gone. She sat in the grass, starring at the screen, unmoved and uninspired. Her attention wandered to a large hawk flying overhead, then back to her computer screen, and then back to a bird singing on a nearby tree branch... and finally back to her computer screen. The pattern repeated over and over again. Within a couple of hours, she had tracked a hawk, some blue jays, a vivid red cardinal, and several birds whose species she did not know. She dug the moss out of the corners of the rock, lay across the grass, followed the route of a strange insect, picked several wildflowers, pulled at the sticky sap oozing down a nearby tree, and became engrossed in the antics of her friends who had recently gathered at the river for some fun in the sun. She was too far away to hear their conversations. She was only privy to their laughter and playful screams.

Her interest peaked when she noticed Travis and Mavis heading towards the river. Mavis carried a picnic basket, while Travis balanced an ice cooler on his shoulder. Mavis waved and called out to the group as she spread two large cloths on the ground and unloaded the food basket. Bronwyn could only imagine the amazing lunch she had prepared for her hungry guests. Mavis finished spreading out the feast and then, without warning, took a staggering run to the dock. Grabbing the thick rope, she swung far out over the river and fell into the water, causing an enormous splash and earning a round of applause from the group. Bronwyn noticed Travis watching Mavis, a genuine smile across his lips. Mavis must have challenged him because he removed his shirt and dove into the water, much to the kids' delight.

Bronwyn felt a tinge of jealousy, which she immediately attempted to suppress and scolded herself knowing she was not that type of person. She should be pleased to see a family so close-knit and a husband who continued to love his wife despite what fate had done. She wondered why Mavis had never replaced the missing tooth. She could understand the scars and even the limp, but a tooth could be replaced. She reprimanded herself again. Isn't this what her script was about?

She turned her straying attention back to the computer screen and began typing randomly:

Does Travis love you, Mavis, because you are beautiful? Hardly, look what tragedy hath wrought. You are now a small resemblance of the girl you once were, the girl that stole his heart. Or my dear Mavis, are you a beauty to Travis because he loves you? Does Travis's heart not see your scars or the gaping hole in your mouth? Does he not see your body lean to one side, swaggering as you pull yourself along? Do they tell of a story deep inside of a woman that only Travis knows? Is it a story full of secrets revealed only to the one that holds your heart? Are they secrets that will not allow Travis to judge this beautifully written book by its cover?

With a sigh, she highlighted the entire paragraph and deleted it. Her thoughts wondered to Ryan and why he had so easily stopped loving her and quickly replaced her with someone else. Thinking of him she clicked on her e-mail. A window immediately popped up on her screen informing her that internet was not available. Figures. I'm cut off from the entire world here. I might as well be on the moon. She laughed at the thought. Moonshine, pretty close.

Her eyes noticed her deleted files. Maybe she could dig up an old idea and run with that. Frustrated that she had resorted to rooting though the trash, she scrolled down a list of her many failed attempts at stories. She clicked on the first.

"My Better Half"

This might have something she could rebirth. She opened the file and read the synopsis:

A story of fraternal twins. "A prince and princess, separated at birth for political reasons. Both taken by different families after their parents' sudden assassination. The two adoptive families fled the country to protect the children, who were the heirs to the throne. These two children were raised in secrecy thousands of miles away from each other, neither knowing the other existed. Until one day...."

Bronwyn stopped reading and closed the file. No help there. She returned to the list of titles. Another caught her eye:

"Birds of Prey" "A group of top secret agents, all possessing bird names, known as "The N.E.S.S.T"

She immediately closed the file. Stupid, no wonder I deleted you. She scrolled the titles again, biting the fingernails on her left hand, stopping at,

"The Eclipse"

"During a lunar eclipse as the world sits in darkness, a warrior who is an extra dimensional being comes to earth as the gatekeeper. Guarding and keeping watch of the forbidden portal...."

"Creepy," she muttered with a shiver as she closed the file. She scrolled the list before clicking again:

"My Brother's Keeper"

"After a tragic accident takes the life of her beloved, a woman finds herself raising her children alone in the new world, facing much more than the severe storms that took her husband's life."

Bronwyn sighed, closing the file. Nothing. She ran her hands through her dark hair, twisting it and pulling it off her neck. She held her hair atop her head for a few minutes, letting the breeze cool her, before allowing it to cascade down over her shoulders. Closing the computer, she sat back against the tree feeling somewhat hopeless. She knew Marcus would expect a re-write by the night's rehearsal. Her attempts for the past couple of hours had produced nothing.

She turned her attention back to the happy swimmers. Everyone was out of the water, eating Mavis's lunch. She longed to join her friends at their festive picnic, but certainly Marcus would inquire about the script. She had no desire to tell him she had nothing. Instead, she opted for an endeavor she had not attempted since she was a little girl. Earlier, she had noticed a perfect tree for climbing. Its branches were thick and low and circled the tree like a spiral staircase. She decided to climb. Leaving her computer on her makeshift rock desk, she entered the edge of the forest and approached the welcoming tree, grabbing the lowest branch and pulling herself up. Within seconds, she found herself climbing effortlessly like a young child playfully swinging across the monkey bars at recess. She climbed a bit higher before stopping.

The view of the river was spectacular. Stretching her neck, she could see some of the many gardens. She wondered if she would be able to peer into the secret garden at this height. She pulled herself up one more branch, but her efforts were futile. The garden was much too far away. She rested herself on a wide sturdy branch, straddling it, allowing her legs to dangle on either side. She leaned herself against the large trunk. The playful screams and laughter of the troupe were barely audible. An occasional burst of laughter from Mavis or one of the children would fill the air.

She watched her friends yet found herself focused on Travis and Mavis. Travis was sitting across the cloth from her, with Molly close beside him, leaning against his sturdy chest. She noticed he kept his arm wrapped around her as she ate. Mavis was sitting near Walt. Bronwyn could tell by Walt's gesturing that he was no doubted re-telling his legendary story. Mavis seemed intrigued and soon took over the conversation. Bronwyn wondered if she was telling the others about her injuries as well. She hoped so, Bethany would be sure to relay the information. Instead, whatever Mavis said caused the whole group to erupt in laughter. Even Wilbur was red-faced, choking as he laughed.

Bronwyn watched Travis's expression as Mavis continued talking. He focused on her every word, paying careful attention to what she was saying, just as he had done with Bronwyn in the cabin. Her heart ached even more. "Where were you Travis, when Mavis was injured?" She whispered to herself. "Why weren't you there to protect her as you were me? Do you stay faithful to her out of guilt?

Or are you faithful because you have never known anything other than Mavis and this small town? Has there never been anyone else to steal your heart?"

The snapping of branches and heavy footsteps, behind her, interrupted her daydreams. Someone was there! Could it be the cloaked figure from the woods! Her mind raced forward, along with her pulse. She could attempt to climb down. No...that would draw attention to her. She could remain quiet, hoping the figure wouldn't notice her so high up in the tree. She could scream for help, but if her friends did not hear her, she would only be revealing herself.

Quietly, she leaned away from the tree trunk to possibly catch a true glimpse of whoever had been stalking her. The heavy footsteps drew closer, the rustling louder. She leaned forward, clutching the branch above her, steadying herself. A dark-hooded figure moved through the trees, the hood obscuring the persons face. What could possibly be going on in this secluded town?

She swallowed a scream that desperately wanted to escape her lungs. Brawny dark hands parted the tree branches, clearing a view of the river. She breathed a small sigh of relief. The shadowy figure was not aware she was in the tree. The figure's attention was fixed on the picnic by the river. She leaned back against the trunk, trying to control her breathing, while collecting her thoughts. Was this man out to harm them?

She had no desire of finding out. She would quietly climb down and make a mad dash for the inn.

Time to take her chances. She stretched out once more to make sure the figure was preoccupied watching her friends before she attempted her self-rescue. Shakily, she rose to her feet, again balancing herself by holding onto the branch directly above her head. She leaned forward.

The cloaked figure was gone! How could it have left without her hearing? She scanned the surrounding area quickly... no sign of him. She leaned as far away from the tree as her body would allow. Nothing.

She sat back down against the tree trunk. The hooded figure was gone. As to where, she had no clue. Still it was time to descend the tree and get out of the woods. Pulling herself up, she glanced above her before grabbing the lofty branch of the tree.

Ebony eyes starred at her from amongst the leaves. Sitting camouflaged on the branch directly above her was another hooded creature! His eyes pierced hers; his face was stoic, stern. Fear overwhelmed her. She let out a powerful piercing scream as her body went limp, causing her grip to slip. She clawed for the other branches, but instead felt herself falling from the tree, plummeting into total darkness.

CHAPTER TWENTY-FOUR

The sandwiches disappeared, along with the soft warm chocolate chip cookies that Mavis removed from the oven only minutes before serving them. She laid out a spread of egg salad sandwiches, fresh tomatoes, slices of melon and a pitcher of ice cold lemonade to wash it all down. The troupe had eaten well and was now relaxing while listening to Mavis' comical stories. The afternoon sun was at its peak, even making the shade of the massive oaks quite warm. As soon as Mavis finished her tale, several members of the troupe planned on returning to the swing and inner tubes and playfully work off any accumulated calories gained by the delicious lunch. Despite Wilbur's earlier warnings that their stay in Moonshine not turn into a paid vacation, the entire troupe, including Wilbur, took advantage of the rest and relaxing activities offered at Sandalwood Inn. A better vacation spot would be hard to find. Moonshine was proving to be one of the country's best-kept secrets.

A bloodcurdling scream from the edge of the woods pierced through the serenity of their afternoon. The unexpectedness of the scream startled the relaxed group. Travis was the first to leap to his feet. Without hesitation, he sprinted across the grounds towards the edge of the forest. The rest of the group sprung to their feet and followed. Even Mavis ran surprisingly fast on her crippled leg. None was able to keep up with Travis, though. When he arrived, he noticed the abandoned laptop lying on the large rock. He quickly charged into the woods, glancing to his right and then to his left. He spotted Bronwyn's body lying on the ground underneath a large oak tree. He sprinted over to where she lay, placed his fingers on the side of her neck, feeling for a pulse.

Bethany made her way to the opposite side of Bronwyn, kneeling on the ground.

"My God, is she okay?"

Travis gave no answer. He lifted her eyelids, checked her breathing, and felt down each arm and leg. Mavis caught up with the group, joining in the circle that now surrounded Bronwyn. She watched intently as Travis examined her.

Within seconds, Bronwyn began to stir. A sigh of relief passed through the group, as she opened her eyes. The darkness cleared as she focused on a face leaning over her, then remembering the cloaked man, she gasped attempting to sit, but a firm hand on her shoulder prevented her, pushing her back to the ground. She fought against it, slapping the man who had a hold of her.

"Relax, Bronwyn, you're alright." She heard Travis' voice instructing her. She focused in on his face, giving into his command and allowing him to gently ease her back to a lying position.

She nervously looked around her. "Where is he?"

"Where is who?" Bethany asked, puzzled.

"The man in the tree?"

"You okay hon?"

She attempted to sit up again, but Travis prevented it. She lay back on the ground but continued to look for the man. She knew he had been there. She had seen his face and locked eyes with him right before she fell.

Trent knelt beside Bronwyn. "What happened, love?"

"I saw something and fell out of the tree."

"Were you climbing it?" He asked, a bit of laughter in his voice.

Bronwyn offered a crooked smile and nodded her head.

"Girl, you are crazy!" Karley said.

"Is she okay?" Bethany asked Travis. "I think she might have hit her head. She seems delirious."

"Are you in any pain?" Travis asked.

She shook her head again.

"No, actually I don't feel anything."

"My God, she's paralyzed!" Lillian gasped grabbing Trent's arm.

"No Lil,'" Bronwyn said attempting to sit once again. "I mean, I have no pain. I'm sure I'm not hurt, just a little stunned....maybe."

Her last words trailed off as she visualized the hooded man.

She glanced cautiously around her.

"Are you sure you're okay?" Bethany asked again, curious about her odd behavior. "Who are you looking --?"

"She's okay." Travis said and his interruption to Bethany's questioning seemed somewhat threatening. "There's no broken bones, no head trauma. She more than likely stunned herself when she fell."

Although Travis answered Bethany's question, his eyes stayed fixed upon Bronwyn. There was something in his face that confirmed her suspicion... he knew of the goings on in the woods. His expression made clear he did not want her to inform her friends of the cloaked man. Reluctantly, she obeyed his stern gaze... but she'd question him later.

"We really need to have a serious talk, love, about the extreme measures you seem to be taking to get attention." Trent said, winking, as he knelt beside her, placing his hand on her knee. "Good God... is this going to be an everyday event?" She smiled at Trent, who turned to Bethany, mouthing the words "stage two."

"Glad you're okay, love." Trent gave Bronwyn's knee a final pat as he stood.

She was glad her friends were there with her. She turned away from Travis, purposely refrained from looking in his direction, and leaned towards Bethany and Trent.

"Enough of this standing around. I'm fine. You guys can go back to your picnic; I'm not going to climb any more trees. I'm just going to finish my re-write."

"If you're sure you're okay love." Trent said, offering her his hand.

She eagerly grabbed it and allowed him to pull her up. An openly touching person, Trent immediately began brushing the dirt from her clothes and plucking a few bits of grass from her hair as well. "You need me to carry you back, love?"

She laughed. "I'm fine Trent. Really I am."

Realizing that she was indeed alright, the group dispersed and casually walked back to the river. Travis stood to his feet and said nothing. He allowed Mavis to grab hold of his strong arm for support.

Bronwyn retrieved her computer, taking her time to place it into her back-pack. She had made eye contact with Bethany, signaling her to loiter a bit. Bronwyn waited until the others were out of earshot before she spoke.

"How did you guys find me?" Bronwyn asked.

"Heard you scream. Pretty chilling if you ask me."

Bronwyn slung the back-pack over her shoulder, "Where was I when you found me?"

Bethany looked at Bronwyn puzzled. "Under the tree." She spoke slowly. "Are you sure you're okay?"

"Did you see anything else?"

"No. Actually Travis got to you first." Bethany said, giving Bronwyn a nudge. "He took off running like a wild animal. His muscles pulsing, his hair flying in the wind. You should have seen that man run. I didn't know a person could run that fast."

"Stop it!"

"But seriously, you should have seen his reaction when he heard you scream. He didn't hesitate one second. He jumped to his feet and bolted. He left us all in his dust... I have this sixth sense, Bronwyn, I can tell when there's an attraction between two people."

Bronwyn remained quiet. It was no use to continue. Bethany was not quiet long enough to listen to anything she had to say.

Bronwyn lounged by the river the rest of the afternoon, staying close to the rest of the group. The rewrites would have to wait. Travis did not return to the river, and was mysteriously absent at dinner.

Marcus cancelled rehearsal once again, completely understanding why the re-write had not been completed. As twilight set, everyone was free to participate in whatever activity they chose.

Bronwyn decided to stay close to the inn and visit her favorite garden, figuring it would be more enticing during the evening hours.

The night was warm and inviting as she stepped off the porch and onto the cobblestone path. Opening the gate she pushed her way through the hanging vines. The romantic scent of night blooming jasmine filled her nostrils. The garden was even more enchanting in the moonlight. Fireflies swarmed around the low hanging branches of the weeping willow tree, displaying their tiny glowing lights. The moon shone down upon the pond, its reflection casting the garden in a deep gray-silver. The quiet rushing of the waterfall accompanied by the croaking frogs and the chirping crickets, provided the night's sounds. She sat in a soft patch of clover growing near the water. She moved her hand gracefully over the leaves, reflecting on how as a child she would spend countless hours searching for a four leafed one. She laid back and gazed at the night sky. It was teeming with millions of stars, more than she had ever seen at one time. The higher elevation made it seem as if she could almost reach out and grab a few.

Moments like this seemed so futile and empty without someone to share them with. Her mind turned to Ryan. Literally no day had passed since their break-up that she had not thought of him, dreamed of him, pictured his face, and heard his voice. She imagined him in the clover, lying next to her, gazing at the stars. There was a time when she could slide her hand over and reach out and touch him, feel him lying next to her.

She passed her hands across the clover once again. The emptiness was so real. Her body longed for him. She wondered if missing Ryan was the reason she was drawn to Travis.

Somewhere in the distance, the faint music of a dulcimer wafted through the trees. The music was beautiful, although she did not recognize the song. Probably some old mountain ballad. She continued staring at the stars, hoping to see a shooting one…on which she could make a wish. The night was peaceful, serene…lonely.

She rose from the clover patch and walked to the pond. She sat on its bank, placing her feet in the shallow waters. She cupped the water with one hand and splashed it further across the pond.

The garden gate swung open. There was not enough light for her to see who entered. Maybe it was Bethany and Lillian. She hoped. Girl talk would be therapeutic right now.

The footsteps grew closer. The approaching figure stepped into the moonlight. Bronwyn's heart leaped.

Travis.

He approached the pond and sat next to her and as much as she hated to admit it she was glad he did. Despite the fact she was trying to convince herself she wasn't interested in him, she longed to be near him. Besides, she intended to interrogate him. She knew that, at the least he was keenly aware of what lurked in the woods. He knew the first day she had questioned him, yet he had avoided the subject, blaming it on kids or curious teenagers.

"What's going on around here? Who are the cloaked men stalking us from the woods? I know you know. I saw you talking with one of them in the garden yesterday."

Travis looked out over the pond.

"There are secrets and mysteries that are not to be revealed to everyone."

Her suspicion rose. "That's unfair."

"How is that?"

"We're obviously being stalked. Am I not allowed to know why?"

"In time."

His words frightened her. "What do you mean by that?"

"Exactly what I said. You will know in time."

Her agitation continued to rise.

"Maybe I won't wait for *your* time. What if I march right into the inn and tell everyone and make a call to the local police?"

"Won't do you any good."

"Are you threatening me?"

"No." Travis hurled a small stone across the water. "I am protecting you."

His words stunned her into silence.

He returned to face her. "How's the re write going?"

Bronwyn would not allow herself to be deceived. There was more to these hooded creatures than Travis wanted her to know...something strangely unusual at work in these mountains. She sensed it from the moment of her arrival three nights ago. If Travis was protecting her, that must mean she was in danger. If the cloaked figures meant her harm, then why was he having a private conversation with one of them?

She looked at him. He was reading her thoughts.

"In time," he said quietly. "How is the re-writing going?"

She stared at him, her emotions waging a war inside. She feared the man that sat before her in many ways, yet her heart ached for him. There was no escaping the fact that she was unwillingly drawn to him. She longed to be near him, yet another part of her desired to run far away from him. She sighed.

"It's not going. I've been staring at a blank computer screen all day, and have produced nothing. I don't know; maybe I'm done with writing."

"Do you think that you're wasting your time writing these scripts, and putting off the story that is buried deep within you? Maybe you're burying it deeper by all the clutter you allow in your life."

"Yes", she answered quickly. "I know that for certain. But, these stories, no matter how trite and sappy, pay the bills."

"Then you might as well be writing for the *National Enquirer.*" His words stung.

She desired to snap off a sarcastic, defensive rebuttal, but she had none. Travis took advantage of her silence.

"You're making a living for yourself, instead of living the life you were born to live."

The heat sensation began rising within her once again, cued by his words. Her heart beat faster. She reached deep into the water in an attempt to cool her arms. She nervously splashed more water over the top of her legs, and then repeated the action by splashing her neck and chest.

He pressed on. "You're attempting to write a love story, yet love is such a vast subject, and one with intense emotion. Science can't even explain it, and you're trying to write about that emotion between two people, yet you have never really loved anyone on this earth except yourself."

Her hands left the water.

"What? How can you say that? You don't know me. I have loved. I loved Ryan deeply."

"You never really loved Ryan." He sounded certain.

She lifted her feet from the water. Intrigued, she turned her body to face him and looked directly into his dark eyes. "Okay...explain yourself."

He stared back, once again his eyes penetrating her soul.

"Can you take it?"

"Take what?"

"The truth."

"Why wouldn't I be able to take the truth?"

"Because truth always sets you free. And some people find it fearful to be totally free. For some reason, they seem to find comfort in the chains that bind them."

Her eyes flashed as she leaned forward, her body closer to Travis than she intended.

"I'm not afraid of anything."

Travis suppressed another smile that pulled at the corner of his lips.

"You're a storyteller. You invent characters. You create them in your imagination exactly how you wish them to be. Correct?"

She nodded.

"You did the same with Ryan. You loved a man who did not exist anywhere but in your ideals. You loved a person that wasn't actually Ryan."

"Not true. I knew him very well. We lived together. You get to know someone that way."

"Then he suddenly changed and turned into someone you didn't know anymore. Right?"

"Yes, in a way he did." She couldn't argue with that.

"He didn't change. You were finally forced to see Ryan for who he really was. The true Ryan. Not your ideal created version of him."

She contemplated his comment. His words seemed so obvious. She didn't want to think that she had actually fallen for a self-absorbed, ego-driven shallow person. She was smarter than that. Now she wondered if Ryan had ever loved her. Obviously he had not.

Sadness gripped her. "I guess Ryan never really loved me. His true love was obviously fame and recognition."

"If all that had been offered to Ryan had been offered to you, would you have taken it?"

She thought a minute before she answered.

"Six months ago, I am sure I would have. I'd been crazy not to. But I'd have taken Ryan right along with me."

"What if Ryan had asked you to turn it all down?"

"I never asked Ryan to turn it all down."

"That's not what I asked you."

Her voice rose, all her suppressed anger for Ryan resurfacing. "It would have been very selfish of him."

"Would you have turned it all down for him?"

"No" She nearly shouted it. "No, I wouldn't have turned any of it down for him. I would have seen him for the self-serving, egotistical, person that he was."

Her voice trailed off as she realized her last statement…*Seen Ryan for who he was…*

Travis was right. She had invented Ryan to be the man she wanted him to be, the man for whom she longed, never seeing him for who he really was.

She looked at Travis, realization shinning in her eyes. He leaned forward and said softly,

"If I say, I love you Bronwyn. Do I mean I love you in the same way as I love these mountains, or the smell of the earth after a good rain, or the way I love music? Do I love you because the way you look ignites a passion inside of me? Is my love for you only contingent on the way it affects me? How it makes me feel? If so, then I only truly love myself. And I only love and want you for how it affects me."

He moved very close to her, his eyes reaching deep into her soul.

"Or do I love you, Bronwyn? Do I love the person who looks at me from those emerald green eyes? Do I love you despite the times you are angry and bitter and unlovely? Do I continue to love you although you freely gave your heart to another? Can I send you away knowing I will never experience you, but you, will experience all you've ever dreamed of? I can if my love is for you and not myself."

She was silent, completely entranced in his words. The heat weakened her body. She wanted to cry, sob tears of regret of wasted time and loneliness. Everything within her wanted to lean against his chest. She wanted him to wrap his arms around her and hold her under the moonlight. If only he would make the first move. If only he would offer.

They sat in silence for a few moments. Despite her inner urgings, she turned her body away from his and back to the water.

"True love is sacrifice," he said.

"Have you sacrificed a lot for Mavis?"

"Love never keeps count."

"Has she done the same for you?"

"Love never keeps count," he repeated.

An unseen tear escaped her eye and splashed into the pond. She quickly stroked the waters not wanting him to notice. The moonlight reflected off the rippling surface.

"I couldn't imagine a more perfect place."

Then feelings and words started to spill. "It's times like these that inspire me. The turmoil of my soul and the strong desire to right all the wrongs. I feel a strong urge to fight against, yet for something. To defy every odd stacked against me. I sense awareness that there is something brewing, a purpose calling me to better things worth living for. The inner turmoil gives me a strange sense of peace. It calls to me, beckons me, out of the mundane and into the remarkable...."

She chuckled. "Wow! Where did that come from?"

"That came from you, Bronwyn. It's what you were truly put on this earth to do." He said it with certainty while peering into her eyes.

Her voice dropped to a near whisper. "I feel it here in Moonshine more than anywhere. This place calls to me, like last night at the waterfalls. I heard a song, music; something was calling my soul, calling to my innermost being. Call it altitude sickness or however you wish to explain it, but I have never felt anything like that before. It was unreal, yet more real than anything I have ever experienced in my life."

Travis listened to her but said nothing. Her words were music to his soul.

Bronwyn quietly pushed open the door; thankful it didn't creak, and crept into the room. Bethany and Lillian were both asleep, more than likely for quite some time.

She had never intended on staying out in the garden so late, but once Travis showed up and their intriguing conversation went from intense to intimate, time melted away. She stole into the bathroom politely closing the door before turning on the light. She quickly changed from her clothes into her sleeping briefs and tank, brushed her teeth and washed her face. Turning off the light, she opened the door and crept into bed.

"Where have you been?"

Bethany's whisper startled her. "Crap! You scared me!"

"It's a guilty conscience that frightens so easily!"

"I'm not guilty of anything! Go back to sleep!"

"You guys can stop whispering. I'm awake" Lillian said, her head remaining on the pillow.

"You see Bethany, you woke up Lil' being all nosey."

Bethany sat up in the bed.

"No, you woke her up, sneaking into the room at an ungodly hour after your late-night escapades."

Lillian sat up.

"You're having exploits with Travis?"

"No, I am not."

"Yes, she is!" Bethany said firmly.

"Be quiet, or you're going to wake up everyone in the inn. Just go back to sleep."

"Not a chance." Lillian fluffed her pillow and leaned it against the head board. "This is too good."

Bethany turned on the lamp. "So where were you? And why are you sneaking in so late?"

"Out with it, woman!" Lillian added.

"I was in one of the gardens…thinking."

"Were you alone?"

"Yes and No."

"What do you mean by that?"

"I was alone for a while, until someone else showed up."

"And who might someone else be?" Lillian mocked.

"Travis," Bronwyn tried to be nonchalant.

"I knew it!" Bethany yelled. Lillian and Bronwyn both quieted her.

"What were you doing?" She asked.

"We were only talking."

"About what?" She demanded.

"Writing, writers block, love."

Bethany's eyes narrowed. "Uh huh."

"It's not what you're thinking. Real love, true love, sacrificial love."

"Sounds deep," Bethany said sarcastically. "He's only playing the game, Bronwyn, setting you up for the moment."

"He's really not like that. There was plenty of opportunity tonight, but he never made a move." Bronwyn felt the disappointment in her voice.

"Are you falling for a married man?" Lillian asked.

"It's not what you think."

"Deny it then," Bethany said, challenge in her voice. "Deny that you're not attracted to him."

"I'll admit there is an attraction. I won't deny that. But it's more than just a sexual attraction. He's like no one I've ever known, yet there is something about him that is distantly familiar and comfortable. Like we were soul mates meant for each other, but for some reason we were born in two different worlds. Travis has been here, hidden away in these mountains, and I've been miles away in southern California."

"Yet fate has brought you two together!" Lillian sighed. "What are the chances of the bus breaking down here... in Moonshine...connecting you two at last?"

Bronwyn sighed. "And who'd ever thought my soul mate would be married, keeping us apart forever?"

Bethany smiled at Bronwyn compassionately.

"I'm sorry. You may not be able to have him, but I think you've found your re-write. Think about it. It has everything. Leading lady meets a handsome mysterious stranger, her ultimate soul mate, who rescues her more than once."

"And they're forced to spend a long stormy night together in a hidden cabin," Lillian said.

"There is a strong attraction between them that they both are denying." Bethany was rolling out the plot now. "He's married and she is forced to stay at the inn he and his wife own."

"He's an honorable person," Lillian chimed in, excited. "Very committed to his wife, despite the fact she's been scarred by a terrible accident."

"But," Bethany continued, "His love and commitments have never been tested, since he's never been out of the small hidden town where he was born."

Lillian blossomed with dramatic flair. "Until, his world is invaded by the ever-beautiful, green-eyed temptress! Will he fall prey to his lusts and desires like every other man on this planet?"

Bronwyn couldn't help but laugh.

"Oh this is good!" Bethany said.

"How will you end it?" Lillian asked

"Time will tell," Bethany said.

"I hope it ends well." Lillian's mood turned serious. "Mavis is a sweet lady and there are children involved. They are real people, not make believe. It wouldn't be right to destroy their lives."

Bronwyn was touched by her thoughtfulness.

"Lil' honey, I'm not going to do anything. I don't want anyone getting hurt. I wouldn't intentionally inflict the pain I have been going through on anyone. Believe me. I need the story to end with Travis as the hero; I need to believe there are some decent men out there."

Bronwyn crawled under the cotton sheets and pulled them over her. Bethany turned off the lamp as the three girls settled into bed. The night breeze blew the curtains back gently. The wooden chimes pealed softly below their window as a rocking chair creaked repeatedly, rhythmically.

It wasn't the wind, however, that rocked the chair, but Mavis who sat on the porch below, rocking, hearing every word from the open window above.

CHAPTER TWENTY-FIVE

DAY FOUR

"Bronwyn."

The summons caused her to stir. She turned over to her side and gave way to her slumber, relaxing to the serenade of the frogs, crickets and the continual hoot of an owl. She had grown familiar with the quiet peaceful sounds of the mountains that filled her room each night.

"Bronwyn."

The gentle whisper of her name fell softly upon her ear.

Her eyes flew open. She glanced about the room. Bethany and Lillian were sound asleep, neither one having called her name.

The room was empty and quiet; only the hum from the rotating ceiling fan penetrated the silence. She lay still; listening, and then decided that perhaps she had been dreaming, so she closed her eyes.

"Bronwyn."

This time there was no mistaking what she heard. It was the same voice that called to her the first night in Moonshine, the voice from the mournful song that beckoned her, into the forest, as it drifted through the trees whispering her name.

The heat began again, permeating upward. Pulling back the feather comforter, she climbed out of the bed, making her way to the open window, hoping the cool night breeze would cause the penetrating heat to subside. A dense fog hung in the air, obstructing her view of the inns grounds and nearby river. Although she could not see if anyone was outside her window, she heard a faint melody of a pan flute, accompanied by the woman's enticing song. Wrapping her silk robe around her, she slipped out of the room, quietly creeping down the staircase, stealing her way outside. She stopped cold at the porch steps, wondering why she would venture out into the dark night alone, in search of the beckoning voice, especially since she knew there were disturbing secrets at play. She had a fleeting thought to go wake Bethany and have her accompany her but decided against it when she heard the woman call again. This time there seemed to be urgency in her voice that empowered her with newfound courage; so she abandoned the thought and entered the thick fog, then sprinted across the lawn. Reaching the edge of the river, she paused and listened. The woman's haunting voice grew louder, and even though the woman sung in a language she had never heard, Bronwyn understood the words of the song explicitly. The lyrics brought overwhelming sorrow consuming her as the fog began to swirl around her while other voices joined the unseen woman in song, all as equally haunting.

"Listen can you hear us?

Can you hear her?

Do you not recognize her call?

Awa is whispering,

Whispering that your deliverance is near.

The vexed voices of many have risen in song.

They inhabit the roar of the ocean;

They howl along with the wind,

Their tears combine with the falling rain,

Their moans give depth to the claps of thunder.

They are singing; Please set us free. Please set us free.

The fog swirled and blew closer, nearly suffocating her in its thickness. It was then; she realized the fog was not a fog at all, but a chorus of pale and ghostly women with strikingly beautiful faces. Their long white hair billowed in every direction, swirling like a vapor along with their flowing silver dresses. The women spun around her their many mystical faces closing in on her, smothering her.

Bronwyn tried to wake, certain she must be dreaming. She desired to step from the fog and run back to the inn, hoping to wake in her bed, but the mist was so blinding, so confusing that she was at a loss as to which way to go. She feared a step in the wrong direction would drop her in the river.

The vapor closed in as one of the ghostly women stretched out her thin white arm and touched Bronwyn's lips with her finger.

"Silent your lips and put an end to you remorseful cries.

Listen to Brijade' whisper,

Your deliverance is near.

Your deliverance is here.

I am Jourgrace', listen to me my dear and begin to remember....

Remember...

Hear my words and remember."

There was a familiarity in the woman's features and for a moment Bronwyn thought she saw herself in her eyes. Desiring to touch the woman's face, Bronwyn reached out her hand just as a solitary tear fell down her ghostly cheek. The woman smiled and then swirled away from Bronwyn's reach. A deep sorrow invaded her heart; the heaviness of it buckled her knees and sent her into the wet grass. Her heart ached deeply for something... but what?

She lay by the water's edge, waiting to wake from the puzzling dream; all the while trying to make sense of it. What did the song mean, and to whom did the mournful voices belong? Why were they in need of deliverance, and what was it they wished her to remember?

The mystical women began fading from her view, dissipating into the air, taking the fog, the song, and her strength along with them. She lay in the wet grass, unable to move, her body weakened from the encounter. Again, she dreamed of Travis surrounded by falling water and in the vision she could see his face, much clearer now. Noise and confusion surrounded him yet he never removed his eyes from her. She wanted to go to him, be near him, but as she reached out, she began to fall, plummeting into darkness, emptiness, loneliness...then strong hands took hold of her, shaking her. She woke, surprised to be lying near the river, and with Travis kneeling beside her. She looked around. No fog, no singing women. Had she been sleepwalking?

She sat up quickly, shaken and somewhat embarrassed to be lying outside in the grass. Her silk robe wet with dew, clung to her body.

"What time is it?" She asked, ignoring his gaze and noticing the sun had not risen.

"Four in the morning."

She didn't want to explain anything. She knew he would offer no insight into her strange experience anyway. He would only remain silent, keeping to himself all the answers to the secrets that haunted her.

"I've always wanted to sleep under the stars," she lied, attempting to stay as secretive as him. "They were beautiful tonight, so I decided to sleep outdoors."

She felt silly for her lame excuse and could tell by his expression that he did not believe her.

"You didn't bring a pillow or blanket?" he asked.

"No. I didn't want to get anything dirty."

"Only yourself."

He smiled as he wiped a dirty tear stained smudge from underneath her eye. Her heart raced at the feel of his hand and she wished he wouldn't entice her. Didn't he know what his touch did to her?

He offered his hand. "I'd feel much better if you slept indoors. You really shouldn't wander off alone." his warning sounded more like a command.

"Why?" She baited him.

"Because, it's not safe for you to be out here alone."

"And why is that?"

He stared at her for a moment and her spirits lifted, thinking now might be the time he would finally allude to the cloaked man, the song of the woman, or any of the unexplained events that had taken place since her arrival. As terrifying as the answers may be, she wanted to know what was going on.

"The bears feed at night," was all he said.

She stared back, exasperated at his answer.

"Bears?"

He nodded.

"They come from the woods and raid the trash. You could be mauled."

She chewed her lower lip in frustration. Why must he continue to give evasive answers, especially when he knew she was aware of something? Why couldn't he just tell her the truth? In the garden last night, he told he was protecting her. Maybe not telling her what was going on in this elusive town was his way of keeping her safe. Maybe it was one of those, I could tell you but then I'd have to kill you situations; and, if that was the case, then maybe it was best for her to play along and act as if she didn't care. But, she did care and her curiosity caused her to wonder why Travis was fully dressed and where was he going at four in the morning? She could hang back and follow him, but she had a sneaking suspicion he would know she was tracking him. She decided to play along; but she wasn't giving up.

"Thank you. I'll be sure to remember that."

She cinched the sash on her robe and headed back to the inn. She'd finish her sleep in the comfort of the grand feather bed, and come sunrise, she'd do some sleuthing and uncover the secrets of Moonshine.

CHAPTER TWENTY-SIX

Bronwyn's nocturnal wonderings robbed her of proper rest, so when Lillian and Bethany woke and went downstairs for breakfast, she thought she'd take advantage of the big empty bed and sleep in. After fifteen minutes of staring at the rotating ceiling fan, she realized her mind was much too preoccupied to rest. Today she would walk into town and do some extensive research, and hopefully uncover what was going on in Moonshine. Who were the cloaked men hiding in the woods, why were they following her, and why did she need protecting from Travis? What secrets was he keeping?

She took a quick shower and then joined the troupe for breakfast. Everyone gathered at the table except for Travis. Mavis was at the stove, flipping whole-wheat pancakes and slicing fresh fruit. She was humming again, as she did almost every morning.

Marcus poured a generous amount of syrup over his pancakes.

"What is on everyone's agenda for today?" He started to fill his mouth. "Bronwyn, I assume you will be writing?"

"Actually, I am heading into town right after breakfast. I have an idea and I'm hoping to do a little research."

"She's hoping to do a lot of research," Bethany said tauntingly.

"Some serious research," Lillian added, trying not to laugh.

Bronwyn gave them both an evil eye. The research she planned on doing had nothing to do with what they were inferring. She could care less about salvaging the lame script, but she would play along and use it as a cover while she did her investigation.

"We have a nice library in town," Carla Jo offered. "They have internet there!"

"What are you writin' about?" Molly asked while maple syrup dripped off her chin.

Mavis brought another stack of hotcakes to the table.

"Now Molly, you're never supposed to ask a writer to tell their story until it is written. It is top secret until then. But I am sure it's something we'll all enjoy reading when it's finished." She gave Bronwyn a gentle pat and then hobbled back over to the stove.

Bronwyn's stomach turned inside of her making her suddenly feeling full. Pushing her plate away from her, she announced she was off to town. Bethany and Lillian jumped to their feet informing her that they were coming along. She frowned at first, not sure that she wanted them along, but thought it might be a good front for her detective work. Besides if she uncovered something, they would be witnesses to it, and that would prove to the troupe that she wasn't losing it, even though she knew they all suspected that she was.

The walk into town did not seem as long and fearful as it had been a few days before. They enjoyed the beauty of the mountains and the peaceful existence it offered, though Bronwyn could not stop thinking about the cloaked man since her fall from the tree. She knew what she had seen; yet felt she should not speak of it to anyone. She also knew that she had never hit ground when she fell. She was still conscious when she felt the strong arms of a man catch her and touch her in the back of her neck, causing her to drift into unconsciousness. She did not fear the cloaked man, or men, as much now, knowing, they had every opportunity of carrying her off yet didn't. Whoever he was, had laid her gently on the ground for her friends to find. Still, there was Travis's statement that he was protecting her, his warning of the dangers of being alone. She was certain he was not really referring to bears.

The girls strolled down the middle the road and still not a single vehicle traveled the winding two-lane highway into Moonshine. This unnerved her as well, and added to the mysteriousness of the place.

As they entered town, she was surprised at the bustle of activity so early in the morning. Many of the local residents lined the main street, constructing booths of various kinds. In the grand courtyard, workers were building a large wooden platform. Several firefighters were stringing up lights and hanging decorations from their ladders. Trays of warm fresh baked pastries and hot donuts flew out of the bakery free of charge for the workers. The coffee shop served mugs of steaming hot coffee and tea. Lively mountain ballads piped through the town's sound system, filling the street with folksy music.

A large banner flapping in the morning breeze explained the activity. The banner reminded Bronwyn of the occasion Gil had brought to her attention the first day. The day of the fateful storm that nearly took her life.

Midsummer's Night Cream

Moonshines Annual Ice Cream Festival

Saturday Night August 16th

The residents merrily continued their duties. Everyone offered a smile, a friendly wave of the hand, a tipped hat, and myriad hellos. Each resident insisted that the girls and the troupe attend their cherished event. Each invitation added the challenge that the girls would indeed enjoy the best ice cream they had ever put into their mouths; yet, in spite of everyone's hospitality, the uneasiness washed over her once again. Moonshine affected her in strange ways. There were times she felt happy and comfortable; however, those moments were fleeting and all too soon gave way to the unsettling anxiety that would overshadow her without warning, like the terror she felt at the waterfalls. Then, there was the matter of her bizarre dreams; last night's being the most unusual. It also frightened her that she had been sleep walking, something she hadn't done since childhood. It was these things that made her desperately wish the bus were repaired, allowing her to ride away and separate herself from this place.

Bethany and Lillian seemed unaffected as always. They did not experience any strange sensations or phenomena's. She wondered if she should try confiding to Bethany one more time about her anxious feelings or about the strange goings on. In times past she had trusted her every secret to Bethany, save the recent pregnancy and miscarriage, yet for some unknown reason, she felt estranged from her friend. As much as she hated to admit it, there was a growing rift between them. She contemplated that once they left this bizarre town, she might leave the troupe and take a long much needed vacation away from everyone. Maybe time away would help her put things in perspective.

It was the elegant woman with the auburn hair that unnerved Bronwyn the most. Stopping her work on a booth covered entirely with decorations of butterflies, the woman approached the girls and grabbed Bronwyn's hand.

"I'm so glad you have finally come to us." She whispered while squeezing Bronwyn's hand. "We have waited for so long. You've renewed our hope."

She held Bronwyn's hand so securely that the ring she was wearing left a deep imprint in her neighboring finger. The woman dropped Bronwyn's hand and returned to her booth; her puzzling words still echoing in Bronwyn's ears causing more uneasiness.

"Did you hear what she said to me?"

"No. What?" Lillian asked.

"She said she was glad I had finally come. That they've been waiting for me a long time. What did she mean by that?"

"Probably meant she's glad they finally have some visitors around here," Bethany said casually. "She probably gets bored of seeing the same people day after day."

Another level-headed, logical explanation. Bronwyn felt angry with herself for even mentioning it. Still, even though Bethany's explanation seemed rational, Bronwyn knew the woman meant more.

Bethany interrupted her tumbling thoughts.

"Hey, you just passed the library."

"I'm not doing my research in the library. Bronwyn said, pointing across the street to the local hair salon. "I'm doing it in the gossip center of every town."

Bethany's face broke in to a large grin. "Good idea!"

"You'd trust them with your hair?" Lillian asked.

"Not my hair, my feet. I could really use a relaxing pedicure."

Bethany examined the ends of her hair. "I could use a little trim."

"Oh I don't know," Lillian warned. "It's such a small, secluded town, I'm not certain they would be up to date on the latest styles."

"I'm not having it cut," Bethany reiterated. "Just a slight trim."

They entered the salon. Any stereotyping of a small town beauty shop suddenly dissipated. The décor was much different than they expected. The ambiance was that of a jungle. Tall shoots of bamboo and various palms grew from large basins scattered about the floor. Water trickled down the smooth black marbled walls, emptying into rectangular pools that housed many colorful fresh-water fish. Overstuffed chairs, upholstered in zebra and cheetah print fabrics, offered rest for the waiting clients. The ceiling was made entirely of bamboo and palm leaves, resembling a thatched roof; recessed lighting gave a twilight feel. A small cabana, housing a reception desk made of bamboo, blocked a beaded curtain, veiling the entrance into the parlor.

The girls introduced themselves to the receptionist, who immediately escorted them into the servicing area where the rain forest theme continued. Three floor length mirrors hung on the walls with styling chairs set beside each one. There was no cumbersome hair stations in sight, just rolling carts equipped with the necessary tools to perform whatever service was requested. Each area had mosquito netting draped over it. Heavy old-fashioned ceiling fans turned slowly, offering a comfortable breeze and ventilation from the smells that accompany a salon.

Bethany was ushered to a styling chair draped, and left waiting for her stylist. The receptionist continued to escort Bronwyn and Lillian into another room, seating them at what looked like a man-made waterfall. On top of the smooth, large boulders were soft cushions. Water fell from underneath their seats into stone basins filled with smooth pebbles of various sizes. Soft, relaxing music played in the background, interrupted by an occasional trumpet of an elephant, a caw of a bird, or the roar of a lion.

Two smiling manicurists entered the room, positioning themselves at the feet of Bronwyn and Lillian.

"Hello!" The overly bleached blond woman said to Bronwyn.

"My name is Ashley."

Ashley appeared to be Bronwyn's age. She was pretty and tanned. Her hair was white from over bleaching. Her companion manicurist, Sherrie, appeared to be the same age as Ashley. Her hair, a very unnatural shade of red, grew in curls that fell well beyond her waistline. Her pale skin was dotted with freckles, continuing on her lips. Her blue gray eyes that seemed to house a freckle or two as well were dancing in excitement, and Bronwyn could see that the two women were thrilled at the opportunity waiting them. Lillian was right; the people here acted giddy, treating them as if they were celebrities.

"Are you enjoying your stay at Sandalwood Inn?" Ashley asked as she went to work on Bronwyn's feet.

She nodded.

"Yes. The inn is very comfortable, and the gardens are breathtaking."

"Isn't Mavis the best?" Sherrie chimed in. "She just adores that inn. It's her way of helping people. All Travis's patients stay there."

"Patients?" Bronwyn repeated the word.

"Uh huh" Ashley casually glanced up at Bronwyn while she trimmed her cuticles.

"Didn't he tell you? He's a doctor."

Bronwyn and Lillian exchanged surprised glances. Her plan was playing out. Not five minutes into the conversation, and already the girls revealed new information on Travis. She was sure to uncover her coveted information.

"He is?" Lillian was intrigued.

"Actually, he is a healer." Sherrie corrected Ashley's statement. "People come from all over the world for his treatments. He has a very high success rate. Most of the patients that come to him have been sent home by their doctors to die. Travis treats them, and soon they return home cured. He hasn't lost a patient yet."

Bronwyn's mind was spinning once again.

"Are you joking?"

Sherrie shook her head. "Why would we tease about that? You've seen the healing gardens where he grows all the herbs and plants to make his oils and medications. That's what the big sheds out back behind the garage are for. They house all this special equipment to distill the oils from the plants. I can't explain the process; all I know is that it really seems to work, better than regular medicine anyway."

Bronwyn was dumfounded. Still it all made perfect sense. Each garden was designed in a special way, each growing strange varieties of plants, offering comfort and vitality just by inhaling their aromas. Bronwyn thought of the night in the cabin when Travis efficiently dressed her wound. He had had used a strange, yet soothing mixture of balms and oils with unique scents; Unique to her, anyway, but apparently not to these manicurist.

"He is very generous, too," Ashley said. "He gives so much of his money away. He has opened clinics all over the world, most of them in very poor countries."

Lillian couldn't withhold her shock. "Travis has traveled the world?"

"Yep," Sherrie answered proudly, as if in some way Travis belonged to her personally. "That man's been all over this world. I'd say he pretty much knows his way across the planet."

Bronwyn was speechless. She sat astounded, as Ashley took the smooth stones from the bottom of the basin and massaged her feet.

"I thought he was some backward mountain man that had never been out of Moonshine," she heard herself confess aloud.

"He just doesn't seem the type," Lillian added.

"The type?" Sherrie laughed. "He's the type, alright. My type. He's pretty near perfect if you ask me. I don't think there's a woman around here that wouldn't take that beautiful man if they could get him. Myself included!"

"Sherrie!" Ashley said, her voice rising, "What would Martin say if he heard you?"

"Oh he'd get over it." Sherrie began to massage Lillian's feet. "Besides, Martin doesn't have anything to worry about. Everyone knows Travis's heart belongs to only one woman."

"Lucky Mavis," Lillian said.

"Yep," Sherrie agreed. "That woman's been through some hard times, but all in all, I'd have to say she's blessed to have Travis."

Bronwyn's heart ached. All this new information, this "research," was proving to be more than she had anticipated. The fact Travis was a doctor surprised her. That he was extremely wealthy, and traveled the world, opening clinics for the less fortunate, shocked her....and stung a bit. The final blow to her heart was Sherrie's statement that he could have any woman he so desired; however, his heart belonged to only one. Again, she reprimanded her pain. She should be delighted in the fact that Travis was proving to be the hero of whom she desired to write. Yet the pain was real, and she abhorred what it was doing to her. For the past six months, Ryan had contributed so much sadness, despondency and sick feelings to the pit of her stomach. Now, she realized she had shoved most of her thoughts of Ryan aside and replaced them with Travis. Could she indeed be falling for him, as Bethany so adamantly stated? Could she be falling for a man she had known for less than three days? She was too smart for that. Yet, there was a strong undeniable yearning for him that far surpassed any silly crush. She could not understand why she desired a man so deeply; especially one she wasn't sure she could trust. She wished Larry would hurry and repair their bus. Then she could flee far away from Moonshine, and never think of him again.

"The people of Moonshine will surprise you," Ashley said proudly. "We have some of the most interesting characters you could ever meet living here."

The girls seemed talkative and eager to give out free information so Bronwyn took the opportunity to explore a bit further.

"Were you both born here?"

Both girls concentrated on their task, dropping their gaze into the pedicure tub.

"No." Ashley answered for them both; but gave no more information. Bronwyn thought it was somewhat peculiar sense she was so chatty only moments before. She pressed the matter some more."

"Where were you born and what brought you to Moonshine?"

Sherrie took over.

"Our families relocated here years ago, and we've been here ever sense."

"You've never left?" Lillian asked shocked.

"We've traveled some. But this is home for now anyway." Sherrie looked over at Bronwyn. "Though I suspect I might be leaving soon." She smiled, and her grin unnerved her, and although their casual banter seemed honest, Bronwyn sensed an underlying meaning.

Bronwyn took a deep breath and asked another.

"I've seen a man around here; he has long hair, which he usually wears back in a ponytail. He's unshaven, has a nice body, cool clothes. He wears dark sunglasses and he smokes. Who is he?"

"That would be Falcon." Sherrie said, blushing. "I'm in love with the thought of that man!"

"Gosh, Sherrie!" Ashley reprimanded her again. "I feel sorry for poor Martin. You're lusting over every man in town but him."

Lillian laughed at the girl's banter.

Bronwyn quickly took back control, not wishing the conversation to phase into frivolity and the topic be dismissed before she found anything out.

"Tell me about him."

Both girls remained silent for a moment, and when Bronwyn noticed them looking at each other out of the corner of their eyes, she knew she had stumbled onto something. Ashley finally spoke.

"There's not much to tell. He's pretty mysterious, keeps to himself. We think he's some kind of secret agent," she said in a hushed voice, as if someone bugged the salon with listening devices.

Bronwyn felt the heat. Her pulse quickened. No doubt about it. This Falcon was the cloaked man! But, if he was some sort of secret agent, why was he following her?"

"He was stalking us," Bronwyn said.

Lillian glanced at her. "He was? When?"

"He was the one following us on our walk the first day into town. It wasn't an animal in the woods. It was him. I saw him. Then he was at the café later when we were having lunch. I saw him staring at us from across the patio. He gave me the creeps."

Ashley laughed. "That would be him alright. He always watches people. I guess no one ever told him staring was rude."

Once again Ashley laughed it off, trying to divert the truth, but Bronwyn knew there was more to him than poor social skills.

"He has friends that come to visit him from time to time," Sherrie added also trying to make light of the subject. "They all have bird names too. I heard him call one of them Hawke, another Macaw, and there's one I heard him call Vulture. Talk about someone giving you the creeps!" Sherrie shuddered. "I guess they're all agents too."

Bronwyn's mind continued to spin. This was all beginning to sound vaguely familiar. She had heard of this before, of secret agents with bird names. But where? She'd recently read about them but remembered dismissing the notion. It seemed so ridiculous. When and where had she encountered these people? Suddenly she recalled the incident. Her deleted files! She'd read that synopsis yesterday while scanning through her discarded writings.

Uncomfortable, she shifted her feet in the water.

"I'm sorry did I hurt you?" Ashley asked.

"No. Just a nervous twitch, I guess. So, do these secret agents live in the woods and wear black hooded robes?" Bronwyn noticed Sheeree and Ashley exchange looks. "Do they? Is there a secret society or cult up here we should know about?" For once, the two girls grew quiet.

Ashley removed Bronwyn's feet from the basin and promptly drained the tub. She toweled them off and then proceeded to rub an agreeable smelling lotion over them.

"Anyone else intriguing?" Lillian hoped to dispel the awkwardness in the room.

"Adam and Alycia." Ashley answered as if she was relieved to discuss a new topic. "They're fraternal twins who were separated at birth."

"You do not know how to tell a story!" Sherrie said. "You left out the best part."

"I'm not a gossip like you." Ashley sounded prudish. "Besides, I won't rob you of the thrill of telling it."

Sherrie leaned in, speaking in a hushed whisper.

"Rumor is, they are supposedly royalty, a prince and a princess in exile from their country. They are supposedly heirs to a throne somewhere. That's the real reason they were separated at birth. Their parents were assassinated. Loyal friends of the family took the babies and fled the country."

Lillian sat on the edge of her cushioned chair, enthralled. Bronwyn remained silent. Her stomach was in knots and her head began to feel light. She wished Sherrie would stop talking. It was if they all had secretly read her deleted files, and then decided to tell the stories back to her. She remembered retrieving that synopsis yesterday as well. *My Better Half.* She could find no explanation over what was playing out. However, she was certain it was not altitude sickness.

Ashley and Sherrie quickly finished polishing the girls' toenails and cleaned up their supplies. They left Bronwyn and Lillian alone to dry.

"My God Bronwyn, why did you ask such a strange question?" Lillian asked. "I think you may have offended them. In any case, you learned quite a bit about Travis. I think your research was pretty successful."

Bronwyn wished the polish would hurry and dry. Her next stop in this town would be Larry's garage, to check on the status of the ordered parts. She wanted out of this place at once!

Her pressing engagement was quickly forgotten when Bethany joined them in the pedicure room. She and Lillian were both caught off guard at the sight of her new mullet.

"Oh my God!" Lillian exclaimed, covering her mouth with her slender fingers. "What happened to your hair?"

"Can we just get out of here before I start to cry?" she asked.

Bronwyn bit her lip in an attempt to choke back her laughter.

Lillian's eyes flashed. "I warned you."

"I just asked for a trim!" Bethany said in a hoarse whisper. "I should have known when she suggested that I would look good in the Jennifer Aniston cut. I told her I used to have that cut, way back when it was in style. Let's just get out of here."

The girls paid and hurriedly left the salon.

Sherrie placed the pedicure utensils in the disinfectant solution and washed her hands. "You really shouldn't smoke in here you know."

"So you're in love with the thought of me huh?"

Sherrie smiled and turned off the water. "So how'd we do?"

Smoking man extinguished his cigarette and stood. "Pretty good. Keep it up and I might let you join the NESST." He flashed his impish grin and disappeared out the back door.

CHAPTER TWENTY-SEVEN

As the day wore on, the outdoor activities in Moonshine shifted from productive construction to gaiety and frivolity. With most of the work completed, the residents enjoyed a pre-festival party. As with every year on the eve of the festival, the café and other local restaurants treated volunteer workers to a free buffet dinner on the courtyard. The bands, taking their turns at a sound check and a brief rehearsal, entertained the dining workers. Dancing followed, along with homemade alcohol and the town soon came alive.

The girls, along with the rest of the troupe, spent the remainder of the afternoon helping construct and decorate, much to the delight of the local towns-folk. Karley and Walt offered to unload the troupe's superior sound system from the bus, despite Wilbur's loud protesting. Bronwyn ran into Larry and questioned him on the status of the parts, only to learn that they had yet to arrive. The eight-to-ten business day estimate was proving to be the actual waiting time.

As the evening wore on, and the strung lights lit the courtyard, the grounds filled with people. They lounged on the ground or danced to the music. Bronwyn soon found herself on the large wooden platform with the others in the troupe, giving an impromptu performance. Marcus had finally relented, due to the pleadings of the locals. He decided on a comedy selection from one of their previous productions, instead of a scene from their current piece, Bronwyn was struggling to re-write.

The locals enjoyed the performance, breaking out in spontaneous laughter at the comedy, and standing to applaud when it was over. Another band took the stage as the troupe descended. The dancing started up once more. Bronwyn joined them on the grass; quickly learning the steps. This dance was obviously a local favorite, perhaps even legendary in these mountains. She enjoyed the fast-paced choreography, spinning from one partner to the next. Each face she connected with, gave her a wide toothy grin. She was spun into the arms of the always-smiling Gil Peverly, the jokester and owner of the market. Sidestepping and shuffling, he gave a slight bow, "Howdy little lady."

This time Bronwyn returned the smile she had withheld at their first meeting. Gil spun her around and passed her into the arms of Larry the mechanic.

"Parts still haven't arrived," he said, grinning as he side-stepped, shuffled and spun her into the arms of an extremely attractive man, she hadn't seen in Moonshine, before now.

He was olive-skinned with dark curly hair brushing the top of his shoulders. His eyes were a deep steel blue. He had a gentle face and his speaking voice matched his appearance. He offered Bronwyn a warm hello and an adoring smile. Slightly bowing his head in a respectful nod, he continued dancing while never removing his eyes from her face. All too soon, he twirled her into the arms of Trent.

"Well hello there, love." Trent's familiar British accent comforted her. Another side step and shuffle, and Bronwyn found herself twirled into the arms of Falcon! Dark glasses covered his eyes. His impish grin frightened her. He said nothing as he twirled her; nor did he pass her on down the line. Instead, he purposely kept her to himself, spinning her out of the dance line, maintaining a tight hold as he whirled her forcefully across the lawn.

She panicked. Why had she let her guard down? Her afternoon with the friendly residents disarmed her to the point of second guessing herself; thinking that maybe she'd been mistaken about the place. But now, locked in Falcon's tight hold, the suspicion resurfaced. She tried to focus her eyes; however, everything was a blur as if she was riding some spinning carnival ride. The heat raised uncontrollably, her heart now in her throat, choking her. She tried to pull away, but his grip remained firm. He kept his body close to hers, moving her along quickly across the grounds. She tried once more to push him away, yet was no match for his strength.

"Stay with me, scribe," his deep voice whispered in her ear. "Don't fight me."

Scribe? What did he mean by that? He moved her swiftly through the crowd, his body creating a shield. Again, she tried to focus and look around for help, yet he spun her with such force she could not.

"Don't try to look around." He turned her head, burying it into his chest. There was no air, she felt it difficult to breathe. She desperately tried to push him away. However, her attempt proved futile against his crushing strength.

Then as suddenly as he had grabbed her, he let her go. Stumbling across the grass she regained her footing and looked around for help. He was not there. Where had he gone? She gazed down the line of dancers, yet he was not among them. She quickly scanned the courtyard; no sign of him. How could he have disappeared so quickly?

The band continued to play, their music blaring from the speakers. She felt trapped in the center of a gigantic carrousel, trying to make her way back to her friends, while everything spun around her. The heat began to rise again, as it did at the falls. Her legs became wobbly, her heart raced at an alarming rate. The twinkling lights faded all around her. She stumbled and lost her footing.

She heard a voice in the distance asking her if she were all right. Then there was sudden darkness as she felt herself falling.

Ashley and Sherrie caught her as she fainted and laid her gently on the ground.

"Someone wanna go get Travis!" Ashley yelled above the music.

Several people stopped dancing, soon a small crowd gathered. Bethany, Trent and Lillian pushed their way through and knelt beside of their fallen friend.

"What happened?" Trent asked. "Don't tell me she was climbing bloody trees again."

"I saw her standing there looking pale," Ashley said, eagerly offering Trent the news. "Then she just kind of fell over."

A sudden gust of wind blew through the crowd, sending paper plates and napkins flying across the courtyard. Booth awnings billowed upward, a couple of makeshift stands collapsed. Bronwyn's eyes fluttered open. She looked around, instantly noticing the sea of faces staring at her from above.

"Bronwyn?" It was Bethany.

"What happened?"

"You fainted, hon," Ashley said.

Bethany leaned in.

"Are you okay? I think maybe you should see a doctor." She whispered her next words, so no one else could hear. "You're not on anything, are you?"

"No!" Bronwyn said, giving her a disgusted look. "Of course not! You know me better than that."

"I just thought maybe you had gotten some anti-depressants or something. You know, because of Ryan."

Bronwyn stood and dust herself off. "Didn't you see what just happened to me? Didn't anyone?"

Bethany shook her head. "No, what happened?"

"I was accosted, that's what! Something's going on around here and I want to know what it is." She made her accusations and demands out loud to the crowd who starred back at her. No one spoke except for Ashley.

"Maybe you should wait for Travis, you know....just to make sure you're okay."

She had not seen Travis since early morning when he woke her at the river. He had not been at breakfast, nor had she seen him in town. Now that the girls told her more about this mysterious mountain man, she decided the less she saw of him, the better.

"I don't need his help."

Her words were too late. Pushing his way through the crowd, Travis approached and stood face to face with her. His hair was wet with perspiration and blood oozed from his bottom lip. His clothes were dirty and torn. Bronwyn noticed blood on the bottom of his shirt as well. His disheveled appearance surprised her while his usual calm countenance gave way to agitation.

"You alight?" his voice demanded an answer.

"I'm fine." She bit back.

Sherrie stepped in close to him. "She fainted. Ashley and I caught her. We didn't let her hit the ground."

He never took his eyes off Bronwyn, much to Sherrie's dismay.

Bronwyn starred back, half angry, full of sentiments she didn't fully understand. She was angry with him for causing most of these emotions and for hiding the secrets she was sure would unravel all of these peculiarities. Yet, he kept these mysteries undisclosed. She had half a mind to shout out accusations and reveal tell-tale information of the cloaked figures that inhabited the surrounding woods. However, she felt as if most of the town already knew. Anything she said might bring a world of dread upon her and the troupe.

"No need to worry about me," she said sarcastically. "It's only altitude sickness, I'm sure."

She brushed past him and headed home. The troupe fell in place, catching up with her on the long walk back to the inn.

Removing the handkerchief from his back pocket, Travis wiped the fresh blood from his knuckles and mouth. He made eye contact with Falcon and with a slight nod Falcon stole into the surrounding woods. Travis remained standing, watching her, until the troupe disappeared from view.

CHAPTER TWENTY-EIGHT

Bronwyn lay in bed, starring at the rotating ceiling fan. Despite her long and adventurous day, slumber would not visit. She realized she was much too tense to sleep. For starters, Bethany had greatly annoyed her on the walk back to the inn. She had launched into a barrage of questions to support her growing suspicion that Bronwyn was on drugs. Against her better judgment, Bronwyn had attempted to tell Bethany of some of the strange events. She mentioned nothing of her deleted stories, realizing it would be impossible to try and explain, seeing she had no explanation for it herself. She confided to Bethany of the peculiar happenings in Moonshine. She mentioned Falcon, the secret locked garden, and the covert meeting between him and Travis. Bethany barely listened, dismissing the stories completely, only to ask more questions about her psyche. It was obvious Bethany had become a recent student of Trent's philosophies.

Feeling defeated, Bronwyn fell into bed, feigning exhaustion and sleep to escape Bethany's constant advice. She listened to the heavy breathing of her two roommates, her mind too active to sleep.

Quietly, she slipped from the bed, tiptoed down the stairs and walked out the back door. The night air was surprisingly cool. The mugginess of the evening had dissipated. She lay on the cushioned porch swing, swaying back and forth with ease, hoping the rhythm of the swing, combined with the chorus of croaking toads and chirping crickets would be the sleeping aid she desperately needed. The fresh air and change of scenery did wonders to relax the tenseness of her body, slowing down the ramblings of her mind.

Unexpectedly, she heard voices coming from far down the cobblestone path. She rose from the swing, descended the porch steps, and crept quietly down the stony path. Making her way, she picked up on the sound of a scuffle and voices engaged in an intense argument. She couldn't tell which garden the disturbance came from, but as she walked, the commotion grew louder. She stopped at the sixth garden. The gate was unlatched. She pushed it open slowly, hoping it wouldn't creak and alert the garden's occupants. A splinter found its way deep underneath her skin, as her slender finger slid across the rough wood, pushing open the heavy door. She pulled her hand away from the gate, recoiling at the unwanted pain. She examined the splinter and realized it would take tweezers and much better light in order for her to remove it.

Nevertheless, she slipped quietly into the garden. Large trees and vines created a canopy at the entrance. This provided her with the perfect cover for her clandestine investigation. If Travis would not tell her what was going on, she would find out on her own. She inched her way past the massive oaks, her slender body slithering through the hanging foliage of the weeping willows. The canopy of leaves kept her hidden, providing her with secrecy, while the soft earth beneath her bare feet allowed no noise, muffling her approach.

The ruckus grew louder. The angry voices now clear. She continued to move from tree to tree, keeping under the weeping willows as she made her way closer to the center of the garden. She could see figures moving up ahead. Reaching out her hand, she slowly parted the hanging branches. The heat rushed upon her, overwhelming her. The man in the road, the night of her arrival, was in the garden.

The warrior stood tall; his features powerful. Emitting from his skin was a faint light creating a golden glow. Poised to fight, he stood alongside Falcon, who forcefully held a man at knifepoint. The prisoner appeared to be composed even though Falcon pressed the knife against his throat. Bronwyn swallowed a frightened gasp. There was something about the man's spiteful demeanor.

A third man stood with Falcon and seemed to be interrogating their prisoner. He too was muscular, well-built and wore his long blond hair fastened back in a ponytail. She hadn't seen him before but like most of the men she had encountered recently, he was pleasing to the eyes.

"Answer me!" The blond man demanded.

"Surely you know." The prisoner choked out his words, with the knife pressed against his throat. "Abaddon's realm is spreading, growing in strength. His power is more than you can imagine. You can kill me but more will come. Your tower of safety is fallen. We found your hiding place and have released the information. We know the scribe is here, somewhere. We will find them, and when we do, they will be destroyed. Then we will find Asa and the other heirs. It's just a matter of time."

Stepping forward, the bronze warrior spoke. His voice was vast and haunting as if some sort of woodwind instrument were playing along with him. The sound of it was captivating, drawing Bronwyn in to each word he said.

"Know that we will not miss a move Abaddon makes. We are aware of every step you take in these mountains. Your sole purpose was to make a name for yourself and receive your reward of power; however, the only reward that the one you serve will offer for your allegiance is death. Your foolish choices have trapped you in a dead end. Death is now the reward you will receive for your betrayal."

Taking a step backward, the warrior gave Falcon a nod. Falcon's hand moved swiftly across the prisoner's neck. Blood spread quickly, soaking into the fabric of his shirt, as he slumped to the ground. Unwillingly, Bronwyn allowed a gasp to escape her lips.

All heads turned in her direction. The warriors' eyes glowed as they pierced across the garden, cutting through the foliage. Ducking, she took cover under the tree. Her legs wobbled nearly giving away. She was witness to a murder! If they found her, would they do the same to her?

She needed to run and wake Marcus along with the rest of the troupe. Without warning, strong hands grabbed her from behind, pulling her beneath the tree and out of view. Terror rose inside of her as she anticipated the cold steel of a knife slicing through her neck. She decided to scream for help; perhaps the noise would wake her sleeping friends.

Before the scream could escape her lips, a hand pressed firmly over her mouth. A voice from behind her, instructed to remain quiet, as she was forced against the tree trunk. She recognized the voice of the one holding her. Her heart pounded hard. The heat continued to rise. Her breathing became labored.

"Sh-sh." The voice was calm. "Don't make a noise, or they will find you."

A moment passed. "I warned you not to venture out alone. From here on out you'd do best to listen to my instructions."

The darkness hindered her view. The only thing visible to her was Travis' dark eyes illuminated by a streak of moonlight penetrating through the foliage. He removed his hand from her mouth and gently pulled her face toward his. Leaning over, he tenderly kissed her on the lips. She felt his fingers press into the back of her neck. Her legs buckled and all went black.

CHAPTER TWENTY-NINE

DAY FIVE

Bronwyn woke to the gentle hand of Mavis on her back.

"Seems you did your sleeping on the porch last night," she said cheerfully. "I've done that a time or two myself. There's nothing like the night air to hypnotize and put you in a deep sleep. The only side effect is the mountain air. It does bring on some pretty strange dreams, and might I say you were definitely having one. You woke me up last night with your hollering and carrying on."

Mavis poured a tall mug of steaming coffee and handed it to Bronwyn. "This should clear up the haziness I suspect is clouding your mind right now."

Bronwyn sat up, confused by her surroundings. She looked over the property. The sun was just making its way over the mountains, striking ground glistening with the morning dew. The pungent aromas from the gardens stimulated her nostrils as they wafted in the morning breeze. She reached for the coffee, and sipped the strong liquid, nearly choking at the bitterness of it.

"I woke you during the night?" She asked.

"Sure did. My window is directly above this side of the porch. I heard you scream. Sounded like you were scared out of your wits. I ran out here and found you havin' a fitful sleep on the swing."

Bronwyn took another small slip of the awful coffee. She vaguely remembered leaving her room last night. Could she have been sleep walking again? As the steam from the coffee filled her nostrils, the events gradually made their way back into her head. The memory of the intense argument began to emerge, and within seconds all the images raced back into her mind...the warrior...Falcon...the blond man...the murder...and then Travis under the tree...The kiss!

Bronwyn involuntarily raised her hands to her lips before she noticed Mavis was watching her intently. She lowered her hand quickly.

"Must have been some kind of dream." A sly smile pulled at the corner of Mavis' lips before she gave Bronwyn a suspicious look.

Bronwyn could sense the distrust and wondered if it stemmed from Mavis' wariness of her and Travis. Maybe Mavis could sense a mutual attraction as well.

"You want to tell me about it?"

Bronwyn's heart picked up its pace. "Tell you about what?"

"Your dream hon."

"I don't think it was a dream." She said boldly. "I think I stumbled on something I wasn't supposed to see."

"Sometimes it helps when you talk out a disturbing dream. Even though it seems so real at the time, you realize how absurd it is when you hear yourself telling it to someone. You suddenly realize it couldn't have possibly happened."

Bronwyn starred back at Mavis in an attempt to see through her pretense. Despite Mavis's outward appearance as a country mountain woman, somewhat beaten down by a hard life, Bronwyn believed she held as many secrets as Travis and the rest of these peculiar town folk.

"I left my room because I couldn't sleep. I was upset about something that happened in town earlier. I came out to the porch and that's' when I heard a heated argument in the garden. I followed the voices just in time to witness an execution."

"An execution! My lands that would cause anyone to scream. No wonder you were scared...who was executed?"

"I don't know. I've never seen him before. But the sight of him unnerved me. He spoke in a foreign language and said a lot of strange things, like a tower of safety falling and finding some heirs and a scribe and destroying them."

"If he spoke in a strange language, how is it you were able to understand what he said?"

Bronwyn felt herself blush as she realized the impossibility of her statement. "I don't know how I understood, but I did."

"You're the writer for the troupe aren't you?" Mavis asked. "Maybe you're stressing over your re-write so much your dreaming people want to destroy you."

Bronwyn remained silent for a moment before speaking again. She was sure what she experienced had not been a dream. However, Mavis friendly interrogation was beginning to cause her to wonder. She shook her head slowly.

"No, it was real. I saw it all. There was this very tall man who was dressed like a warrior...."

She stopped cold, realizing how absurd her story sounded. Nevertheless...

"The man who did the killing was someone I have seen here in Moonshine. I think they call him Falcon."

Mavis remained unaffected. "What happened in town earlier that upset you?" She sounded like a psychiatrist.

"Falcon got pretty forceful with me last night."

"How so?"

"During the dance, he pulled me away from everyone and spun me into the crowd. When I tried to get away, he called me 'Scribe' and told me not to fight him."

Mavis smiled. "But he didn't hurt you. That's the way some of these mountain men are, but you bein' from the city wouldn't understand our ways. No wonder you had such a frightful dream about him."

The diplomatic stare down between her and Mavis continued, while each one's distrust for the other seemed to hover just beneath the surface, unspoken. Bronwyn broke her gaze and looked over towards the gardens and then back to Mavis before she stood.

"It seemed so real."

"I'm sure it did." Mavis smiled. "How did it end?"

She sipped the coffee, only to hide her face. How could she tell the part where Travis kissed her? Mavis made her uncomfortable. Despite her supposed concern for her, she felt Mavis already knew the answers to the questions she was asking.

Bronwyn forced the bitter coffee down and handed the mug back to Mavis.

"I don't remember. It's all still a little sketchy. I guess you're right; it was just a dream. Thanks for the coffee. I think I'll go take a long hot shower to work out the kinks in my neck."

Mavis waited for Bronwyn to disappear inside of the inn before pouring the remaining coffee in the grass. She grabbed the shovel leaning against the side of the inn, and limped out into the gardens.

The steaming shower relaxed Bronwyn, soothing her aching neck and back. The porch swing hadn't made a comfortable bed. She hated to think she was sleep walking again after all these years. It used to be a problem for her as a child; resulting in her parents taking such extreme measures as alarming their house and adding bolt locks on every door. Her dreams as a child were night terrors, and although she could not remember any of them, her mother had documented almost every one. She prayed they weren't returning, but her dreams of late had been quite vivid and disturbing, and she hoped that maybe the cause was the higher altitude. Once they left this God forsaken place, she hoped the nightmares and sleepwalking would end.

Massaging the shampoo into her hair, she felt a painful stinging in her finger and discovered a splinter embedded under her skin. The events of last night had not been a dream! The splinter was proof she'd witnessed a murder! Her mind reeled with questions. She let the warm waters run over her as she tried to calm and focus. She thought back to the garden, the words of the murdered man. He spoke in another language, yet she understood…even though what he said made no sense to her. However, he had definitely evoked the wrath of his three captors when he mentioned a tower of safety falling, and that his people had found the hiding place.

His next words unnerved her. He mentioned finding a scribe and destroying them along with a man named Asa and other heirs. Heirs of what? Could he be referring to Adam and Alycia? And, who was Asa and the scribe? Could he have possibly been referring to her? After all, that is what Falcon called her, and Travis admitted he was protecting her. When he caught her under the tree, he warned her not to make a noise or they would find her. Who are "*they*?" She was more confused than ever.

However, the events in the garden were powerfully overshadowed at the recollection of his kiss. He had kissed her! She remembered him pulling her face to his and tenderly placing his mouth on her lips. It had been quick and unexpected, yet more passionate than any kiss she had ever received from Ryan. The kiss was given by Travis. He had not stolen a kiss from her under the privacy of the weeping willow. He had not satisfied his desire by taking a kiss; rather, he had *given* her a kiss. He had placed a kiss on her lips, for her. Then he'd placed his fingers on the back of her neck causing her to slip into unconsciousness, just like the cloaked man when she fell from the tree.

CHAPTER THIRTY

The only reason Bronwyn showed up at breakfast was to see if Travis was present. He wasn't. She picked at her food, her inner anxiousness suppressing her appetite. She ignored the idle chatter at the table and gazed out of the window, thinking it would be a smart move to return to the garden and collect any evidence of last night's slaying. Surely there would be blood in the grass... something to prove to everyone she hadn't dreamed it all up.

Marcus interrupted her thoughts to ask again about the re-write. She sighed. Her mind was far from the plot of a cheesy romance. However, to satisfy him, she mentioned that she had been contemplating the idea, of instead of doing a simple re-write, she would rather scrap it and try an entirely new script. To her surprise, he endorsed the idea. He lovingly confessed that her latest script had not been one of his favorites. He went as far as to say that he absolutely abhorred it, finding it was full of cynicism, bitterness, and a bit apathetic, and admitted he would be delighted in rehearsing a brand new script.

Then, he told her he was actually pleased with their recent turn of events. He was happy that the bus broke down when and where it did. Despite the fact they had lost their biggest venue of the summer, he realized that the troupe needed this sabbatical. Had they plowed through their summer schedule, attempting to perform the ill written script, he felt they may have lost more than just the revenues of one missed engagement. Bronwyn appeared to be listening to his ramblings, responding with an occasional smile and nod, but her mind was far away.

After breakfast, she slipped away from the group and settled on the porch swing. The grand veranda provided a pleasant view, and a large spinning ceiling fan that generated a nice breeze the summer day would not.

She opened her laptop, to reveal her dormant files, the last place she visited. Her mind returned to the pedicure room, the stories told by Ashley and Sherrie. She paused a moment or two, debating on whether or not to open the file again. If the stories the girls told were identical to those she had written some time ago, she wasn't sure she could muddle through the strong emotions.

She felt desperate for more information about Falcon. After all, she had witnessed him commit a murder. If there was some clue in her files as to what was going on, she was intent on finding it. Her slender finger clicked on *Birds of Prey.* The file opened once more, displaying the short synopsis. Taking a deep breath, she scrolled down to her character list and read the typed names:

Falcon, Macaw, Hawke, and Vulture, All agents of an elite top secret organization known as the N.E.S.S.T, a group of top secret agents, all possessing bird names. Falcon, the leader of this group, is sworn protector of a Prince who is being hunted by an evil assassin. Falcon, and the other birds of prey, have made their NESST in the branches of The Tree of Life.

Leaning into the swing, she thought back to when she received the inspiration for this story. A vivid dream jolted her awake at 3 a.m. one morning. Its images so real, that she stumbled from her bed and sleepily typed the brief synopsis. By the next morning, she had forgotten about the dream completely. A few days later, the vision of the dream invaded her mind. She read her rambling notes and dismissed them as incoherent babble.

She read the brief synopsis again. If this was true, then possibly Falcon killed in order to protect a Prince. But how could this be? How could she have known this and written of it? And what was the tree of life? Some kind of fountain of youth? Could this be what the cloaked men were guarding? Could the Bible's mysterious Tree of Life be hidden somewhere in Moonshine?

She shut her eyes and took in a slow, cleansing breath. She closed the file and nervously clicked on *My Better Half.* Once again she skipped over the short synopsis and scrolled down to her character list. Jumping off the screen were the names the girls mentioned yesterday: *Adam and Alicia.*

With a trembling hand, she closed the file. The heat rose within her. How could she have written of people she had never met, nor knew existed until now?

She closed the page and clicked on, My *Brother's Keeper,* and read the synopsis once again:

A woman is forced to face life, raising her children alone, when a tragic murder claims the life of her beloved husband....

Nervously, Bronwyn scrolled down to view the character list; letting out a small gasp when the name *Mavis* appeared on the screen. Her heart pounded. How could the people in her stories be real? What did all this mean? Was Travis foreordained to die?

She felt as if she would vomit at any minute. Realizing she was hyperventilating, she gasped for air. She needed to breathe; she needed to talk with someone. But who? Who could begin to understand the craziness of all this? Bethany? Maybe she should try talking with her again. This was too much to take in alone. Maybe she should talk to Marcus. Show him the files. Her stomach churned. She knew the person she must talk to; the person who hid volumes of secrets behind his dark eyes. The same person, who had pulled her to safety last night, whispered a warning before kissing her.

Travis.

Closing her laptop, she decided she would find him and demand an explanation. If not, she would threaten to write a disparaging story, revealing the location of a supposed fountain of youth, the whole world would read, blowing wide open the deep secret of Moonshine and the clandestine deeds they were hiding.

A strong wind swept across the back lawn, toppling over chairs and vigorously ringing the chimes hanging overhead. The back screen door slammed shut, as a cold chill raced up her spine. An overwhelming feeling of terror washed over her, as an unseen presence swept across the gardens. The sudden fear was almost paralyzing.

"Here you are!"

Bronwyn spun around, startled at the sound of Bethany's greeting.

"You ok?" Bethany asked. "You look pale."

"I'm alright," Bronwyn said, relieved at Bethany's arrival on the porch. However, she still felt the malevolent presence roaming about.

"You're shaking!"

"I'm cold."

"You're kidding me!" Bethany laughed. "How could you be cold, it's at least 90 degrees in the shade. Are you sick?"

Bethany walked forward and placed her hand on Bronwyn's forehead. "You feel fine. Are you sure you're not taking some kind of meds?"

"Damn it, Bethany! Quit asking me that. I am not nor have I ever taken anything!"

Bethany's eyes widened at Bronwyn's reaction. "Alright! Calm down! I won't ask you again. It's just that you haven't been yourself lately. You're not sleeping at night. You leave the room at all hours, you have fallen from trees, and last night you fainted. Now you look terrified and are shaking. I just want to know what's up with you."

"Do you really want to know?"

"Yes, please tell me."

Bronwyn glanced above, remembering Mavis' comment about her window being directly over this part of the porch.

"Come with me."

Bronwyn led Bethany off the porch and into the gardens. Confused, Bethany followed her down the cobblestone paths until she stopped at the sixth garden. Bronwyn took a deep breath and pushed open the gate.

"What…"

Bronwyn held her hand up to silence Bethany. She passed the weeping willows and headed toward the open grass, where she witnessed the slaying. She focused on the spot and sighed.

"I should have known."

A freshly planted tree stood where the condemned man's death sentence had been carried out. There was no evidence of blood. The ground had been broken and the soil turned.

"What?" Bethany repeated her question.

Bronwyn looked about her cautiously before whispering. "Beth, I saw someone killed in this garden last night."

Bethany stared at Bronwyn, at a loss for words.

"I know it sounds crazy, but I saw a man get his throat slit right here. Right where this tree is. I think it was planted to cover up the spot where he bled out."

"I'm sorry," Bethany said. "But I have to ask it again. Are you taking pills?"

"Damn it Bethany! You insist I tell you things and when I do, you completely disregard it. Why do you do that?"

Bethany suppressed a laugh. "Come on Bronwyn. You really don't expect me to believe you witnessed a murder. I'm not Lillian you know."

"Yes I do." The frustration seeped in her voice. "Why wouldn't you? Have I ever lied to you before?"

"No. But before you weren't…."

Bronwyn's eyes flared. "Weren't what?"

"You weren't depressed and upset, and going through the phases of a break-up. C'mon Bronwyn. You have to admit you've not been yourself lately. Even Trent…."

She rolled her eyes. Bethany had truly succumbed to the philosophies of Trent. "Beth!"

"Well sometimes he makes sense! Besides, if you did see someone get murdered, why did you wait so long to tell me? Why didn't you wake me during the night? How could you have simply fallen back asleep after something like that?"

She couldn't disclose to Bethany that Travis kissed her under the willow tree. She paused a moment before offering a feeble answer: "I fainted."

Bethany looked intently at her, suspicion pulsing from her eyes.

"Okay" Bronwyn sighed. "Someone grabbed me from behind and did something that caused me to lose consciousness. I woke up on the back porch swing early this morning."

Bethany still looked skeptical. "And you never told anyone about this? You were just going to let all of us be bludgeoned to death in our sleep?"

"I didn't think any of us were in danger. They could have killed me too, as an eye witness. Instead they laid me on the porch swing."

"And they didn't think you would tell when you woke up?"

Bronwyn dropped her voice to a whisper. "Mavis tried to dismiss it as a bad dream. She said I woke her during the night screaming. In her words, I was having a fitful night sleep. I think she is in on it."

Bethany sighed sympathetically. "In on what Bronwyn? I am sure Mavis is right. You were having a dream. I hadn't mentioned it earlier, but I've noticed you have been leaving our room during the night. Maybe you're sleepwalking again like you did when you were a kid. Dreams can seem so real at times."

Bronwyn ran her fingers through her long dark tresses and surveyed the garden. The splinter in her finger was more than enough proof that what she witnessed had not been a dream. A definite cloak and dagger conspiracy was unfolding among the residents of this puzzling town. Should she dare mention the fact she was suspicious that the tree of Life may be hidden somewhere in Moonshine? After all, she had not seen one senior citizen her entire stay, and no one in the town looked any older than forty. Bethany's reaction to everything else answered that question. She couldn't blame her for her. It did seem absurd to say the least. However, she knew it was very real. She would continue to keep it to herself, and only discuss it with those who knew what was truly going on. At the festival, she would search for Travis. Once she found him, she would demand answers.

CHAPTER THIRTY-ONE

The girls spent extra time dressing for the whimsical festival. Lillian appeared as a mountain blossom coming to life, wearing a soft pink halter dress, cascading into several layers of powder pink and white airy fabrics. The sheerness of the fabrics would have undoubtedly been see-through, had they not been layered one over the other. Her luxurious platinum hair hung loosely down her back, with random strands of pink ribbon braided periodically throughout her massive mane. She did her make up to its usual perfection. Silver sandals adorned her dainty feet.

Bethany's greatest challenge was disguising her new haircut. Lillian and Bronwyn both suggested several different styles, yet nothing seemed to work. Much to their surprise, Carla Jo entered their room with a pair of razor-sharp scissors, and quickly and artistically turned Bethany's mullet into a classic stylish bob. Even though Bethany grieved over losing her long locks, she much preferred the bob to the hideous mullet. She quickly chose a turquoise tank style dress, accessorizing with silver bangle bracelets and hooped earrings.

Bronwyn plugged in her three-barrel waver and spent an hour crimping her long black hair. She gently pulled it over her left shoulder, securing a very loose low ponytail. Several pieces escaped their clutches and fell around her face. She chose a simple white linen halter dress, and accessorized with turquoise jewelry and silver sandals.

The troupe trekked into Moonshine on the two-lane highway. The more frequently they walked this path, the less the distance seemed. The melodious tune of a dulcimer drifted over the mountains and through the trees, as at it had throughout the week. The night was clear, beautiful. The magnificent moon gave off enough light to illuminate the dark road. Millions of stars filled the sky like loose diamonds scattered across a piece of dark purple velvet. The cool breeze, swept gently over the mountains, stirring against the trees and casting the aroma of spruce, firs, pine and cedar into the air. It evoked a sense of protection, a sacred feeling that seemed to empower Bronwyn and fill her with renewed strength.

As the troupe walked down the center of the crooked highway, they each took turns recanting events of the past five days. Spontaneous stories of the curious people they had met thus far. Trent occasionally pointing out the unique lifestyle and forgotten dialect of the mountain. Bronwyn enjoyed this moment, listening to her friends telling of their adventures. Their stories gave some sense of normality to her situation. What she did notice, was that all their stories were typical, average. Not one of her friends spoke of uneasiness, or gave mention of any peculiar events, apparitions, cloaked figures or murders in the gardens. Everyone simply experienced every day common behavior. She envied them in a way.

Country mountain ballads could be heard on the outskirts of town, along with laughter and gaiety. The festivities were in full swing. As the troupe rounded the final curve, they saw streets and courtyards ablaze with activity. Each decorated booth erupted with color and offered a tasty treat or trinket of some sort. Strung lights and blazing lanterns gave off a fairy tale ambiance. Vendors were dressed in some sort of medieval masquerade, most of their identities hidden by peculiar masks. To Bronwyn, it felt like a combination of a Renaissance faire and Carvenale in Venice. In keeping with the midsummer's night theme, young children, dressed as charming fairies, ran through the crowd throwing glittery fairy dust, and giving out small bags of delicious candies. Molly, a winsome little fairy, eagerly brought her bags of goodies to each one in the troupe.

Delicious aromas of sweets and baked goods overpowered the natural scents of the mountains. Booths offered home-made waffle cones, warm baked brownies, and oversized cookies, all of which could be covered with mounds of the delicious frozen treats.

The troupe dispersed as they entered the festival. Wilbur stopped at the first ice cream booth he approached. Marcus and Anna headed to the courtyard. Ashley, who overdressed in a revealing low-cut ensemble, spotted the troupe right away. She immediately, sauntered over with a friend, eyeing Trent and Daniel. Soon the boys were whisked away. Karley and Walt challenged each other to games of skill, heading over to the recreational booths.

Bronwyn, Bethany and Lillian were left alone. They strolled amongst the kiosks and various stands. Everyone eagerly offered them ice cream samples. Not yet ready to begin gorging, the girls graciously declined.

Tiny lights blazed all over the hills, giving indication of homes hidden deep in the trees. Judging by the enormous turn out, Moonshine appeared to be much larger in population than Bronwyn had originally thought. All these people, hidden from view, nestled in the mountains and still she saw no one over the age of fifty,

The courtyard bustled with activity. A group of dancers, dressed in silver and blue angelic costumes, performed a beautiful interpretive dance in the grass outside the church grounds. Another large group of people danced to the lively tunes of the band.

A masked figure approached the girls, offering them each a single rose. He bowed slightly, and without a word, gaited back into the crowd, giving away more flowers. This carnival-type atmosphere was nothing Bronwyn had ever experienced before. It was as magical as a page out of a fairy tale book.

Lillian grabbed Bronwyn's arm, "Look! Is that Falcon?"

Bronwyn's heart leaped in her throat. He was leaning against a tree with a cigarette clenched between his teeth, and appeared to be in deep thought, unaware of each drag he took. He kept his attention on the crowd, not watching anyone in particular; yet, it was difficult to tell, seeing he was wearing his sunglasses despite the late hour. He seemed totally indifferent to the fact he had recently slit someone's throat. She shuddered at the thought of his forcefulness last night and the extreme fear and discomfort he hurled upon her. She definitely did not wish to draw his attention her way.

"It's him," She said emphatically, then steered their small group in the opposite direction.

The girls continued to walk past the booths, stopping only once for a giant blue cloud of cotton candy. Bronwyn unwound a strand of the fluffy confection from the paper stick.

"I'm really missing Ryan tonight," she confessed, before popping the sugary substance in her mouth.

"Really?" Bethany was surprised, yet somewhat joyful that Bronwyn had opened up and shared a rational feeling. "Why?"

"I don't know. The ambiance maybe, the sultriness of a warm summer night. The fairy tale atmosphere of the festival. The perfect night sky. It all seems so surreal. Like some sort of a dream. It's moments like this I wish I had someone special to share it with."

"What are we then?" Bethany attempted to sound offended.

Bronwyn laughed. "You know what I mean. I enjoy spending time with you both. In fact I am glad we're here together. It's just…"

"There's no need to explain," Bethany confessed. "I totally understand. I am desperate for some sort of romantic interlude myself."

The girls spent the majority of the night sampling ice cream, feasting on sweets and baked goods, even trying their luck at several challenging games. They took in a few impromptu performances of various dancers, magicians, poets, and watched the strange antics of a mime.

Masked figures would approach from time to time, presenting the girls with flowers or placing colorful beads around their necks. Some simply took their hands and kissed them. Occasionally, Bronwyn would glance over her shoulder to keep a close eye on Falcon, who dutifully maintained his attention on the crowd. She'd also glance around, searching nonchalantly for Travis. He was not among the crowd. She bit her lower lip in disappointment. She had not seen him since last night. She feared he was staying hidden, more than likely avoiding her, so he wouldn't have to answer any questions concerning the events in the garden.

Three nervous teenage boys approached them, interrupting her musings. Timidly, they asked for a dance and soon the girls were being whirled about the grass. Although she was dancing and laughing, she felt it impossible to relax and enjoy the evening. A bitter feeling gnawed in the pit of her stomach, as her attention was drawn to the large banner hanging over the bandstand. She had seen this banner her first day in Moonshine, and had read it several times since. This time a certain portion jumped right off the canvas and punched her in the face.

Saturday August 16th

There hadn't been a day in the past year, especially the past six months that she hadn't thought of August 16th. It was embossed on hundreds of discarded invitations. The day she and Ryan were to be married. Her stomach knotted, a lump formed in her throat, blocking a cistern full of tears that would certainly burst forth if given the slightest chance.

She left the dance floor, making her way through the crowd, and across the busy courtyard, heading as far away from the festivities as she could. Another masked figure approached her, placing a small decorative cylinder in her hand.

"I am delivering a message just for you my dear," He whispered in her ear.

Blowing her a kiss, he bowed slightly and twirled away, disappearing into the crowd.

She shoved the small cylinder in her dress pocket, before she discovered a small path leading towards the lake. She followed the trail until the music and laughter transformed into croaking frogs and singing crickets. Tears stung at her eyes, yet she defiantly held them at bay. She refused to cry. She would not allow herself to give Ryan any more of her tears. She picked up her pace, wanting to run for miles and never stop.

Removing her low-heeled sandals, she contemplated whether or not to toss them into the lake. They were one of her favorite pairs, but at this point she didn't care. She hurled them one at a time into the dark silvery waters and continued to run. Soft pine needles provided a carpet, cushioning her bare feet most of the way. Still, a few splintery sticks and sharp pine cones pierced her bare feet. She didn't feel the stinging, since the pain in her heart overcame all other senses in her body.

Then from behind her, she heard the sound of snapping branches. Thoughts of her mourning disappeared; burned away by the realization of what she had done. How could she have been so careless? Why did she put herself at risk by running through the woods late at night alone? Should she dare stop and look behind her?

A cold chill snaked its way up her back. She had no idea where she was, or how far away from the festival she had run. She wanted to turn back, but realized running back might bring her face to face with Falcon and imminent doom.

Snap!

Terror consumed her as she ran. She did not know how much longer she could go; she was running out of breath.

Relief overcame her as she came into a clearing and saw a cabin. She knew this place...*Travis's cabin!* It was dark; no lights glowed from the inside.

Bolting up the porch steps, she headed for the door. On the night of the storm, Travis opened it without a key. She doubted these mountain dwellers ever locked their homes. She would seek refuge inside, bar the door, and perhaps find a knife or something she could use to defend herself.

She grabbed the knob and turned, pushing hard. The door didn't move. She turned the knob again and pushed harder. Nothing! Maybe there was a back door. She whirled around. A scream escaped her lips as she ran into Travis.

"I told you not to wander off alone."

She tried to catch her breath. "Were you following me?"

He nodded.

"Why?" she panted.

"I've already answered that question," he said firmly. "Yet you still disregard my warnings...why did you leave so quickly? You seemed to be enjoying yourself."

He had been watching; but from where? She chose not to answer him right away. She looked into his dark eyes. She had a myriad of questions she intended on asking him before the night was over. However, before she interrogated him she would play along and answer his questions first.

"I was having fun... until I happened to look up and see the banner. And for the first time, I actually read what it said. And there it was starring me in the face: August 16th. My wedding date."

She paused a moment when she noticed his expression change.

"Ryan and I were supposed to be married today." Her voice dropped until it was nearly inaudible. "A day hasn't gone by for the past six months that I haven't thought of that date. And now, for some unexplained reason, it slips my mind and I don't think of it for days, and then suddenly, there it is mocking me, staring at me in the face from a ridiculous ice cream banner."

Her voice rose. "Now instead of being surrounded by my family and friends at my seaside wedding, I'm surrounded by strangers in a small town somewhere in the southern Appalachians at an ice cream festival. And you know what, Travis? I don't even like ice cream." She watched his stern expression melt into a slight smile.

"I contemplated going to the beer garden and getting drunk. But I knew that would solve nothing so I decided to go for a walk and have a good long cry. But for some reason I couldn't cry. All I could think about was Ryan, and I was wondering where he was tonight and if he remembered what today was, and I wondered if his heart was aching at all. Then I decided to run, to run and run until I fell off the face of the earth, or ended up somewhere else. That's when I heard someone behind me, and despite the fact you do not think I listen to your warnings, I remembered what you said last night. I was scared, so I kept on running. Before I knew it, I was here, and you know the rest."

She studied him as she finished her long discourse. There was something about having a conversation with him that kept her eyes engaged. He was always attentive a rare thing in her social circles. She remembered so many events, being introduced to seemingly nice men. As she spoke with them, she would notice how their eyes would either wander below her face, only interested in one thing, or wander completely over the top of her head, surveying the room, to see if someone more important had entered. Someone, who they felt would be better to talk with.

Travis was different. His eyes absorbed her every expression, her every syllable. She appreciated that. Deeply.

He reached for her hand.

"Come with me."

She took his hand. It was large and strong, surprisingly rough for physician. It made perfect sense though; he worked with his hands, growing and distilling the many plants he used to treat his patients.

Favoring her bleeding aching feet, she carefully descended the porch steps, following him on a path leading to the lake. A boat rocked in the waters, softly knocking against the dock. He helped her into the vessel. It was very inviting, with plenty of nice cushioned seats. She chose one near the back of the boat, slightly behind the captain's seat. He opened a cabinet door and removed a plush blanket, handing it to her.

Gracious, she took the blanket and wrapped it around her bare shoulders. She had no idea where he was taking her, or his plans. Nor did she care. Her life had been changing so much recently that everything was completely opposite of what she anticipated. Tonight was supposed to be her night. Her wedding night; the night she was supposed to wear the white dress. The night all eyes would be on her. The night she danced in celebration with her friends, the night she was to become Mrs. Ryan Reese.

Her hopes had not come true. Her dreams of her future had been disrupted. So tonight, she had no plans. She was not in control, nor did she desire to be. Tonight she would allow life to happen.

Travis started the engine and guided the boat across the glassy waters. As he pushed the throttle back, the boat picked up speed. She was grateful for the blanket. He had been thoughtful; the night air was quite cold. She pulled the blanket closer and eyed him. His hair was blowing away from his face and for the first time, she noticed a small silver earring in his ear. She quickly turned her attention away before he could catch her looking at him.

The lake was much larger than she had anticipated, with no end in sight. Travis had been driving full speed and there was still so much ahead. The water reflected the glow of the moon, while the hills and trees were black silhouettes against a deep purple sky. He pulled back on the throttle, steering around a corner and into a large hidden cove. He drove the boat to the center of the inlet and turned off the engine. There was complete silence except for the woodland noises and gentle kisses of the waves against the boat as it rocked slowly, the wake continuing to dissipate.

Her head raced. What would happen next? He turned and looked at her, offering his hand once more. She stretched her hand out to him, apprehensive. He led her to the center of the boat, saying nothing. He stood next to her and then released her hand.

Suddenly the whistling sound of an object being hurled across the sky broke the silence, followed by a thunderous pop and explosion. She gasped. Colorful embers of fireworks exploded directly overhead, raining down around them and falling into the waters. The night sky shimmered. Another whistle tore across the sky, followed by another explosion, and more colorful embers. She was stunned at the brilliance and beauty of the firework display and by her host's graciousness. Travis had brought her to the best spot in Moonshine to see the festival's firework show. Another explosion as blue, lavender, silver and green embers burst around them. The experience was magical, breathtaking, exhilarating. The kindness Travis had shown was amazing. He showed no selfish ulterior motives, only the desire to give her a magical moment.

Her emotions began to overcome her. The tears she had held back inside of her heart for months stung at her eyes. The dam broke. A single tear escaped, trickling down her cheek, followed by another, and then another. Soon she was sobbing uncontrollably, her soul cleansing from the pain and disappointment, the shock, the betrayal, the bitterness, the abandonment...the miscarriage. Each tear seemed to have a name as it poured down her cheeks and splashed off her face. She felt a heaviness leave her body. She sat on the cushioned bench, shivering as she watched the enchanting display through tear-filled eyes. She pulled the blanket tighter around her. Travis sat down next to her, and wrapped his strong arm around her, pulling her against him. She gratefully scooted in closer to him, leaning her head upon his shoulder.

The fireworks continued to fall, and Travis continued to hold her as she cried. He never moved, spoke, or interrupted her personal moment of healing. He simply sat there, patiently, his powerful arm around her, offering her a shoulder to lean on, and a private place in which to escape.

The night grew quiet once again. The fireworks stopped, the music no longer played in the distance. The sounds of laughter and carefree frivolity dwindled away. The festival had come to an end.

The only audible sound was the gentle rocking and creaking of the boat. The lake had become somewhat darker, the moon now high in the sky. Bronwyn felt heavy-eyed, fatigued. The steady swaying of the boat nearly rocked her to sleep. She knew she should move, to allow Travis to take the boat back to the dock and return home before Mavis worried. He had been so kind to bring her here, to allow her the privacy to grieve. She did not intend to take advantage of his thoughtfulness, yet she wished to remain exactly where she was as long as possible.

Her mind ventured back to earlier in the day, the uneasiness, her desperate need to speak to him and her urgent desire for answers. That was one of the mysteries of Moonshine. Some experiences were so bizarre, supernatural, leaving her weak and in an emotional panic. Yet within moments, the episodes would give way to the ordinary, almost causing her to forget the urgency she had felt earlier.

Finally, she broke the silence. "You're a doctor?"

"A healer."

She smiled at the strange way he responded. Then, "Who did Falcon kill in the garden last night?"

There was no reply.

"I know what I saw was real. I wasn't dreaming."

Still no reply.

"Part of me tells me I should fear you, yet another part wants to trust you completely. I am not sure which one I should listen to."

She could not see his face from her leaning position. She could only feel his body. It tensed when she asked the questions. She pulled herself away from him and looked at his face. His eyes were fixed across the water.

"How could I have written about people I never met? Am I the scribe the murdered man spoke of?"

He continued to fix his gaze across the lake. His mood was somber. She studied his expression, contemplating his silence.

Time to press the matter. "I know there is something very out of the ordinary going on here. Something supernatural. I have felt it from the moment I arrived. From the moment we met on the bridge, I've experienced strange sensations. I'm not sure what they are, but I know what they aren't. They are not symptoms of altitude sickness, so please don't insult me with that explanation again. I need answers and I know you have them."

"Not tonight," he said softly.

"Why?" She pressed.

"Because you've gone through an incredible amount of emotion tonight. You could not handle what I would tell you."

Although his words frightened her, she found a reason to trust in them. His eyes shown with sincerity and truth. He was right. Tonight had been emotionally exhausting. She knew she couldn't take much more. Her body was drained. She had a sense of satisfaction in knowing that there was something going on. At least she wasn't losing her mind.

Only one question left to ask. "When? When will you tell me?"

Travis took his gaze off the water, and turned his eyes back to her.

"Soon."

CHAPTER THIRTY-TWO
DAY SIX

Bronwyn's intention of sleeping late was clapped aside by rolling thunder and a gentle rain tapping on the window screen. Fluffing her pillow and re-adjusting her position, she dozed back to sleep, only to be reawakened by the continual slamming of the door, as Mavis and the kids headed out to church. She lay in bed for another half hour, attempting to fall back to sleep, her mind suddenly crowded with thoughts of the boat, the lake…Travis.

She crawled from bed, grabbed her laptop and headed downstairs. Mavis left behind a continental breakfast for her guest, so she poured herself a cup of coffee, grabbed an oversized blueberry muffin, and headed for the back porch. She curled up on the swing, sipping her coffee and enjoying the smell of the warm summer shower.

Bethany joined her on the porch before she had an opportunity to write, and settled down in a rocking chair along-side the swing. Bronwyn laid her computer aside, realizing there would be no writing as long as Bethany was there. She could sense Bethany was full of questions. She had been so overcome with the realization about her wedding night; she left without thinking, and without giving Bethany or Lillian any notification.

Bethany rocked in the chair, sipping coffee and nibbling at her croissant, while Bronwyn relayed the entire story of the walk, how she ended up at Travis's cabin, the boat ride, and the spectacular fireworks display. At that point, Bethany removed herself from the rocking chair and joined Bronwyn on the swing.

She curled her legs up underneath her, anticipating a more secretive accounting. However, that's where Bronwyn ended her story.

"So, you're saying nothing happened between you two?" Bethany asked skeptically.

"Nothing at all. I told you he is a good man. He is in love with his wife. Even Ashley said it at the salon. Everyone in town knows

Travis's heart belongs to only one person." She ended her last statement with a sigh.

"It just doesn't make sense. He definitely seems to be attracted to you. He's always following you around or at least showing up where you are. He followed you up to the top of the waterfalls. He obviously was watching you at the festival, because he followed you to his cabin. Then he took you out on his boat to a secluded private cove on the lake to watch fireworks... and he doesn't make a move?" she shook her head in disbelief. "Something's not right here."

Bronwyn smiled. "Just admit it, Bethany. There may be a few good, trustworthy, faithful men out there."

"That's just it." Bethany pointed out. "He's not that faithful, or he would have taken Mavis out on the boat, and had some happy times away from the kids. Maybe you intimidate him."

"I don't think so." Bronwyn chuckled at the thought.

Bethany was wrong. Travis was faithful. What was faithfulness anyway? Being loyal? Steadfast? Dedicated? Committed? Travis was certainly all those things to Mavis.

"You promise me, nothing happened?" Bethany asked again, eyeing Bronwyn suspiciously. "He didn't hint at anything; accidentally touch your leg or something?"

Bronwyn laughed again. "No, he didn't. He did put his arm around me when I started crying. He literally gave me his shoulder to cry on, but that was it."

"AH HA!" Bethany yelled, nearly spilling her coffee. "I knew there was something! He's just a slow mover, but he's making his moves alright, setting up opportunities, getting you to trust him, to relax around him. That scoundrel!"

She shook her head, feeling she'd achieved an inner victory.

Bronwyn smiled, unmoved.

"You're wrong Beth. You're way off on this one." She reached for Bethany's mug and exited the porch to refill their coffee, only to return to more questions.

"So what happened after the fireworks? You didn't come back to the inn for a long time after the festival was over. I'm seeing a time gap here. How did you fill it? Bury more victims?"

Bronwyn gave a courteous laugh and proceeded to tell Bethany how her sobbing had taken its toll, leaving her heavy-eyed and drained. She explained how the stillness of the night and the gentle swaying of the boat nearly rocked her to sleep. How Travis had sat there patiently, allowing her all the time she needed. Then when she was ready, he brought the boat back to the cabin and returned her to the inn. She purposely neglected to tell Bethany of their conversation that transpired, understanding it was not for Bethany to know. She could never comprehend the meaning of it all.

Bethany leaned her head back against the swing, watching the light rain falling outside.

"I'm glad he was there for you last night. I'm proud of him for behaving himself. He could have easily taken advantage of a distraught bride, abandoned on her wedding night. For that, he's a good man."

Bronwyn watched her friend sipping coffee and contemplating. She knew Bethany's concern was entirely for her well-being, combined with her own heartbreaking experience. Even though Bethany's relationship had only last a short three months, Bronwyn knew her pain, from that experience of deception, was more than she showed.

The rain began to lessen, the clouds having completed their duty of giving the thirsty earth its morning drink. The sun broke through the gloom just as the local church was dismissing. The few dedicated worshippers, faithful enough to attend services on the morning after the festival, exited the sanctuary, and milled about outside. They discussed various topics, from the relevancy of the sermon, to the antics of the previous night's celebration. Mavis descended the steps of the church, carefully holding tightly to the pastor's hand.

"How are those big city guests of yours?" The benevolent minister asked, as he helped her off the bottom step.

"Doin' just fine." Mavis said, smiling. "The kids are enjoying all the activity going on at the inn, and I think Carla Jo has developed a crush on the handsome one."

The pastor smiled. "They seemed to be enjoying themselves last night."

"Didn't we all!" Mrs. Meer, a hefty woman, eagerly wedged herself into the conversation. "I think it was the nicest festival we've had in a while."

Mavis forced a smile, excusing herself. She yelled to the kids to head to the car. She knew if Doris Meer joined the conversation, there would be no getting away anytime soon. Her guests would be sure to starve before she would be able to return and prepare a meal. However, Doris had other intentions.

"Mavis dear!" she lumbered to catch up with her.

"Where are your guests this morning?"

She was panting, her chubby face already red with the energy she exerted to catch up with the hobbling Mavis.

"Not church goers I assume? That's how it is with big city folk. They're so busy; they never make time for God and spiritual things."

"I suppose." Mavis continued limping to her car.

"Well I can only assume they were plenty tuckered out from last night," Doris continued. "As pastor said, they all did seem to enjoy themselves quite a bit. Especially one of them. I'm sure you know of whom I am referring. I saw Travis taking her in his boat late last night."

"Really?" Mavis answered, somewhat perturbed. "And how could you have seen that, seeing as Travis's boat is docked at his cabin, which we all know is not visible from the courtyard?"

"Charles and I weren't at the courtyard. We had taken a little walk." Doris said, trying to sound naïve. "We were near the cabin when I noticed Travis helping her into the boat. It just surprised me is all I'm saying. You know I think the world of you and that man Travis! I'm just lookin' out for the both of you. She may seem sweet and innocent but....."

Mavis swung her car door open and climbed into the front. She glanced back to make sure the kids were inside. Molly was safely buckled in the back seat. Carla Jo, was standing outside of the car, still talking with her friends.

"Thank you Doris." She grabbed the door handle.

"Travis is a wise and decent man. I am sure he knows what he is doing. I trust his judgment completely."

With those words, she slammed her door shut.

"Carla Jo! Let's go!" she yelled.

Carla Jo jumped in the car. Mavis sped away leaving a disappointed Doris behind her.

Mavis returned from church, prepared a quick simple lunch, and disappeared for the rest of the afternoon. Bronwyn and Bethany decided to clean up their room, and do some much needed laundry. Sunday was the one day of the week that Mavis neglected to make the beds, and clean the rooms. It was her day of rest. Usually, when the girls returned to their room, they would find the bed made, clean towels in the bathroom, fresh flowers in a vase by the window, and some sort of treat on their pillows. Once, they received a plate of her famous chocolate chip cookies; on another day, it was a bowl of chocolate dipped strawberries. Then there was a plate of chewy brownies. It was always a treat to see what Mavis would leave. In all of Bronwyn's travels, she had never stayed in a place as inviting and comfortable as Sandalwood Inn.

She tossed the last pillow back onto the bed and then retrieved her dress from the floor. She'd come back to the Inn so late last night, and with no desire of waking her friends, she quickly disrobed, leaving her clothes on the floor. As she grabbed the dress to add it to her pile of laundry, she noticed a small bulging in the pocket. She retrieved a small cylinder tube. Examining it, she noticed the cylinder was carved from a smooth wood. She studied the beauty and antiquity of the object in her hand. Detailed carvings were etched around the tube. An elegant letter E was carved in the center. A golden cap sealed the tube. She barely remembered the masked figure that placed it into her hand. "I am delivering a message just for you," he whispered before he kissed her hand, bowed and backed away, disappearing into the crowd.

She'd been so overcome with emotion at the time, that she paid little attention to the event, let alone remembered it. Curious she pried open the end of the cylinder, emptying out a parchment rolled into a scroll, and tied with a blue ribbon. Her slender fingers carefully uncurled the paper. Handwritten in beautiful calligraphy were the words, *Isaiah 42:9*.

"A bible verse?" she said out aloud. Probably a gimmick of the church, she thought, handing out scriptures and telling everyone to repent or they will go to hell. She spoke from experience, having been a victim of that methodology before.

"What did you say?" Bethany asked, as she sorted through her clothes, deciding what items needed to be laundered.

"Sorry. I was just thinking out loud. I opened my cylinder, thinking it was Moonshine's version of a fortune cookie. All that was in it was a Bible verse. Probably a gimmick of the church."

Bethany looked at the ornate cylinder. "Where did you get that?"

"One of those masked, trinket bearing figures, gave it to me. He said he was delivering a message just for me."

"Weird," Bethany said. "I didn't get a cylinder."

Bronwyn twirled it around her fingers, wondering if there was significance.

"What's the message?"

"Just a Bible reference," she replied. "Probably telling me to repent or go to hell."

Bethany laughed. "They're on to you and your late night escapades."

Bronwyn tossed a soiled towel Bethany's way.

"Look it up and see what it says."

"You got a Bible?" Her voice matched the sarcasm of her question.

"As a matter of fact I do," Bethany said smugly "But it's packed away in the bus."

"A lot of good it's doing you there."

She didn't mention it to Bethany, but she also had a small Bible packed away on the bus that she read from time to time.

"Go look it up," Bethany urged. "I'm sure Mavis has a Bible somewhere around here."

"I'll do it later." She returned the scroll to the cylinder, which she placed it in the pocket of her shorts.

CHAPTER THIRTY-THREE

After supper, Bronwyn retired to the back porch swing to work on the new script. Bethany and Lillian sat with her, relaxing in rockers, sipping iced tea with lavender, and enjoying a calm Sunday evening. Mavis joined the girls, occupying another rocking chair, and reading the paper. Bronwyn was listening to her iPod in an attempt to drown out any conversation on the porch.

"You girls enjoy the fireworks last night?" Mavis asked from behind her paper.

"Yes, they were amazing." Bethany answered, somewhat startled by the randomness of the question.

"What about you Bronwyn?" Mavis asked, her face still hidden behind the paper.

The music piping into Bronwyn's ears prevented her from hearing Mavis's inquiry.

"Bronwyn!" Bethany raised her voice trying to overpower the music.

She was busy searching the Bible, attempting to look up the message in Isaiah 42:9.

"What?" She pulled out her earbuds.

"Mavis just asked you if you enjoyed the fireworks last night." Bethany said, glints of warning in her eyes. Bronwyn quickly glanced at Mavis, whose face remained hidden by the paper.

"Yes I saw them. They were beautiful."

"That's good." Mavis casually turned the page. "I was hoping you had a good view."

Bethany's eyes widened as she looked at Bronwyn. Bronwyn felt as if her stomach had fallen on the floor. Mavis had to be suspicious.

Why hadn't she asked Lillian the same question? Bronwyn wanted to blurt out "Nothing happened!"

Instead, she returned to her search for Isaiah 42:9. She flipped through the many smaller books, Psalms, Proverbs, Ecclesiastes, Song of Solomon, and Isaiah. She found the book. Her hands began to tremble from the adrenaline rush that had accompanied Mavis's question. She was only seconds away from reading, "The message that had been delivered just for her" Bronwyn wouldn't at all be surprised if it said something to the effect of, "Adulterers will burn!"

Her finger scanned the pages, Isaiah 39...40...41...42... Verse 9. Bronwyn read silently:

"See the former things have taken place, and new things I declare. Before they spring into being, I announce them to you."

The heat sensation began to invade her again. The message was nothing more than another riddle; another enigma to muddle through.

She scribbled the verse on the back of the scroll before returning it to the cylinder.

The melodies of the late evening dulcimer player began drifting through the trees, as they did every evening. This was becoming clockwork. The winsome melody was soon accompanied by the song of the woman, drawing her attention away from the crowded porch and into the woods. Curious, she decided to follow the voice. She laid the Bible and her computer aside. Standing, she stuffed the scroll back into the pocket of her shorts, and left the porch.

"Where are you going?" Bethany asked.

"I'll be back in a while," she called over her shoulder as she hurried away. Bethany and Lillian both watched as Mavis slightly lowered the paper, peering at Bronwyn as she headed for the river.

Bronwyn found the small trail that led to the waterfall. She was sure she could easily follow the path and successfully find it on her own. She glanced over her shoulder and looked back at the inn, relieved she was already too far for anyone to see her. The distance, accompanied by the dark of the night, hid her completely from the view of the porch.

Stepping into the woods, she began following the soft path, thankful for the moonlight that glistened through the trees, providing enough light to illuminate her way without the need of a flashlight. She walked confidently at a brisk pace, following the trail for quite a ways before the crackling and snapping of leaves and twigs caught her attention. She picked up on movement to her right. Her heart hugged her throat, as a frightened deer bolted across the path and disappeared in the darkness. She stopped a minute to regain her composure and catch her breath. For a second time, she remembered Travis' strict warning not to venture out alone. She had done it again, when was she going to learn?

Her mind began to taunt her with thoughts of dark-hooded, knife-wielding men, hiding behind every tree. She even conjured up the visual of hungry grizzlies descending to feed. She began to scold herself for running off without thinking first or at least grabbing a flashlight. The trees had thickened during the course of her walk, causing the light from the moon to decrease dramatically. She attempted to adjust her eyes. With the aid of her hands, she felt her way down the winding path continuing on her determined walk, but unfortunately at a much slower pace, uncertain if she still remained on the path. She stumbled over rocks, low lying branches and felled tree trunks, groping her way along as a seed of terror began to grow inside of her. The fear was not brought about by her present situation, despite the fact she wished she had ventured out a bit more prepared. The fear that manifested within was of a threatening horror overtaking the woods. The same malicious presence she felt at the falls seemed to be manifesting before her. Her courage dissipated. She decided to abort her mission and return to the porch.

Desperately trying to get her bearings, she questioned which direction to go. She was disoriented and unsure about re-tracing her steps. Within a few minutes, she decided it was impossible, although she continued to feel her way through the dense forest, grabbing at branches, hoping for a break in the trees, which would allow the moon to give her a bit of light.

She groped along a little further before the trees cleared, releasing the bright glow of the moon, and just as she had the confidence to scout around and look for a better direction, the path beneath her feet dropped off, causing her to lose her footing. She toppled over the side of a deep gulch, turning several summersaults as she careened down the side of the hill. Sharp branches sliced into her arms and legs tearing at her flesh. When she crumbled to the bottom of the gulch, she was drenched by dirt and in complete darkness. She lay there stunned. The distant hoot of an owl pierced the black silence surrounding her, for the dulcimer and the song of the woman suddenly stopped.

She sat up slowly, fully aware that she needed to climb back to the top of this ravine before she could determine which way to go, though she knew for certain she would not be able to retrace her steps.

"Damn it!" She cursed out loud, angry over her weakness and extreme stupidity. She rarely ever cursed, unlike most of the people with whom she hung out. She found cursing to be the sign of a poor vocabulary, and as a writer; she preferred more descriptive appropriate words to describe life events. However, there was always a time and a place for everything, and this certainly was the time to curse. In fact, she realized, she had cursed more in the past few days than she had in years.

She crawled to her knees, feeling around for a root or a stone, anything that would help her climb up the steep embankment. Her fingers tore into the wet clay, but the slippery mud could not hold her. Her feet slipped, causing her to slide a few feet further down. She exerted every effort, but the slick ground made it futile. She would not give up. She reached her hand into the darkness, feeling the side of the cool muddy wall for a solid root, a rock.... anything. She grabbed a protruding root and attempted her climb once more, only to become part of a mudslide, the soaked wall giving way and escorting her to the bottom once again.

Her heart beat loudly in her head. She'd heard stories of people hiking in the mountains, becoming separated from their party, never being heard from again. These mountains were massive. The woods were vast. If she could just lie there for the night, perhaps in the morning there would be enough light to find her way out; yet, her mind taunted her with thoughts of a bear or a mountain lion, or some other hungry animal that would soon feast upon her as their midnight snack. She feared she wouldn't survive till morning, and that distress compelled her to make one more attempt to climb out of the horrible pit.

She reached out into the forbidding darkness, grasping for anything. Her hand touched something slick, warm, and soft. She screamed hoping she had not grabbed a sleeping snake but before she could pull away, the object wrapped itself around her wrist and with incredible strength, pulled her up out of the pit, placing her on level ground.

She was too shocked to scream again. She could barely make out the outline of a shadowy figure. It uttered no sound, but continued to hold onto her wrist, guiding her deeper into the woods. She stumbled along, trying to keep her footing as she was led through the pitch darkness, wondering if this creature possessed some sort of night vision. It seemed to walk through the darkness with ease. The figure dragged her along for some time before coming into a very small clearing, cast into soft silver light by the moon.

Her heart sank. She could see his body before her, draped in the black robe, his face concealed by the side of the hood. His masquerade gave an eerie presence. Her heart climbed into her throat, she was in the custody of one of the cloaked men.

He led her to a broken down shack, camouflaged into the side of the mountain. A dilapidated front porch housed a single weathered rocking chair. A dulcimer lay nearby. Her pulse quickened, she had no desire to enter the dirty shack. The cloaked creature's grip had lessened during the duration of the walk. She contemplated that a sudden jerk of her hand would surely release its grip, allowing her to escape. But where would she run? Back to the pit from where she was pulled? She took in a deep breath and uttered a small prayer, as the cloaked figure led her into the darkness of the cabin. A smoldering wick of a candle offered little light, but she could make out a small fireplace, a cot type bed with worn coverings, a rustic wooden table and a single chair.

Keeping his grip on her wrist, he led her into the back of the small shack. The shack was built much deeper into the side of the mountain than she thought. What could be waiting for her in the deeper recesses of the room? She stopped walking and planted her feet firmly. The cloaked figure stopped only for a second, never turning to face her. He continued to walk, gently pulling her along. They stepped into darkness, in the back of the room. The air was cold and stale as if they had just entered a cave. She watched the cloaked man reach high above his head and pull some sort of lever.

The ground beneath her feet shook, as the entire rock wall began to slide to her left. A sudden gust of cold air blew through the opening, sending shivers through her body. A dimly lit corridor of some kind appeared in front of her.

Again she planted her feet, this time much more firmly. She feared if she ever entered that corridor, she would never see the light of day again.

"No!" she shouted forcefully as she tried to pull her wrist from his grip.

The cloaked man turned his head slightly. Only one saffron eye was visible behind the fabric of the hood.

"Trust me," he said quietly. She recognized the distinctness of the voice. This was none other than the warrior from the garden.

The pleasant sound disarmed her some; however she still wasn't convinced.

"Why should I?"

He gave her another sideways glance.

"Isaiah 42:9."

His answer was a password of some sort, and she thought that possibly the key to every riddle and secret lie just on the other side of this passageway. So, against all reason, she followed the cloaked man into the corridor. Her heart fell when the rock wall immediately closed behind them. As they descended deeper underground, the cavernous tunnel grew dark. The cloaked man grabbed a lit torch fastened to the wall, and held it out in front of him to light her way. By the light, she could see an underground river in a bed of white marble, cutting through the deep passageway, the icy cold waters of the stream rushed over her aching feet.

The two continued to descend until the path grew rocky and suddenly elevated at an increasing rate, like the shaft of a coal mine. The cloaked man lifted her from boulder to boulder with great ease.

Nearing the top, she noticed a faint beam of moonlight in the distance, announcing the end of the corridor.

The cloaked man placed the torch in another holder, and led her through the opening. An immense silver lake lay before her, reaching as far as her eyes could see. The calm and tranquil waters were surrounded by trees of every variety. Two gondolas, carved to represent some sort of angelic cherubic, floated near the shore. The cloaked man removed his dark robe and placed it at the entrance of the cave.

Stunned, Bronwyn's knees bent beneath her, causing her to take a few steps backward. Her guess was right. It was the warrior; the man she'd seen the night of their arrival and then again in the garden with Falcon two nights ago. His skin was dark golden brown; he wore long flowing white linen pants. His toned chest was bare, revealing his muscular arms, no doubt the source of his amazing strength. His hair hung to his waist in dread locks, neatly fastened into a pony tail. His saffron eyes smiled as he offered his hand.

Her fear and apprehension vanished in the glow of his presence. She climbed aboard the floating vessel and relaxed in the comfortable cushioned chair, as the mysterious man pushed off from shore. She could only guess what awaited her, and what was soon to be revealed. She was more certain than ever, that the answers she had been seeking, the answers Travis had promised, were coming.

The ride was silent, both Bronwyn and the warrior immersed in deep thought. The warrior stood at the back of the boat; paddling through the placid waters. Bronwyn rested comfortably, taking in the view that lay before her. The lake narrowed on several occasions, once taking a thin passageway behind a magnificent waterfall, another time entering a dark cave and riding the swift current until they emerged from the other side. Her fears had long subsided, she trusted the warrior now; certain he meant her no harm. Her only anxiousness lay with what she still didn't know, and her part in the whole of it.

Half an hour later, the boat arrived at its destination. The shore line was splendid. Snow white sand covered a small beach. Tall trees grew in rows, providing a leafy archway over a smooth stone path, each tree trunk covered in leafy vines, producing colorful exotic flowers. She noticed many rare and beautiful plants that were not indigenous to these mountains. The warrior led Bronwyn through a sandy path, winding through even more exotic plants. At the end of the trail lay tall sculptured hedges, growing in a vast maze with numerous entrances, she saw five or six. The warrior led her to one of the many openings. They proceeded down another path, surrounded by a hedge wall, taking many sharp turns and corners. The only visible sight was green leafy walls, and the night sky overhead. She continued to follow the warrior feeling somewhat like Alice falling down a rabbit hole, caught in some crazy maze.

The warrior stepped through the end and she followed, stunned and speechless at what her eyes beheld. A majestic castle made of smooth white stone and glass sat directly in front of her. The architect of this dwelling had created a masterpiece. The warrior led Bronwyn through a courtyard housing bubbling fountains, ornate statues, and sculptured bushes, all landscaping the front lawn. Within minutes, they arrived at a large blue door that barred entrance to the astonishing fortress. The warrior pushed opened the door, allowing her inside this magnificent citadel.

The interior of the home was just as awe-inspiring. The floors and walls were fashioned from white marble. The furnishings were elaborate, from intricately carved tables, to chairs covered in a luxurious midnight blue fabric. Ornate mirrors adorned the walls, as well as paintings of beautiful scenery, just like the ones hanging at the inn. Lush green ferns hung from the ceilings, and plants of every kind grew from large planters.

The warrior escorted Bronwyn to a comfortable room.

"You can clean up here. Make use of anything you find. If you wish to change from your soiled clothing, there are gowns in the wardrobe. We will begin when the council arrives."

With those words, the warrior exited her room and disappeared down the hallway.

She walked about the large suite. An artistically carved canopy bed, covered in colorful pillows and satin blankets, stood invitingly in the center of the room. A bombe' chest, with a hand-painted swollen front, sat near the bed. Large glass doors led outside to a courtyard filled with giant palms and ferns. In the middle of the courtyard an overflowing fountain emptied its water into a pond filled with beautifully colored fish. On the opposite side of the room, marble steps spiraled down into a sunken tub, hewn right into the marble floor.

Turning a golden lever, she watched in awe as a water fall poured from the ceiling down into the basin. Reaching over, she pulled a small lever to her right. Violet colored cream squirted into the tub, causing the water to foam taking on a lavender-scented, milky appearance. Delighted at her discovery, she pushed the lever to the left. The waters bubbled and threw off a hot, steamy, Jacuzzi feeling. She hurriedly removed her torn filthy clothes and made the spiral decent into the warm milky waters.

"I'm in heaven." She said aloud, and then thought that maybe this was the entrance to heaven, and Mavis must have shot her in the back when she left the porch. She thought that maybe she died on the grounds of the inn, and didn't know; like in the movies, when a person dies and is not aware of their demise for some time.

Maybe the warrior was some type of gate keeper and just as the thought entered her head she recalled her deleted story.

"The Eclipse" The world sitting in darkness during a lunar eclipse as an extra-dimensional arrives as the gate keeper.

Her stomach turned within her. The heat sensation rose and her mind began to scramble. She needed answers now.

Quickly washing up, she paid close attention to the gaping cut on her leg. It stung in the scented waters. Grabbing a thick cloth from the basket, she gently dabbed at the sticky blood. She washed her hair in the sudsy waters, and quickly exited the tub. Wrapped in a towel, she picked up her soiled clothes. She dreaded putting them on again now that she was clean. Then she remembered the warrior mentioning the gowns in the wardrobe. She pulled out a long silk robe and held it out. It seemed to fit so she pulled it over her head and gazed at herself in the mirror. She resembled some Greek mythical creature, her long dark hair falling over the aqua silk empire waist robe. This is crazy, she thought; removing the robe, she returned to her soiled clothes, deciding not to buy into anything just yet. Once dressed, she ventured out of her room in search of the warrior, and for an explanation as to why she had been brought here.

CHAPTER THIRTY-FOUR

Bronwyn managed to lose her way just as completely in the castle as she did in the woods. Just as before, the warrior found her and once again offered his hand.

"Are you ready Bronwyn?" he asked kindly. "The council is waiting."

"I think I am," she said, and wondered to whom he was referring when he mentioned the council.

He led her outside, through a grove of trees, and into another courtyard that contained several palms and ferns, along with many other plants that didn't seem to be from the mountains. They passed a reflecting pool, which was home to several geese and a couple of elegant swans. She followed him up a set of stairs, to a large patio. A low fire burned inside a rectangular fire pit, running the entire length of the terrace. Five ornate chairs sat in a circle near the fire. Three of the chairs were currently occupied by the council members. The two remaining chairs were reserved for the warrior and Bronwyn.

Her pulse quickened when she noticed the occupants in their chairs.

The warrior introduced her to the first council member. He stood to his feet; a pleasant smile spread across his face. She remembered seeing him before. He was the beautiful man, with whom she had briefly danced, the night of the pre festival activities. She had been twirled into his arms for a brief moment.

"This is Adam," the warrior said. Adam took Bronwyn's hand in his, raised it to his lips, and gently kissed it. He bowed, and when he did, a silver chain with a white stone pendant, like the one Travis wore, fell from his shirt.

"It is my extreme honor to meet you," he said, tenderly.

She smiled, so this must be Adam, the fraternal twin she wrote of, in her attempted story, My Better Half; the exiled prince. Adam remained standing as the warrior introduced Bronwyn to the second council member.

Crushing his cigarette underneath the heel of his bare foot, Falcon removed his dark glasses, allowing Bronwyn to get a glimpse of his entire face. To her surprise, his eyes were quite pleasant. However, there was a deep scar under his right eye. He grabbed her hand and pulled it toward his lips. He too kissed it, more gently than she had imagined him capable. Dropping her hand, he gave her a slight wink. He also remained standing as the warrior introduced the last council member.

"I am sure Travis needs no introduction."

Standing, Travis took her hand as if it were the first time he'd ever met her. He lifted it to his lips, keeping his eyes engaged on hers, and kissed it tenderly. At the touch of his lips on her skin, the air escaped her lungs, and she found it quite difficult to breathe. He dropped her hand, and reverently bowed his head.

He remained standing as the warrior took Bronwyn's hand, and for the first time announced his name.

"I am Barak," he said, before kissing her hand.

The four men all bowed and then returned to their seats.

She swallowed hard and sat as well. Her heart continuing to pound, as her anxiety grew.

"Do you know why you are here in Moonshine?" Barak asked.

"Walt took a wrong turn and now I'm stranded here until the parts to fix our bus arrive," she said wondering why he would ask what they already knew.

Barak asked another.

"What do you know about Moonshine?"

"Actually I had never heard of it until six days ago."

He questioned her as if she were lying, "Never?"

"Pretty sure never. I would certainly remember a place like this."

He looked away from her and up into the night sky.

"How long have you been writing?"

"I began writing stories when I was nine years old."

"What do you write?"

"Plays, scripts, short stories. I hope to write a novel someday."

"Why haven't you?" His voice was suddenly stern.

"I have attempted several times, just never completed any of them."

"Why not?"

She sighed; first Travis, now this Barak. She was growing weary of answering this question. The answer always resulted in depressing her, making her feel as though she were a failure as a writer.

"Because," she sighed, "I'm not sure that I can. Every time I try the story always seems to fall short of what I know it should be. Just because it's a dream of mine, doesn't mean I have it in me to do it."

The council remained silent, making her extremely uncomfortable.

Now her turn, whether or not they agreed…

"Why the interview?" Her voice walked a tightrope between demanding and frustrated.

"You're not explaining anything to me. I want answers, not questions. I want to know where I am, and what this place is, and why I was brought here, and who you all are."

"Who we are? You don't remember us?" He asked, bringing his eyes back to her.

She felt weak; no words would come to her throat. Her head began to swim.

"This beautiful town of Moonshine," he continued; "you wrote of it when you were ten. You made the setting of that story here, and gave it the name of Moonshine, because of the way the moon shines down thru the trees, and onto the lake."

A memory surfaced; clawing its way through the years of suppression, finally defeating the force keeping it hidden. He was right, she partially remembered this story! Her pulse quickened. Her breathing became labored. The intensity of the heat rose within her along with a familiar terror. There was a reason she had forgotten about it...why? And then, as if he were privy to her thoughts he answered the question.

"Disturbing things began to happen as you wrote your story. Things you haven't spoken of since. Things your parents forced you to forget."

No, she wouldn't listen to this; she couldn't listen. Everything inside of her forbade her from remembering. Panicked, she covered her ears with her hands but his voice penetrated her barrier.

"After extended counseling," he continued, and she wished he wouldn't. "Your parents took your story away, and insisted you discontinue writing. It was then they enrolled you in dance and acting, steering you toward theater, keeping your mind off of writing."

She wanted to wake up from this ridiculous, haunting dream. Who was this man, and how did he know so much about her? A whirlpool of thoughts ensued. Barak was right in what he was saying. It had been twenty-four years, and she hadn't thought of the story, or its aftermath in all that time. More memories began forcing their way back into her mind. Terror pushed its way forward, along with a deep sorrow filling her soul, as the tears pooled in her eyes, spilling over and streaking down her cheeks. She wanted to leave, to get on the bus and go back to a normal life traveling with her friends. She would much rather choose the pain of Ryan's betrayal, than the craziness she was experiencing now. She stood to leave, intending to bring an end to this bizarre confrontation. The emotion was proving to be too much. Her legs buckled beneath her. Each council member reacted quickly in an attempt to catch her before she hit the ground. Adam, the nearest to her, reached her first.

"Maybe it's not the right time," he said kindly. "It's proving to be too much for her."

"It will never get any easier," Travis said. "We all knew she would have to go through this. She needs to hear what Barak has to say; no matter how traumatizing it may become. She has already heard and seen too much to stop now."

The sound of his voice soothed her troubled spirit. Something in her heart told her he was right. It was for this reason he refused to tell her anything on the boat last night. Whatever Barak was attempting to tell her was immense. It was much more significant than she had anticipated, yet, she wanted answers. Deep inside the bottom of her soul, she knew she was meant to be where she was tonight.

"Travis is right." Her voice quivered. "I'm sorry, I just became overwhelmed. I can continue."

Adam helped her sit back in her chair before returning to his own.

"If you certain you're alright?"

She nodded; smiling at his kindness.

"I suggest we take a less threatening approach," Falcon said. "Why not let the lady scribe ask us the questions? We can take it one step at a time. The whole story should unveil itself."

They agreed that this might prove to be the best way to approach the subject.

"Alright," Barak said. "What would you like to ask us?"

She contemplated where to start. There were so many questions. She leaned her head back and closed her eyes, to block out all distractions.

"You asked me if I remembered you, and I know I wrote of each of you at one time. I found your stories in my old writings. Does this mean you all are figments of my imagination? Am I schizophrenic?"

There was a brief pause as Barak deciphered the best way to answer.

"Excellent first question."

Falcon lit up another cigarette, proud how successful his way of interrogating was proving.

"In a way we are a figment of your imagination." Barak said. "But no, you are not schizophrenic. We actually do exist outside of your mind."

Bronwyn digested the answer, relieved. She continued on with her eyes closed. It seemed to work better for her that way.

"Did I create you then?"

"No, we existed someplace else. We came into your mind, and then you wrote of us, bringing us into this world."

She expelled a slow cleansing breath before she posed the next question.

"Where did you exist before I brought you here?"

The silence was much longer. So long, that she opened her eyes to see if they all were still there.

"This is difficult to answer," Barak said. "I will answer your question by telling you a story. You may feel free to interrupt me anytime."

She nodded in agreement.

"The place we existed before," he began, "is another earth, somewhat like this one."

"You're aliens?" Bronwyn was certain she was dreaming now. Falcon laughed heartily.

Barak smiled, "No, we are not aliens. We are all human just as you. We are from earth, but from another dimension. We are what you would call, extra dimensional beings. Our world is existing right now, right here, just in another dimension."

Satisfied with the answer, she leaned her head back, closing her eyes once again.

Barak shifted in his chair.

"Without getting to deep into the study of quantum physics, allow me to surf shallow waters by explaining to you, that there are many other dimensions. Your space program stumbled onto a portal to one of them. You know of it as area fifty-one. Even the Almighty mentioned it in the book you know as the Bible. *In my father's house are many dwelling places. If it were not so, I would have told you.*

Our world has existed for millions of years. We were peaceful, happy and content. Our world is almost identical to yours, as far as the earth is concerned, but our way of life is completely different. We continue to exist in a garden state. Just as it was with your Eden, in the beginning of your time. But our world had never fallen as yours did. Until recently, we still existed in a utopian type paradise, communing with celestial beings. Our children were born into a society of giving, learning and sharing. They were never forced to attend a government school system from ages five to eighteen; instead, they lived freely, learning everything from parents and community. There was not the drive to attain a career with the sole purpose of acquiring more and more possessions. Our lifestyle held all things in common. We owned nothing, yet possessed everything. We were driven by the beauty of art, literature, music, dance, song and verse."

Bronwyn felt peacefulness with the sound of the Warrior's voice and the description of his world. The turmoil in her soul melted away as his explanation continued. What earlier seemed bizarre and unnatural, now for some reason seemed to make perfect sense.

"Each person," he continued, "contributed and administered their talents and gifts to others. Every one considered the other person more highly than they did themselves. We all lived, learned and loved."

"You speak in the past tense." she said, realizing something dire must have happened, because they were here, in her dimension, and not theirs. There had to be a reason. "Why is that?"

"We were governed by three brothers," Falcon said, taking over the story. "The three Princes of Eden. They were great men, governing our world with compassion and mercy. However, a coup arose among a group known as the Barons. The dark dimension crept in, and the desire for power and possessions consumed the leader of the Barons."

Falcon's voice took on an intensity that caused Bronwyn to open her eyes once again.

"He promoted himself and his ideas among the people. He extolled himself higher than the Princes, betraying and assassinating his best friend, Ariston, the eldest of the three ruling Princes. And, for the first time, blood was spilled in Eden. This wicked Baron spoke lies to the people, tainting Ariston's character, making untrue charges and accusations against all three Princes. Unfortunately, he happened to be a very well-liked and popular man, so his worthless promises, words, and ideals seemed intriguing to many. Our world became divided. His selfish ambition produced nothing but chaos and dissention. A war broke out, and many good people lost their lives. The tumult was so magnificent that the balance of our world was ripped open, creating a portal into this one. Upon this opening, the wicked ruler exiled all the heirs of the royal city Eden, to earth. It was a death sentence, barring them from the tree of life. Thousands fled, and have been living here, in your dimension for years, waiting for the time when they could return to Eden. The remaining peoples of our earth, who were not citizens of Eden, were forced to become followers of the destroyer and his new ways. If they refused, they were immediately executed."

Falcon lit another cigarette and leaned back into his chaise, allowing Barak to take over the story again.

"Three prophecies were given to us by the virtuous realm. The first one stated that one day a writer would emerge, and write a story that would exonerate the character of our Princes, against the false charges of the destroyer. This story will validate something very important to all the inhabitants of our world and beyond. This story, once written, will allow us to reclaim our world and our way of life. What the writer writes will happen."

"See the former things have taken place, and new things I declare, before they spring into being. I announce them to you."

"Isaiah 42:9," Bronwyn whispered.

There was complete silence. All council members relieved that the story was out, the story they had contained within themselves since their exile.

Bronwyn attempted to wrap her mind around the entire thing... a futile effort.

"So you believe I am the writer?"

"We *know* you are the writer" Barak said. "You fulfilled the prophesy to the very letter. You are the one who wrote of Moonshine, causing it to come to be, calling us to dwell here, providing us a safe place of refuge while we wait."

"But I thought you said the people were sent here in exile, so how did I bring you here?"

Many of the royal families of Eden were exiled to earth through the portal, a few of us were held back pending execution. When you wrote of us, you called us through the portal to Moonshine and for that we will be forever grateful."

She scanned their faces.

"How many of you roam the earth?"

"Too many to count," he admitted sadly. "Literally thousands were sent over. Unfortunately the longer they exist on earth, the more their memory of their former life becomes erased. Most eventually die having no recollection of Eden. Only those who reside in Moonshine and the other safe havens still remember."

"There are other towns?" She asked.

"Yes. Some are hidden ranches and villas, much like the Citadel here. We call them towers of refuge. As long as our people dwell there, then they are kept safe."

"Are they allowed to leave?"

"Only for short periods of time. After two weeks they begin to forget who they are, if that happens, and then they do not eat from the tree of life, so they die."

She knew it! The tree of life was here, and that is what the cloaked men were guarding.

"So the tree of life is here somewhere in Moonshine?"

Barak's smile answered her question.

She nodded, affirming his answer but somehow felt the council feared she wasn't grasping any of the magnitude of what Barak had just said.

"So you say I fulfilled your prophesy by coming here. If so, then what's next?"

"You start writing." Falcon sounded demanding.

"What lies ahead is the quest of a lifetime," Adam said tenderly.

"You will receive inspiration, write, and things will take place, allowing us to return to Eden. We do not know the way. Only you do. You will be our guide."

She felt a heaviness fall upon her shoulders. The heat sensation was replaced by a cold chill. Her teeth began to chatter.

"You mentioned being governed by three brothers. You said one was murdered. Where are the other two brothers, the remaining Princes of Eden?"

Again the council grew quiet, an aching silence, deep remorse, and sadness spread through their faces.

"Sadly Ariston wasn't the only Prince who lost his life. We lost another one as well," Barak said. "There is only one Prince of Eden remaining. Prince Asa."

"Where is he?"

Barak smiled. "He resides in Moonshine, and he is here among us tonight. You know him as Travis."

Her eyes immediately cut over to Travis. His dark eyes looked back; there was helplessness in them that confirmed his need for her. Her body grew numb; her mouth speechless, her stomach in knots, her heart aching more than ever.

"Maybe I'm not the one," she said shaking her head. "I don't begin to know where to start writing. I've had severe writers block for some time now. I can't even produce a simple sappy re-write. On top of that, I know nothing about your world. How could I ever be expected to expose the false charges of this wicked baron, defeat him, and return Travis to the throne?"

Barak smiled.

"The story is in you Bronwyn, it is a part of your soul. That is where it has been buried for years. You know the story. You've known it your entire life."

She sighed. "Why can't you just go back through the portal yourselves?"

"It has been closed for many years. It closed when you stopped writing your story. However, when you fulfilled the prophesy by returning to Moonshine, the portal was re-opened. Unfortunately, we do not control it. Abaddon does. He possesses the key, which is the first prophesy."

Her head continued to swim as thoughts raced across her mind. "You said there were three prophesies. What do the other two say?"

"Unfortunately we do not know that either," Barak confessed. "No one has ever seen them. They are veiled from us. We believe the second prophesy may be hidden in your original manuscript."

Travis had remained silent for most of the meeting. Not now.

"We must warn you that writing the story will be extremely dangerous. Our enemies do not want it written; neither does the dark realm. They will be defeated if it is. Once you began to write, adversaries will come looking for you. Their solitary goal is your destruction. The storm that hit your first night was one you wouldn't have been able to track on the weather radar. The portal was re-opened. Spies were sent. Once they find you, they will kill you. Your life will never be the same again."

This time she heard him in an entirely different light. He was no longer the soothing voice in the cabin, garden, waterfall or lake. No wonder he always spoke with such wisdom and authority. He was royalty, a Prince, once ruler of an entire world.

She grew frightened as she realized the severity of his words, the night he caught her under the tree: Be quiet or they will find you.

Falcon noticed the distress on her face.

"Not to worry, lady scribe" That's where I come into play. I will be your personal body guard, your secret service; so to speak. I will give my very life to save yours."

His declaration took her off guard. The distrust she felt for him earlier began to dissipate. He was nothing more than a rebel rogue, a fighter for a world and way of life stolen from him. He was a bit unorthodox, but the ultimate in passion for his cause. *I will give my very life to save yours.*

"That's why we danced so close the other night." He explained, flashing his impish grin. "They were searching for you, asking questions. The fat man in your group pointed you out. I shielded you and hid your face, so they could not identify you. But not to worry, my lady scribe, as far as those spies are concerned. Travis and I disposed of them. You saw the last one lose his life in the garden."

She sat in silence, dumbstruck. The victim did say they will find the scribe and destroy them. Fear began rising within her. He and Travis actually killed someone to protect her. Her stomach knotted. She was finished talking. She didn't want to hear anymore. She longed to lay down somewhere and bury her head under a soft blanket and sleep for hours.

"One last warning," Barak said. Her heart sank even further, if that were possible.

"There is another enemy at work that will keep the book from being written."

She sighed. If there hadn't been enough at play here. Now she had to hear of yet another enemy.

"The enemy is you." He said it resolute, yet kind. "As I mentioned before, the longer our people reside on this earth, the more they lose the memory of who they are. They forget about home. The same can happen to you. If you leave Moonshine, you can once again be caught up in the mundane routine of life. You can easily forget Moonshine and everything that has happened here, and avoid your true calling. Days will turn to weeks, and weeks to months, months to years... Soon all will be lost. The enemy knows this and can conquer you by distractions."

"Be certain of who you allow in your life," Falcon continued. "You will not always be able to discern the trustworthy from the enemy. You could very well befriend the adversary, unaware that their only intention is to stop and destroy you."

Barak stood, and offered Bronwyn his hand as he bowed slightly.

"Think on all these things that have been spoken to you."

Content that the councils work was done for now, Barak suggested that Bronwyn retreat to the room for a few hours of sleep before heading back to Sandalwood Inn. She didn't object. She was exhausted, her mind full. She needed to withdraw to a quiet place, where she could meditate on all that had been said to her.

Barak graciously escorted her back to her room.

"Sleep well, my dear Bronwyn. In a few hours you will be escorted back to the inn. You must return before sunrise, to dispel any questions or suspicions."

He smiled and closed the beautifully ornate door behind him as he left.

She undressed and climbed under the silk covers, extinguishing the small lamp on the bedside table. The room remained filled with the glow of the moonlight filtering through the glass doors. She lay there sinking deep into the feather mattress, the silk coverings feeling heavenly against her bare skin. She stared at the ceiling, listening to the low murmurs of Barak and the council continuing their meeting outside. She somewhat hoped to fall asleep and wake up back at the Inn, realizing the whole thing had been a dream. She could imagine re-telling the events to Bethany and Lillian as the most bizarre insane dream she had ever dreamt. She sighed, realizing she could never breathe a word of this to either of them. She knew she would more than likely have a lot of explaining to do in the morning. Bethany was a light sleeper and certain to notice she had been out again all night. Bethany would profess without a doubt that she and Travis were having "escapades," as she so often called it.

Her heart fell. For the entire week, she allowed the girls to convince her that Travis, with all the time and attention he devoted to her, was somewhat romantically interested. Now she realized the entire reason for his concern. He was only protecting his interest in the whole equation. *She* was his gateway back to Eden, and as a Prince of Eden, it was his duty to protect that passage. His heart did only belong to Mavis. That is why he never took an opportunity or made an advance when they were alone together. Even the kiss under the tree was nothing more than a tender gift. She and Travis were literally from two different worlds, and he was not interested in her in any romantic way.

A tear escaped her eye, finding its way down her cheek, rolling onto the silk satin pillow case. She'd never felt more alone. She desperately missed Ryan and the normalcy of what they once shared. Another tear slid silently from her eye, onto the pillow that cradled her head. Her eyes became heavy and she soon fell asleep.

Falcon entered her room. A small amount of moonlight streamed across her bed, giving light to her ivory skin, as she lay sleeping. A smile moved the corner of his lips. He picked up her discarded clothes from the floor and tossed them onto the bed.

"Scribe," he whispered. "It's time to head back."

She stirred but remained asleep, spellbound in the comfort of her bed.

"Scribe." This time he was much louder.

Opening her eyes, she groaned at the sight of him.

"Good morning to you too," he said sarcastically. "Get dressed. It's time to head back."

Making sure the covers were pulled high enough to cover her nakedness, she reached for her clothes.

"Turn around!" She demanded, before rising to a sitting position. Falcon laughed lightly as he turned his body to face the opposite direction.

"Why don't you wait outside the door?" She suggested.

"You must begin trusting me scribe. You're going to be seeing a lot of me." He opened the door and gave the command, "three minutes," before leaving the room.

She dressed quickly, her body shivering from the coolness of her chamber. Heaviness invaded her with the realization that last night's events had not been a dream.

She joined Falcon. Together they headed outside into the damp darkness of the early morning. He led her back through the hedge maze, effortlessly, knowing every turn to take, navigating just as expertly as Barak the night before. They reached the line of trees, walked through the leafy tunnel, and arrived at the white sandy shore-line.

Approaching the lake, Bronwyn noticed Adam and Travis waiting beside the gondola. She was relieved to see them, pleased she wouldn't be taking the thirty-minute boat ride alone with Falcon.

Adam offered her his hand, helping her into the vessel.

"Were you able to get some rest?" He asked.

"Yes," she managed to smile. "I did sleep well, thank you."

He returned her smile. "Good to hear it."

He did seem princely. She smiled at the thought of what Lillian would say if she met Adam. He was strikingly handsome, not to mention royalty.

Travis remained silent, offering no greeting as she and Falcon arrived at the water. Her heart ached over it. Just as well, she thought.

She shivered in the early morning air, as a gentle wind blew across the water. She pulled her bare legs up into the seat, attempting to curl them underneath her for added warmth. Noticing her discomfort,

Travis, removed a blanket stored in the compartment below and draped it over her shoulders.

Their eyes met briefly.

"Thank you," she muttered softly then looked away.

Falcon steered the vessel across the still lake; all the while, his eyes searched the waters, watching for anything that would threaten his passengers. They glided along in silence; the only sound was the oar quietly cutting into the water. The tranquility of the early morning ride caused her eyes to grow heavy. She shifted in her seat fighting the drowsiness, but the comfort of her blanket, and the gentle swaying of the boat rocked her to sleep. She was just dozing off, when the short harsh cry of a nighthawk ripped through the silence. Had she been alone she would have thought nothing of the bird call, but when Falcon cupped his hand to his mouth and sent back a series of convincing whippoorwill cries, she knew otherwise. Within a matter of seconds the call was returned. As usual, no one offered her any information, and no words were exchanged among the men. Yet, when all three smiled at once she could tell they were communicating in some way. Her heart dropped, hoping that they were not able to read minds. If that was the case, then Travis knew every thought she had about him. The assumption made her sick.

"How do you do that?" Her sleepy voice broke the silence. "How are you communicating with each other? Can you read minds?"

Falcon cocked an eyebrow and grinned; but it was Adam that put her mind to rest.

"We can read minds, but only if the other person allows it. We call on each other through meditation, much like you do when you pray. When the other person responds to the beckoning, we exchange information with our thoughts."

She was intrigued. "Then why the bird calls?"

Falcon grinned and again Adam answered.

"Because, Falcon has been talking to Travis the entire ride; and their conversation cannot be interrupted."

His answer annoyed her although she tried not to show it. If she was expected to fulfill the prophesy and write their story of redemption, then it might be nice to be let in on what was going on. The time of confidentiality should be over; and the fact that they continued to hold secrets caused her to distrust. She hadn't agreed to write their story and even if she wanted to, she doubted she could. How can you write about something you know nothing about? Once more, how can you learn if others refuse to inform you? A flame of anger ignited inside her. As soon as the bus was repaired she was boarding and leaving this place and never giving it another thought.

Once they arrived at the opposite shoreline, Falcon grabbed a torch and led the way into the mouth of the cave. The descent seemed a bit more treacherous in this direction. As Bronwyn recalled, there had been several different levels of boulders upon which Barak had actually lifted her. Falcon led, jumping from the first one. His movements in the dimly lit cave resembled those of a mountain lion. He jumped the great distance with little effort, landing lightly on his feet. Adam also gracefully descended the lower levels, always landing noiselessly on his feet, exuding minimal effort. Travis followed suit. Same prowess, same result. Without hesitation he turned back and raised his arms high, offering his help to Bronwyn.

She wanted to descend to the lower levels as the men had, and was almost certain she could make it. However, she feared she might slip on the muddy surface, landing hard on her face, possibly breaking a bone, and then needing to be carried the rest of the way. To save herself from extreme embarrassment, she decided to take Travis's offer. He placed his hands firmly around her wrist, and with amazing strength and control; he lifted her into the air and then steadily sat her on the ground below. This act was repeated seven more times as their trail descended deeper underground.

Before long they arrived at the marble riverbed. The icy water on her shoeless feet caused her feet to cramp. Sensing the pain, Travis scooped her into his arms and carried her across the watery path. Grateful, she held on tight, wrapping her arms around his neck. She was too emotionally drained to care about the awkwardness of the situation. However, she did notice he continued to carry her once they had crossed the river bed, and up the steep slippery path. She was grateful. She was extremely tired from the heavy emotion of last night. Not to mention the dire lack of sleep. She longed to reach her room at the inn, and lay in bed for hours.

The four continued to walk in silence until they reached the end of the long tunnel. Falcon replaced the torch, and then climbed a few feet up the side of the wall, where he pulled a small lever. Once again, the ground beneath them trembled as the rock wall slid slowly to their right. The musty dirty smell of the shack façade greeted their noses. All four crossed through. The wall closed slowly behind them.

Adam retrieved a hidden sword, then donned a black hooded cloak, as he stood on the broken down porch of the cabin. He took Bronwyn's hand in his.

"Bless you lovely Bronwyn. It has been an honor. Until our paths cross again." He kissed her hand, and then nodded to Travis and Falcon. He jumped from the porch; running into the woods, disappearing like a frightened deer.

"I'm turning the scribe over to you. You have it from here," Falcon said to Travis. He gave Bronwyn a slight wink. "I'll be seeing you around, Scribe."

He too slipped into his hooded robe, darting off into the woods, disappearing into the thickness of the trees.

Travis and Bronwyn were left alone on the porch. He took her hand.

"Stay close beside me."

They made their way through the woods back to the inn. Neither one saying a word.

CHAPTER THIRTY-FIVE
DAY SEVEN

Bronwyn woke earlier than she planned. Despite her body's protests, she climbed from the bed, desiring to take advantage of Bethany and Lillian's absence. She was glad they weren't in the room. She had no desire to try and make up a story explaining where she was last night, and why she had snuck back into the room at five in the morning. She quickly splashed cold water onto her face, brushed her teeth, ran a comb through her hair and dressed. While the others were eating, she quietly took her leave.

The sun was at work again, radiating its warmth, making her grateful for the beauty of the morning. The gently moving ripples of the river glistened under the rays of the sun, and seemed to smile at her as she walked past; uplifting her spirits some, from the feeling of dread that overwhelmed her last night. She skirted past the river scouting for a place to escape. She needed a place of solitude, a place to collect her thoughts and pen the many questions invading her mind. She made her way across the property and onto the small narrow highway. This time instead of heading into Moonshine; she decided to venture in the opposite direction. She strolled on down the highway until she arrived at the old covered bridge where she and Walt took shelter the night of their arrival; the same bridge where she first laid eyes on Travis. The place was perfect. No one would ever think to look for her here.

She hiked on down the grassy hill, leading underneath the bridge, and found a nice place near the river's edge to sit and collect her thoughts. Her mind had been jumping from one subject to another since she escaped the inn, and now as she sat in solitude, she thought of the implausibility of last night's events. What Barak and the others told her defied all physical laws, all logic, all sense, and yet, for some bizarre reason, she believed it; her heart did anyway. Throughout her life she usually followed her heart rather than her head. She'd learned from experience, if her brain told her it was impossible, then her heart knew it to be true; and right now, her heart was telling her this was the very reason she was here.

She reflected on her earlier writing of Moonshine. Thoughts of the old manuscript evoked an anxious feeling that did not set right with her; and as she continued to mediate on the subject, she noticed she twisted at her fingers in nervous agitation. Her memory of the story was vague at best. Barak was right when he said her parents insisted she stop writing. She hadn't thought of the incident for twenty-four years. A gnawing dread surfaced making her realize there were suppressed memories concerning the story, events she'd been forced to forget. With her curiosity peaking, she desired to find her old writing and shed more light onto all of this. Besides, as Barak mentioned, the second prophesy might be hidden somewhere within the pages. Hopefully, her mother had not destroyed the book, but stored it somewhere in the attic. She decided to make a surprise visit to her parents on the way home from touring, and search for the manuscript. With the conclusion of that matter, her mind settled on the subject, and then sporadically jumped to the next....Travis.

He was a Prince, the ruler of another world, a man of wisdom and power. He was the very definition of compassionate, caring for everyone alike. She felt silly for thinking he had been attracted to her in any way. His concern lay in who he was; his solemn duty, it was what he did as a benevolent ruler. She should've never read any more into his actions other than that simple fact. This thought caused her heart to ache. She immediately forced it from her mind; but it didn't leave willingly. Instead, it attached itself to thoughts of Mavis, and Bronwyn began to speculate why Mavis asked about the fireworks show. Did Mavis know she had watched them with Travis?

She felt a tinge of guilt then dismissed it. Nothing adulterous happened between them. She pondered once again about Mavis's injuries, wondering if they had happened during the uprising.

There were so many more questions. She thought of the troupe, and Marcus, and the re-writes she had yet to start, let alone finish.

Today was their seventh day in Moonshine. It was just a matter of time before the parts arrived and Larry repaired the bus, accelerating their departure.

Leaving seemed like an escape back to normality. The idea of getting on the bus with the troupe, and heading back to civilization, to their next engagement, seemed like a visit from an old friend. The thought of being home in her condo on the beach, visiting her favorite coffee house with her friends, and the other activities that usually consumed her life, seemed so appealing. She stared across the flowing river smiling at the thought of it all.

"How's our Lady Scribe today?"

A voice startled her, breaking her gaze from the river. She cast her eyes on Falcon sitting on his motorcycle.

"I never heard you drive up."

"You need to become more aware of your surroundings. I followed you the entire way."

He lit a cigarette, took a draw, and expelled the smoke slowly, all the while keeping his eye on her.

"Didn't Travis warn you about going off alone? Yet, for some reason you continue to neglect his instructions. Why is that?"

Bronwyn gave a defiant chuckle.

"I'm not used to asking permission to take a walk."

He drew on the cigarette.

"Get used to it."

She scowled.

"Am I in danger?"

Her question was nonchalant. There was no fear in her voice, and she could tell her relaxed attitude on the subject didn't set right with him.

"Always."

"It was you following me the night we arrived, wasn't it? I saw you moving in and out of the trees."

He took a long draw exhaling the smoke slowly before he answered.

"I knew you noticed me, I saw the fear in your eyes, as I do now."

He wasn't taking his eyes off her and his stare was cold.

She swallowed hard.

"I'm not afraid of you."

"Yes you are."

The smoke billowed from his mouth as he spoke. A shudder crawled up her back and for some reason a seed of distrust began to take root inside of her.

He took one last draw, and then tossed his cigarette on the ground.

"You don't trust me?"

The heat wrapped around her neck. Was he reading her thoughts? She swallowed hard again and tried to dismiss the accusation.

"I have a hard time trusting men in general."

He stared at her for a few seconds longer, and then continued on with the previous conversation, as if they had never strayed from it in the first place.

"Abaddon was awaiting your arrival that night. He sent many of his men through the portal as soon as you opened it. It took all of us to fight them off."

She shuddered again at the thought. "How did they know I was coming? Our arrival was an accident. Walt took a wrong turn that night."

"According to you." He dismounted his bike.

She studied him. He was in excellent physical shape, as were all of the men she had encountered from Eden. Moreover, like the others, he wore his hair long. She noticed that a small part of his scar was visible from underneath his dark glasses. He had no facial hair, save for a slight five o'clock shadow. In addition, as with every time she had seen him, he was barefoot, dressed in jeans and a muscle shirt. He also wore the same white stone pendant around his neck as she saw on Adam and Travis.

"What's the necklace for?" she asked. "I noticed you all wear one."

"It reminds us of who we really are."

She knew she would not get any more information than that elusive offer.

"Tell me about your world. What's it called?"

"It's called earth same as yours. Remember we're of another dimension not another planet. Only a doorway separates the two, not a universe."

She had read of portals, worm holes and black holes and was aware of the possibility of other dimensions. But, she also read that it would take millions of years for technology to advance to the point of accessing them; if ever. If that was the case then their world must be extremely advanced, yet Barak spoke of it as a garden state, like the original Eden of the Bible.

"Where's the portal?"

Falcon lit up another and took a quick draw before he answered.

"The waterfall."

Her eyes flashed in surprise. The peculiarity she experienced that night now made sense and she trembled inside at the thought of being so close to another world.

"Something happened to me there. Travis said it was altitude sickness but I know it wasn't."

He expelled a long line of smoke.

"You climbed to the top where the veil between the two worlds is very thin. You felt the pull."

"The pull?"

"There's a presence there that will call to your spirit. Some people never feel it, but if you're sensitive to it, you will hear it."

She'd heard a woman singing now three different times since her arrival and each time the song had beckoned her, drawing her away from where she was and into the unknown. This must be the presence he was referring too. Was it attempting to call her through the portal? The thought was paralyzing, causing her to shiver despite the mugginess of the morning. She hugged her arms with her hands hoping Falcon wouldn't notice her trembling.

He knocked the ashes from his cigarette, and then took a seat on the rock next to her. Again, he spoke as if he was reading her thoughts.

"The presence will speak to your spirit, not your mind so don't waste your time trying to find the logic in everything, and don't waste time being frightened. Listen to it, it will empower you, give you courage, guiding you into the truth."

He took another draw and expelled a long slow trail of smoke. His eyes were reminiscing, and she could tell his thoughts were literally worlds away.

"Eden's beauty is a lot like that of Moonshine." He changed the subject attempting to steer her thinking away; and although the description of his world was intriguing she couldn't stop thinking of the portal.

"There are many lakes, rivers, streams, oceans… there is a lot of water. All of it is pure and unpolluted. Eden's climate is tropical with much vegetation. The rest of our earth is a lot like yours, with different climates in various regions. It's all very beautiful. We eat only the food we get from plants. We never consume meat of any kind. We have many species of animals, none that we have lost to extinction. We live among them in no fear. There are no wild beasts; all are tame, existing among humanity. We communicate with them through our thoughts. We have the same ability with each other if we choose to communicate in that way. We have no need of cell phones; we summon each other with our minds. If I wished to speak with Travis right now, I would simply concentrate and call on him in my thoughts. Much like this worlds attempts at praying except you all are not tuned into the listening part of it."

His words interested her. She had always found praying to be a difficult task and as Falcon described it, a one ended conversation.

"How do get your mind to tune into the listening?"

He flicked the burning ashes onto the ground, took a small draw and expelled the smoke.

"That's the problem; you try to accomplish things with your mind. God will never speak to your brain, Scribe. He will only speak to your heart. When you learn how to listen with your spirit, you will hear his answers."

He took another drag of his cigarette, this time expelling the smoke very slowly, letting her contemplate his answer, as he watched a hawk glide overhead. Again, his mind seemed very far away.

"In Eden, we possess the ability to fly."

Her heart leaped with that statement. Often in her sleep, she would have dreams of flying. She would be running and without warning, her feet would leave the ground in flight as her body soared higher and higher, past the tops of trees, higher than the clouds. The feeling was always euphoric. She reasoned that is probably what Falcon missed the most, hence the bird name.

Both were quiet for some time. Nothing but the sound of trickling water touched their ears. The light lessened as dark gray clouds began to fill the sky, obscuring the brightness and warmth of the sun. A sudden gust of wind blew, stirring up a few fallen leaves and bringing the smell of rain. Within a few moments, Falcon jumped to his feet. Again, he tossed the butt of his cigarette on the ground, crushing it under the heel of his bare foot.

"Let's go, Scribe."

"Go where?"

"I'll give you a ride back to the inn before it rains."

"I like walking in the rain."

He climbed on his bike and stared at her through his dark glasses.

"I'm going to have a lot of trouble with you, aren't I?"

"That depends on you. You give me trouble; I'll give it right back."

She sighed and softened her voice. "Honestly, I'm not ready to head back. There will be so many questions. My friends know I was out all night."

He considered the magnitude of what she said. "Let's go for a ride, then. I won't take you back just yet."

She studied him perched upon his sleek high-speed motorcycle. Just a few days ago he terrified her, spinning her across the lawn, and all the while he was protecting her from a would be assassin. His ways were a bit unorthodox and although she wasn't sure she trusted him completely she no longer feared him as she did before.

She broke into a smile then climbed on behind him, wrapping her arms around his hard stomach. He quickly placed his hair in a ponytail, to keep it from whipping into her face, and then started the engine. He raced down the narrow highway, taking the curves at tremendous speed. At any other time, she would have screamed in fear, protesting, demanding the driver slow down. However, she felt very confident in his ability to maneuver the heavy bike. Besides, if it was his sworn duty to protect her, he wouldn't risk her life by crashing his bike, so she rested in the fact that he knew what he was doing, and before long found herself enjoying the intense thrill of the ride. He drove for a while longer before he made a speedy U-turn and stopped on the side of the road.

He looked back.

"You alright?"

"It's great," she said.

"Rain's coming. You ready to get back, or do you want to go somewhere else?"

Bronwyn had much rather go somewhere else, but she knew she should not delay the inevitable. The longer she was gone, the more intense the questioning would be. She sighed.

"I guess I'd better go back."

"To the inn it is." He took off at incredible speed once again. The rain began to fall just as he whipped the bike into the Inn's driveway. Bronwyn was surprised to see a strange car sitting out front and everyone crowded on the front porch. Carla Jo was jumping up and down; her hands were covering her mouth. The entire troupe stood gathered around the driver of the car. The sound of the approaching motorcycle drew everyone's attention. All eyes focused on her arriving with Falcon. Pure perplexity stretched across Bethany's face.

Climbing from the motorcycle her eyes suddenly fell upon the driver of the car, her heart raced...

Ryan.

The one person she never expected to see at Sandalwood Inn.

She stood by the bike, her strength escaping her. Unwilling to move her feet, she remained where she was as the rain fell on her face.

"Look who showed up," Bethany announced sarcastically, breaking the silence.

"I can't believe he's here, on my porch!" Carla Jo squealed as she continued her jumping.

"Hello, Bronwyn."

The sound of his voice knotted her stomach.

"What are you doing here?"

"You weren't returning any of my calls, so I came in person."

"How did you know where to find me?" She demanded suspiciously while remaining planted by the bike.

"Who is this man?" Falcon interrupted then stepped in front of her to block Ryan's view.

"You don't know Ryan Reese?" Carla Jo exclaimed, shocked.

Ryan bravely descended the porch steps and stood directly in front of Falcon.

"I'm her fiancé," he said, sizing up the beefy motorcycle rider.

"Ex- fiancé," Bronwyn said.

Falcon stood his ground, unmoving.

"What do you want with her?"

"What business is it of yours?" Ryan bit back. "Are you dating her now?"

"And if I am?" He said while lighting up another cigarette. He removed his dark glasses revealing his penetrating eyes and deep scar.

"Look. I don't want any trouble from you mountain people. There's no need to pull out your sawed-off shotguns, I just came to speak with Bronwyn."

Falcon took a long draw, keeping his eyes locked on Ryan in a threatening gaze.

"Do you wish to talk to this charlatan?"

"I have nothing to say to him."

Falcon gave Ryan a satisfied grin as he replaced his dark glasses, then blew a cloud of smoke directly into Ryan's face. Ryan backed away choking on his next words.

"Did your girlfriend tell you she is carrying my baby?"

Collective gasps sounded from the porch. Bronwyn's pulse quickened. Her stomach became suddenly sick.

"You're pregnant?" Bethany asked.

"No!" Bronwyn said. The word collided in mid-air with Ryan's "Yes!"

"That bloody well explains the mood swings," Trent said.

"And all the fainting," Lillian added.

Bronwyn couldn't believe what she was hearing.

"Come on guys do I look six months pregnant to you?"

"Did you abort my child?" Ryan pressed the matter.

"I lost *my* child," She said angrily.

The rain poured down. Bronwyn looked up at Travis, disheartened. He was the only person she had ever told about her pregnancy. Had he betrayed her confidence? What reason could he have in doing that, unless he had told Mavis, and Mavis in hopes of getting rid of Bronwyn had phoned Ryan? Bronwyn knew that would be impossible. Almost every woman on the planet wanted to call Ryan Reese. How would Mavis have discovered his private number?

"Who told you about the baby?" She demanded.

"I got a call," Ryan answered smugly.

"Who called you?" She was nearly screaming her words.

"Wilbur."

She glanced at Wilbur who was watching everything unfold from the comfort of a rocking chair. His lower abdomen hung over the top of his thighs. He disgusted her.

"You shouldn't leave your personal journal up on your computer," Wilbur said in his thick voice. "It becomes public access for anyone who happened to pass by. I made the call to Ryan for your own good."

Her head began to swim. All eyes were on her. Bethany looked somewhat wounded and insulted. Lillian appeared shocked and sympathetic.

"I want out of here." she whispered to Falcon.

"Can we go someplace private?" Ryan asked. "I really need to talk to you."

"You sure pick a fine time and place to talk. There's no place private. It's a small town; everyone will recognize you."

"You can go to my cabin."

Travis' offer surprised her. He had descended the porch and was now standing directly behind Ryan.

"You can go there. You will have privacy." He said, directing his words to Bronwyn only. "It's up to you though; you do not have to go with him if you don't want to."

She looked at everyone watching her from the porch and sighed defeated. "I'll go. I think I need to."

"That's my girl." Ryan said, eyeing Falcon. Falcon took a firm step forward, Ryan, retreated to his rental car.

Bronwyn continued to stand in the pouring rain, her mind and stomach reeling. She could not believe this strange turn of events. Bethany shook her head in disgust and disappeared inside the inn, slamming the screen door behind her. Bronwyn wanted to climb on the back of Falcon's bike and ride down the road until he'd taken her far away from everyone and everything. She even contemplated returning to the waterfalls and being sucked through the portal only to avoid her present situation. Instead, she climbed in the rental car.

Falcon and Travis watched as the car left the driveway and disappeared down the highway towards Moonshine.

"Do you trust him?" Falcon asked.

"I never trust a man who would leave his lady," Travis said. "However, the only threat he possesses at this point, is convincing her into taking him back, and returning to California. If they re-unite, she could leave and soon forget about all she has learned."

Falcon could hear the sorrow in Travis's voice and knew Travis's concern was far deeper than he was showing.

"Then why did you offer your cabin? We could have gotten rid of him pretty easily."

"You can protect her life, Falcon, but you cannot protect her heart. She must work through these matters. There will be many obstacles facing her if she chooses to write. This is very small in comparison to what lies ahead. She needs to draw upon her inner strength. Still, I wouldn't be opposed if you kept a close eye."

Falcon replaced his dark glasses and gave Travis his impish grin.

CHAPTER THIRTY-SIX

The intense rain tapped hard on the blue tin roof. Ryan walked around the cabin, surveying it. Bronwyn took a seat on the sofa and curled her feet beneath her while waiting for him to turn his attention to her. He seemed so different from how she remembered him. He had definitely changed. Or something had changed him. On the other hand, maybe Travis had been right. Maybe she was finally seeing Ryan for who he really was, not who she had invented him to be.

He stood at the front door looking out over the lake.

"This is a really nice place he has here."

"Uh huh. I rode out the storm of a lifetime here."

"Cool." He answered dismissively.

"I'm not so sure it was cool. It was pretty scary to me."

He continued to survey the lake. "Wonder what kind of fish they got in there."

She sighed and waited.

"Ryan? Why did you come all the way to Moonshine? I don't think it was to check out the bass and trout in the lake."

Ryan broke his gaze and closed the door behind him; taking a seat on the couch next to her.

"I came because I've been missing you, babe." He paused for a moment, studying her face for impact.

"Life's been, wow! You know. It's totally insane. I'm constantly surrounded by people. I have my own security guards. It's a wonder I got away to come here. There are so many people advising me, telling me what to do. All of them are trying to control my career and my personal life. It kind of bugs sometimes. I'm not sure I like all this attention. It's great, don't get me wrong, but everywhere I turn, there are cameras and screaming girls, like that kid at the inn. It's so annoying. It gets old, you know? Most guys would love to have girls screaming after them, but not all of them are pretty."

Bronwyn sat stoic, offering no sympathy.

"I miss you babe. I've been around all these sexy actresses with killer bodies and everything, but man, are they shallow! They are so into themselves. All they want to talk about is how thin they are or how they look. I haven't had one decent conversation. I crave it."

He scooted in a bit closer, "Remember, babe, how you and I could talk for hours, planning out stories, and characters and backgrounds? Together we came up with the best scenarios. I miss that."

She smiled; she couldn't help herself, those were good times. Ryan relaxed; her smile putting him at ease. He continued his long-winded rambling.

"I miss you. I miss that amazing smile, those deep green eyes, I miss coming home to you and the way you made our place on the beach so nice and comfortable. I miss our relaxing evenings and dinners out on the deck, overlooking the ocean. I miss the way I feel when I am around you. I realize that I am still in love with you...Do you know what Saturday was?"

She knew but offered no answer.

"I was supposed to marry the most amazing woman in the world, and there I was, out at another publicity party, surrounded by flashing cameras and women throwing themselves at me. I was so tired. I wanted you so bad right then. Then I got the call from Wilbur, telling me about the baby. I thought, wow, how's that for publicity. A baby, just what I need. A great excuse for me to settle down."

"There is no baby, Ryan." She spoke the words quietly. "I miscarried."

Ryan moved in tighter until he practically sat on her lap, "No problem, babe. We can make another one, here, tonight. I love you. I never wanted to end things but it was like I had no choice ya know. My agent kinda controls my life. He's always looking for ways to keep me in the spotlight. Gabriella was his idea. He said if we were in a relationship it would help promote the movie."

The rain continued to tap on the roof overhead. Thunder rolled softly outside.

She sat, silent. Stunned. She had been waiting for so long to hear all the things that Ryan was saying. For those nights, she had longed for an opportunity to be with him, wanting him to desire her again. Now he was practically begging for her, offering himself to her, and she knew there was not a woman in the world that would not give everything they had to be where she was right now.

He surprised her by moving from the couch to the floor. Kneeling before her, he grabbed her hand and slipped an enormous diamond on her finger

"I love you babe. Take me back and marry me. This time it will be for real. I won't let anything get in the way again. I promise. You're the best thing that ever happened to me, and I want the best. I need the best. I love you."

It was his way of saying "I love you." that made her mind up on the matter. Suddenly, her decision was right there, final. The last time she had heard those words, Travis uttered them in the garden. He was not confessing his love to her, only offering an example of what true love really was. She remembered his final words that night: "True love is sacrifice."

She fumbled at the diamond on her finger.

"You have no idea how many nights I have prayed and dreamed for this moment."

Ryan moved in closer. "Me too, babe. Me too."

"And now that it is actually happening, I realize it's not what I want at all."

She turned the ring and pulled until it slipped off her finger.

"What?" He was shocked, taken aback by her rejection.

"You don't love me Ryan, Not really."

"Babe!" He protested.

"It's Bronwyn."

He looked at her confused.

"My name is Bronwyn, not babe, Bronwyn."

"Okay!" he said, flustered. "Bronwyn, Bronwyn, Bronwyn. I do love you. It took me awhile but I realize now that I need you."

She shook her head.

"Ryan, I have no desire to be needed by you or anyone. If you're not a whole person without me, you will never be a whole person with me. Everything you said, all your reasons for loving me, were for you, based entirely upon your feelings."

Her voice rose.

"My God, you were even excited about the baby because it was an excuse for you to settle down… not because you loved it."

"I would love a baby once it came. It's just hard to love someone you don't know."

"Exactly. So how can you love me, when you don't really know me? Me, not babe. Me."

"God, Bronwyn, how many times do I have to say it? I do love you. I left all that Hollywood stuff to come back for you. My manager will be livid when he finds out what I've done. I've taken a huge risk. How can I prove it to you any more than that?" He practically yelled the words.

She smiled softly.

"Then you're willing to stay here with me?"

Pure surprise sprawled across his face. "Here, in this town?"

"Yes. I'm inspired here, I can write here and I want to write more than anything."

He stood from his kneeling position, agitated, while running his fingers through his blond wavy hair.

"Babe, I can't stay here. I gotta get back. I'm on contract. We can visit here from time to time so you can do some writing, but my career has me there. You know that."

"I thought you were leaving it all behind for me?"

"I would if I could. Contracts, babe."

She remained silent.

His voice turned whiny.

"Awe come on, this isn't fair. I'm not leaving you behind this time. I'm offering to take you with me."

"I don't want to go," she said quietly. "I was unfair to you, Ryan. I loved a man who never existed anywhere but in my own mind. I imagined you to be someone I wanted you to be, instead of seeing you for who you really were. And I'm sorry"

Her voice softened with compassion.

"I can't go with you, because I do not love you."

He stopped his pacing and stared at her.

"Is it because of that bad ass on the motorcycle? Are you in love with him?"

She almost laughed at the thought.

"No. I am not in love with him."

Ryan didn't say a word. He walked to the front door, and stepped onto the porch, his hands in his pockets, watching the rain.

"What do I do now?"

"Find yourself. Know who you are and become a whole person, so when you do find that someone to spend the rest of your life with, it will be two whole people walking side by side, sharing their lives together."

"You see, you're so deep," He said. "I miss that."

She smiled.

The summer rain continued soaking the earth, the sky doing what her soul longed to do. Cry and cleanse. She was sending Ryan away, and rejecting his love, and companionship. Yet, she felt peaceful.

"So this is what it feels like," he said pounding his heart with his fist.

"Man, it hurts."

"I know," she whispered.

He leaned over, kissing her on the cheek.

"I'm sorry. I really am."

She watched as he headed to the car, and climb into the driver's seat. He gave her a slight salute as he pulled away from the cabin. She watched until the car was out of view, and then sat on the porch swing, pushing off slowly with her feet, hypnotized by the falling rain. Only a few tears escaped her eyes.

She was not sure why, but she was not heartbroken. She was not in love with Ryan. Spending the past hour with him confirmed that. Spending the past week with Travis had given her a more certain picture of what she desired. A love she not only wanted to experience for herself, but what she longed to be able to give. Could she ever love someone so selflessly? Could she, as Travis said, send a person away, who she truly wanted and loved, never experiencing them, yet knowing they would experience all they ever dreamed?

She sat there for hours, swinging and thinking, never moving, just swinging, and thinking. She thought of how trite and superficial Ryan's world appeared in contrast to the men with whom she had communed last night. They lived for a much nobler purpose. She thought of Barak and his final words to her. He had talked of the opportunities to return to a normal life, a comfortable life. However, he had warned her not to settle for good, when her destiny was to be great. True, she could have returned with Ryan and lived an amazing life. But now, she could follow her destiny and be a part of something profound. Barak had also warned her that there was much pain and suffering on the path to greatness.

Her mind dwelt on these things.

A warm steam rose from the lake, the golden sun showing its face for the first time in several hours. However, it appeared for only a few minutes before dipping behind the mountains, allowing the moon and stars to take over. She sat in the darkness, watching the fireflies as she listened to the crickets and croaking frogs. She inhaled the aroma of the wet earth; remembering her first night in this cabin, and how she was given a second chance at life. She remembered Travis's response when she asked why he had braved the storm to rescue her, a person he had known less than twenty-four hours. He had simply said, "Because you were born to live, not to die."

His words warmed her, touched her. He was right. There was a life to be lived, a purpose to fulfill, a destiny waiting.

She entered the dark cabin and knew what she must do. She'd made up her mind. She approached the antique desk sitting in the corner of the living room. Turning on a small lamp, she sat at the computer. She opened a new file, typing on the keyboard with speed and accuracy. Marcus would get his re-write. She didn't care if it was her best work. She would not spend valuable time worrying over it. What would it matter in the whole scheme of things anyway? She would write only one more simple, sappy, love story for the troupe. She would not write herself as a character in this script. There would be no part for her to play. She intended instead to play a part in a much greater story. Perhaps one of the greatest stories ever written.

She wrote all night finally finishing her work early the next morning. She stretched, exhausted but invigorated, yawned and sent the document to the printer. Soon, she held a stack of warm papers in her hand. She laid them aside, picked up a pen and paper and wrote a long letter. She placed it in an envelope, sealed it, and then headed into the bedroom to sleep.

Should she sleep in Travis's bed? She hadn't yet seen the bedroom. She turned on the lamp and looked around. It was simple, yet masculine. Beautiful scenic paintings adorned the walls; no animal heads or antlers hung over the fireplace. Bronwyn now understood why. In Eden, man and animals co-existed. They never considered the flesh of an animal as food, so there would be no reason to kill an animal and hang his head. Quite a barbaric act, once she thought about it. Furthermore, she had never seen meat on Travis's plate at any of their meals. He ate only fruit, vegetables and nuts.

Exhausted from yet another emotion-filled day, she crawled onto the comfortable bed and tugged at a blanket that lay folded neatly at the foot, pulling it up over her. As she reached to extinguish the lamp, she accidentally knocked a small beautifully hand carved box off the table spilling its contents onto the floor. Lazily, she crawled from the bed to retrieve the items lying scattered on the hard wood. She picked up the first item, a silver chain with a white stone pendant identical to the one she had seen Travis and the rest of the council wearing. She draped it gently across her fingers, examining it. Turning the stone over, Bronwyn read the word *Kenalycia* carved into the back of the white stone. She gently laid it back onto the velvet lining of the box. The second item was a dark amber vial of some sort. She carefully pried off the lid. An amazing aroma rushed into her nostrils and filled the room. It was a distinct scent acting as a key, unlocking a deep memory, a feeling lost in the secret places of her mind. The aroma attempted to take her back to an amazing joyful occasion. What was it? She sat on the floor, stunned. Of what did that opulent scent remind her? Where had she smelled it before? What wonderful buried memory was it attempting to unlock for her? She lifted the vial to her nose once more, and inhaled, accidentally touching the tip of her nose. A portion of the oily substance clung to the bottom tip of her nostril, keeping the scent alive. She replaced the lid slowly and put the vial back into the box and then carefully placed it back on the table.

Turning off the light, she lay in bed, with the scent of the oil still permeating the room. Her eyes grew heavy; and as she drifted off to sleep, the scent pried open a suppressed memory…

CHAPTER THIRTY-SEVEN

DAY EIGHT

Marcus hung up the phone on the kitchen wall.

"Bus is ready!"

He expected triumphant cheers, cries of relief, excitement to get back on the road. It didn't work that way. His supposed good news was not met by a round of cheers from the troupe. Instead, their reactions were more subdued. Each member hating to see their week of rest and relaxations come to an end. However remote and quaint, Moonshine had crept its way into their hearts. Marcus returned to the table and continued his announcements. He informed the troupe that Larry would be delivering the bus to the inn within a few hours. He suggested they pack all their belongings so they could be on the road before one o'clock. Then he asked Travis to get their bill ready, desiring to take care of their debt immediately. To everyone's shock, and Wilbur's delight, Travis informed them that there was no charge, stating that one should never take advantage of someone else's misfortune. Those were the first words Travis spoke all morning.

Stunned, the troupe sat in silence.

"Anyone heard from Bronwyn?" Lillian interrupted the sudden quietness. "She never returned to the inn last night."

"She probably stayed out all night making another baby with Ryan," Bethany said bitterly.

Travis shot her a sharp look. She blushed. She spoke out of turn, but she didn't care. She was angry. Bronwyn had been so different since her break up with Ryan. Bethany had accepted the distance, figuring the pain in Bronwyn's heart was causing the change in her behavior. Now she understood the distance. When you withhold a secret of that magnitude, it builds an invisible wall. No matter how hard Bethany may have tried, she could have not broken through that barrier. Her anger with Bronwyn stemmed from the fact that she had kept the pregnancy quiet purposely. She could have been there for her. She could have helped her through it all. To her, it was a loud proclamation stating that Bronwyn didn't want her help or encouragement.

"You have to be happy for her," Lillian said, jumping to Bronwyn's defense. "This is what she has dreamed of for so long. I find it terribly romantic that Ryan would come all this way to find her."

"She'll have it made now," Karley said, biting into her bagel. "Being married to Ryan Reese, she'll never have to work again. Lucky girl."

"She is so lucky," Carla Jo nearly drooled the words into her cereal.

Travis stood and took his dishes to the sink, exiting the kitchen in silence. Bethany and Lillian exchanged glances; each knew what the other was thinking. Travis appeared sad, yet angry, not to mention agitated. Bethany was glad Ryan had come. She had not trusted Travis from the beginning. She could not see in him this integrity that Bronwyn insisted he possessed. Furthermore, if Bronwyn had kept something as big as her pregnancy with Ryan a secret, then she'd certainly withhold the truth about herself and Travis. It didn't make sense for two people to be out all night, sneaking back into the inn at ungodly hours, only to insist that nothing was happening. No two people who had just met have that much to talk about.

Bethany made a mental note and recounted how many nights on this short trip Bronwyn had been away. There was the first night during the storms, when she and Travis spent the entire night in his cabin's basement. Then there was the second night, when they both disappeared for some time at the falls. There was the third night, when she and Travis had supposedly sat in the garden until midnight discussing her writing. The night before the festival, Bethany woke to see Bronwyn leave the room. She didn't return until sunrise the next morning. Then there was the night of the festival, when they were out on the lake watching the fireworks together, not returning to the inn until three that morning. Then there was Sunday night when Bronwyn mysteriously left the porch to take a walk and did not return to the inn until just before sunrise. And what about yesterday afternoon, riding up on a motorcycle with that Falcon guy? What was that all about?

Bronwyn was definitely keeping secrets. Bethany's anger began to fester and rise. Of course she had been lying. Her best friend, who she thought she knew very well, had turned into someone altogether different. The Bronwyn she knew would never intentionally have an affair with a married man.

Now on the eve of their departure, Ryan shows up. Bethany found herself thinking Bronwyn didn't deserve Ryan, either. She pushed away from the table angrily, stomping up the stairs, to pack her belongings.

CHAPTER THIRTY-EIGHT

Bronwyn woke with the sun. She was quite refreshed; despite the fact she only had four hours of sleep. She refolded the blanket returning it to the foot of the bed, smoothed out the comforter, re-fluffed the pillows and left the room. She washed her face, brushed her teeth with her finger, and combed her hair. Realizing she had not eaten in almost twenty-four hours, she scooped up the completed script, and headed back to the inn for breakfast. As she passed Larry's Garage on the way, she noticed their tour bus parked directly out front. Larry whistled as he finished up the final repairs.

She stopped in and complimented him on his skilled work, and as she entered the bus, the familiar smell greeted her nose. She walked down the aisle, stopping in her area, sitting in the seat where she'd traveled and slept. She thought back to the fateful night of the breakdown, the storm, riding to the inn in the back of a pick-up and dodging hailstones. She smiled at the recollection. She walked back down the aisle, allowing her hand to gently rub the back of the seats. She pulled a small envelope from her stack of papers and placed it in Bethany's seat.

With that done, she left the bus. She wasn't sure how she would return home to retrieve her belongings or where she would go to begin writing the story. She desired to stay in Moonshine. However, there was one problem. Travis. She knew she needed to distance herself from him. He was married and she had no intentions of interfering any further and as much as she hated the thought, she knew it would be best for her to leave Moonshine altogether.

The Inn was quiet when Bronwyn entered the kitchen. Only Marcus and Anna sat at the big wooden table, mulling over a map, trying to decide the quickest route to their next destination. Bronwyn was happy to find the two of them together. She proudly turned the new script over to Marcus, who was extremely delighted to receive it. He scanned the pages, speed reading, happy with their new story.

She then tendered her immediate resignation. After several questions borne of deep concern for her, Marcus and Anna accepted.

Not finding Bethany or Lillian in the room, and after querying Molly, Bronwyn decided to search for them in the gardens but her hunt was futile. Every garden was empty with no sign of the girls. She continued on, following the small cobblestone path until she approached the final garden; the door was slightly ajar. The secret garden was now accessible. She pushed the heavy door and eagerly stepped inside. Thick massive trees, overtaken with moss and hanging vines, guarded the entrance. She pushed her way past, following the path as it led to a wooden bridge crossing over a medium sized pond. Koi and other colorful fish swam gracefully in the waters below.

After crossing the pond, the bridge led to another cobblestone path. She followed the trail through many more flowering plants and trees. This garden, though seemingly un-kept and extremely wild in nature, proved to be the most beautiful of all; and as she made her way through, she felt a sense of the sacred and wondered why this garden was special. Why did it have a locked door when the others did not? And then she had a thought. Could this be the place where the legendary tree of life is hidden? Her heart pounded at the assumption; and as she looked over the many massive trees growing near her path her eyes fell upon Mavis, on her knees working the soil, planting and pruning. Gardening tools and a basket filled with plants lay beside her.

She stopped, not sure if she should continue her approach or back away slowly. She was not at all prepared for a one-on-one conversation with Mavis. She could only deny any involvement with Travis should Mavis question her. The fact that she indeed had feelings for him might surface, which she could not refute. So, she decided to back away, retracing her steps quietly.

"Leaving so soon?"

Caught! Her heart skipped a beat.

"I was looking for Bethany and Lillian. I thought they might be here."

"No, it's just me."

She took the information as her opportunity to leave, but Mavis' request stopped her cold.

"Can you stay for a minute?"

Mavis continued to dig in the dirt. She grabbed a flowering plant from her basket and placed it into a small hole; keeping her back to Bronwyn.

"Would you like to know how I got my injuries?"

The question surprised Bronwyn and made her stomach churn. She had been curious, wanting to know, yet for some reason she feared the answer. She didn't have a chance to respond however, for Mavis's continued on anyway.

"I think you need to know. Why don't you sit there in the nice cool grass? My stories tend to get lengthy."

Despite her inner urge to run, she felt somewhat of an obligation to hear her out. Besides, whatever story may unfold, she was certain it would provide some sort of insight into Travis, his heart, and depth of his faithfulness. So she sat in a patch of cool green grass, in the shade of a Maple tree, and waited for the story to unfold.

As though she had eyes in the back of her head, Mavis waited until Bronwyn settled before beginning her story.

"It happened when we came through the portal. The call was swift and unexpected, but we were thrilled to find ourselves here in Moonshine, safe at last. What we didn't know, was our enemy followed after us. They were desperate and couldn't lose Travis to this world, seeing he is our Tree of Life. They needed him in order to remain immortal."

Bronwyn's head grew dizzy with Mavis' statement. However, Mavis allowed no time to question.

"The opening of the portal always causes a horrific storm, like the one that hit the night of your arrival. We all ran for the basement. Once we got down there, I noticed my husband wasn't with us. I waited, but he never came."

Bronwyn's heart began to race as Mavis continued to dig, plant, and speak. All the while her back was still turned.

"I gave Molly's hand to Carla Jo, and told them to stay put down there. I headed back up the stairs. To my surprise, half of the inn was gone. The rain was pouring down, the wind stronger than I had ever seen. I saw my husband lying on the ground. Blood was pouring from a knife buried in his chest. I ran over to help him. I tried to pull the knife out, to help him to safety. The force of the wind working against me made it impossible. He yelled at me to go back underground with the kids. I couldn't leave him there. He was the love of my life. I adored him. This was the man I loved more than I loved myself."

Bronwyn hung her head and closed her eyes.

"The next thing I knew, I was hit in the side of the head. It was if the entire half of the inn blew over on top of me. The last thing I remember hearing was my husband screaming. When I woke a few days later, Travis was there with the kids. As usual, he was doctoring me, seeing to my every need. I could tell by the look on his face that my husband hadn't made it."

Bronwyn's eyes flew open, as she raised her head. What had Mavis said? Her husband hadn't made it?

Before she could interrupt with her question, Mavis answered it.

"I lost the love of my life that day."

Mavis turned around to face Bronwyn, sorrow hollowing her face. Pulling herself up from the ground, she grasped onto a large embellished stone for support. A stone that had been blocked from Bronwyn's view was now plainly in sight. Bronwyn stood from her spot in the grass, slowly, reverently, walking towards the grave marker. Moving her lips she read almost inaudibly.

"Brennan John Colton

Beloved husband,

Amazing father, brother, and friend.

Prince of Eden

"On this earth, but not of it."

I don't understand," she stammered. "I thought..."

"You thought Travis was my husband." Mavis finished the sentence for her. Speechless, Bronwyn swallowed and gave an affirmative nod. Mavis smiled.

"Travis is Brennan's brother, my brother in law. He and Brennan were extremely close, especially since the death of Ariston. Travis came along side me during the horrible tragedy, rebuilt the inn, helped me raise the kids, and gave them a father figure."

"You two never married?" Bronwyn thought she knew what shock felt like, but this revelation brought it to an entirely different level.

Mavis smiled. "No, our hearts both belong to only one person. Mine to Brennan and Travis, well he lost his heart to someone many years ago, and I suppose he'll wait a life time for her if it comes to that."

"Who is she?" Bronwyn asked curiously, color flooding into her cheeks.

Mavis noticed and smiled sweetly, the gaping hole in her mouth not near as unappealing now.

"Travis might get upset with me, if I share secrets from his personal life. You'll have to ask him about her yourself."

"Is she from Eden?"

"Yes, she is from Eden, and that is all I am at liberty to tell you."

Bronwyn wasn't sure how to feel. All the guilt she had for being attracted to Mavis's husband was suddenly lifted. Her heart had betrayed no one. Yet all the bliss of that freedom was overshadowed by the new realization that Travis had a lover in Eden. Undoubtedly she was someone breathtaking, a flawless ethereal goddess, with whom she could never compete. Now it was her duty to write the story that would return Travis to Eden; and to the arms of his lover, another world away.

For a fleeting moment, she thought about running back to Marcus, retrieve her resignation and head back to normal life, forgetting she ever set foot in Moonshine. However, her heart would not hear of it. Now that she had heard the story of Eden and met some of its people, she could not turn back.

She observed Mavis gazing at the stone marker, her eyes lost in thought. The darkness that took her beloved must have been the same force that came looking for her the first night. The enemy of Eden, riding on the wind, to kill and destroy, devouring whatever lay in its path or posed a threat. A cold chill sent a warning to her soul.

"I'm sorry," she whispered to Mavis, placing her arm around the innkeeper's shoulder. They stood silently for some time, starring at the marker, until their solitude was interrupted by the hissing sound of the tour bus air brakes. A loud honk of a horn announced the bus's arrival.

"Looks like your ride is here," Mavis said.

CHAPTER THIRTY-NINE

Bronwyn left Mavis in the garden and headed to the front of the inn where she found Bethany and Lillian loading their luggage, along with the rest of the troupe. It didn't take long for her to sense Bethany's anger. She wanted to talk with her but Bethany refused, stating that there would be plenty of time for them to talk on the bus, since their next engagement was in Texas, and the ride would be a long one. Bronwyn honored Bethany's request and said nothing about staying behind. She regretted parting ways with things still unresolved, but took comfort in the fact that she had left a letter on Bethany's seat, explaining some of the events of the week, combined with her sincere apologies of never confiding about the miscarriage. She excelled in writing her thoughts anyway; so a letter might indeed prove to be a better way of resolving the hurt feelings.

"Where's Ryan?"

Bronwyn startled. Travis was standing beside her and looking more desirable than ever, now that she knew he was not a married man.

"I sent him away."

"Why?"

"Because I don't love him."

Travis continued to stare at her and she thought she saw a hint of a smile in his dark eyes as the words left her tongue.

Walt slamming the luggage compartment shut drew their attention back to the bus.

"One last chance." Marcus said approaching her; making sure she was certain of her resolution to remain behind. Her face grew warm feeling Travis's gaze as she convinced Marcus once more of her decision. She hadn't told Travis she was staying behind, and she wondered what he was thinking now that he knew. She longed for him, she couldn't deny it, and even though he wasn't married, he was still completely unavailable to her. She ignored his gaze and watched the heavy black bus make its way out the long driveway and disappear down the lonely two-lane highway without her. A wave of loneliness swept over her along with a slight panic that possibly she had made an impulsive and irresponsible decision. She quickly reprimanded her thoughts. She would not allow herself to doubt. Her decision had been well thought out, hours upon hours on the porch swing last night. Deep inside her soul, she knew she was doing the right thing; still, there was something about watching the bus disappearing around the corner that evoked a deep feeling of loneliness.

"Want to go for a ride? There's something I'd like to show you."

Her heart raced at his offer.

"Sure," she tried sounding nonchalant hoping he didn't see the sheer excitement spread across her face.

She climbed in his truck and before she could shut the door he had it rolling toward the highway, heading back into Moonshine. He drove down the main street, past the church and courtyard, past the lake and road that turned off to his cabin. He drove for some ways before the two-lane road narrowed into a single-lane. She realized now why there was never any passing traffic on the highway. The road actually dead-ended in Moonshine. It would be impossible for anyone to be passing through the town. If one traveled this forgotten highway, it was for one reason only; they had business in Moonshine. She realized now that her arrival was no accident, but instead was a prophesied event beyond her control just as Falcon had said.

They were some distance past the city limits of Moonshine now. Large trees grew close to the road, their foliage making a tunnel over the pavement. Travis drove down the narrow road for quite a way, offering no conversation. She studied his side profile not sure if he felt her gaze. If he did, he didn't turn to look her way. His eyes remained straight forward, his thoughts unreadable.

He turned onto a narrow dirt road. They bumped along over the uneven terrain, the truck making its way across rocks, holes, and large roots of trees protruding through the ground. He drove until the road nearly vanished, finally stopping near an abandoned cottage, camouflaged within the dense foliage. He crossed over and opened her door, offering his hand, he led her to a narrow footpath leading up to the secluded cottage.

She looked past the worn wooden fence and surveyed the overgrown dwelling place. Lush vines with blooming flowers covered the roof; cascading down over the large picture windows. Leafy bushes hugged the exterior of the house, wild and unkempt to the point of blocking the steps to the porch. Two weeping willows stood vigil on both sides of a cobblestone path that lay buried by overrun grass and weeds. A tall Elm grew near the cottage; she noticed a weathered birdhouse hanging from the lowest branch.

"Looks like your real fixer upper. Who lives here...or who lived here?"

Travis picked up a piece of the fallen fence and leaned it against one of the posts.

"No one has ever lived here. It's remained empty ever since it's construction. Legend says, one day it's owner will arrive and will have they key to open the door."

The heat rushed over her again, weakening her legs and for a moment she thought they might give away. She had a haunting suspicion that Travis thought she was the owner of the small cottage, and a gnawing dread that he was right. But, she didn't have the key.

"Would I be trespassing if I went in?"

He smiled and she knew the answer. She grasped the smooth wood of the small gate, her slender fingers fumbling nervously with the rusted latch. The bolt loosened and the handle lifted much easier than she imagined it would. She pushed it open, and stepped inside the much overgrown yard.

Travis remained silent, his eyes fixed upon her; watching her as she high stepped through the tall grass. Her pale slender body resembled a beautiful flower wafting along with the afternoon breeze. She was not aware of his observations as she made her way up the porch steps; pushing aside the hanging vines blocking her entrance into the cottage. She took in a deep breath, placed her hand on the doorknob and turned. It was locked.

"So is there a magic word I should say?" She asked while placing both hands against the door.

The corners of his mouth formed a slight grin, and she wondered if he knew she was not ready to enter the cottage. He nodded to the weathered porch swing and she immediately took his invitation. He courteously dusted the dirt from the faded cushion before allowing her to sit, and then he took the seat beside her. She pushed off with her feet, the swing swayed gently. A noticeable creak sounded from the eroded chain connecting to the wooden roof overhead. A cool gust of wind stirred the dust and dead leaves on the porch sending a chill. The smell of oncoming rain combined with the strong scents of the earth permeated the air. The sun slowly started to withdraw and hide behind the approaching gray clouds, covering most of the sky. Large raindrops began falling on the tall grass flattening it to the ground.

"It has sat empty for years, a little longer won't matter."

She smiled, "I do want to go in, it's just that...."

"No need to explain. I understand."

She wondered if he could understand. The emotions of the past week continued to overwhelm her. The secrets of Moonshine were unraveling slowly, each revelation taking its toll on her. Now, Travis was expecting her to walk into a two hundred year old cottage that supposedly belonged to her, and for some reason she was afraid her mind could not handle what was beyond the door. It was Travis's unexpected question that finally gave her the courage.

"What made your decision to stay behind and write the story?"

There was only one answer to his question. Should she give it? She knew she could play it safe and give a reason such as, she thought it would be a great adventure, and her chance to write the story she always dreamed of writing.

However, she didn't say that. Instead, she decided to answer honestly from her heart.

"Because, I want to do this for you. I want to help you get back what was taken away from you. You saved my life, if I do this, I can save yours."

What she neglected to say was that she believed she was in love with him and this would be a test of her love. Would she be able to write the story that would send him back into the arms of his love in Eden? She could if her love was only for him, and not herself. Her heart ached at the thought.

The rain continued to fall, tip toeing gently across the overgrown yard. A soft rumble of thunder sounded in the distance.

She stood, resolute. "Let's see if the roof leaks."

Travis' dark eyes locked on hers. She could see her disclosure had touched him. She nodded to the weather-beaten birdhouse hanging from the branch of the large Elm.

"It's always been a habit of mine to keep a spare key in a bird house. If this truly is my cottage, there will be a spare key in the bottom of that house."

He watched her as she exited the porch and approached the Elm. The gentle rain kissed her face as she reached her willowy arm into the small birdhouse. She moved her hand about and then a smile suddenly formed, as she gracefully pulled her arm from the small wooden abode, waving a small brass key in the air

She passed the key to Travis and watched as he turned the lock and pushed open the weathered blue door. Bronwyn took a deep breath and stepped inside. The peculiar heat sensation once again began at the souls of her feet and permeated upward through her body. Her pulse quickened. She was home! The sights, the design, the furnishings, were all so familiar. Every part of the cottage was a blaze with her personality. She toured the tiny cottage reacquainting with every detail. The entrance hall gave way to a small cozy living room. A large three-sided bay window with a soft cushioned seat faced outside on the east side of the property. A soft red couch with fluffy throw pillows faced a beautiful stone fireplace with an oversized hearth. A thick woolly white rug lay in front of the fireplace taking the chill off the cold hard wood. Beautiful paintings of scenery adorned the walls and she noticed that each picture was of a night scene and all with a full moon. She smiled at the sight of a dark cherry baby grand piano standing in the corner of the room.

The kitchen gave off a warm intimate feeling. Pale yellow walls and white cabinetry circled the entire room. Another ample sized picture window, covered with white lace curtains, faced the back yard. A small country table with four chairs sat in the middle of the inviting room. An antique hutch full of beautifully painted dishes rested against the far wall. A comfortable love seat faced yet another fireplace. Bronwyn surveyed the room and then walked toward a small antique roll top desk facing the picture window. She lifted the cover of the desk, rolling it backwards. On the inside lay a single thick book. Its leather cover and antique lock gave it the appearance of a secret diary. She picked it up and ran her fingers across the soft leather cover. She glanced across the kitchen taking inventory of the window above the sink, the mantle of the fireplace, and the antique hutch. Her eyes fell upon the object she was searching. Cunningly placed amidst the colorfully painted dishes was a miniature birdhouse. She approached the hutch, opened the delicate glass cabinet, and retrieved from the tiny abode a miniscule key hanging on a delicate silver chain. Crossing back over to the desk she anxiously placed the key into the lock and turned it. The latch clicked as the leather strap fell from its casing. She opened the book reverently; all the pages were blank, save for the first one. Hand written beautifully across the front page, in her best penmanship, was the words:

"A Story of Deliverance"

By Bronwyn Sterling

She sat down hard; the heat rising, her heart racing, her head spinning. Had the keys hidden in the bird houses not been enough, the book she held in her hands, her name and handwriting occupying the pages, more than confirmed this was indeed her cottage, and she was certainly where she was destined to be.

"I found it." She whispered cradling the heavy book in her arms.

Travis walked to the desk accepting the book from her hand. His eyes grew troubled as he noticed the key laying on the desk and the opened lock on the cover. He glanced at Bronwyn and then back to the first page. He skimmed through the blank pages of the book, as if he were looking for something. His dark eyes closed as he reverently latched the cover. She knew this book meant everything to Him. It was his redemption, his release from the confines of this dimension, the story would place him back in his Eden, and back in the arms of the one his heart belonged to. The thought weighed heavy on her.

She left him alone with the book and stepped out onto the back porch inhaling the scents of rain and wet earth; replacing the musty stale air of the cottage. Her head was spinning; she needed the fresh air. Just like the front, the back was overgrown with vines and plants, dried leaves, dirt and cobwebs. Two eroded and splintered rocking chairs sat upon the porch.

The yard was a nice size, a walnut tree, along with an apple tree and a couple of Elms, grew tall, giving ample shade on a hot day. She noticed a small pond fairly hidden by the overgrown brush. A two-tiered cement birdbath full of green mossy water sat near the back porch. She leaned across the wet railing. Despite the rain, she could hear the rushing water of a small creek cutting across the back of the property, and disappearing into the dense woods.

The rain began to increase in intensity pounding on the roof, the sound of it so deafening that she didn't hear Travis join her. He removed a knife from his boot and began cutting back some of the vines growing wildly over the roof, and cascading downward.

She continued to lean across the porch railing, not minding at all that the rain was blowing into her face. Her mind was entertaining a thousand thoughts, and now that she discovered the book, she was more than ever eager to begin writing the story. This call on her life was irrevocable. There would be no turning back. However, there were still things that needed attending to before she could begin. She needed to locate her previous writing of Moonshine, no matter how painful it may be. She hoped her parents had not destroyed the book, but knowing her mother, Bronwyn was certain she had it packed away and hidden somewhere in the attic. She felt that if she could locate the old manuscript, it would shed some light upon some of the mysteries still veiled to her.

She also knew she needed to go back to California and retrieve her things. If she was leaving everything behind to pen the story, then there were certainly things that needed done before she could settle down and write. She needed to turn in her notice at the beach condominium she and Ryan once shared. The place was luxurious, expensive and something she could never afford on her own, but when Ryan left her he graciously paid for the remainder of the lease which gave her another 10 months. Still, she stayed away as much as possible and the thought of leaving it all together made her feel as if she were moving on in some way.

Her eye caught sight of Travis intensely cutting back the overgrown foliage with his knife. She watched him prune back the vines for a while before she spoke. The skill he displayed in using his knife, and the strength in his arms impressed her. Everything about Travis Colton appealed to her.

"You're pretty good with that knife."

He threw a handful of cut vines into the yard. "I prefer it. It does the work much more quietly than a gun."

This time Bronwyn was taken aback. She had never sensed a violent side to him, and while watching him hack away at more vines she wondered how futile it would be to shoot them down. She knew that he didn't carry the knife for pruning and landscaping. She recalled her fourth night in Moonshine when he approached the pre-festival dance, agitated, bloody, and dirty. Later that same night in the gardens, she witnessed Falcon slit a man's throat with the same type of knife. During her meeting with the council Falcon had mentioned how he and Travis had *taken care* of a couple of spies from Eden. She thought back to the grave marker in the secret garden baring the name of Travis's brother Brennan, and how Mavis confessed that her husband's death was caused by Abaddon's men. Even though Travis seemed like a peaceful, composed person, she admitted to herself that she had only known him for a little over a week, and while some mysteries of this place were revealed to her, there were still multitudes of secrets behind his dark eyes, and what he was capable of, she was not sure. However disturbing this may be, she knew he was carrying the knife for their safety, and the thought sent a chill through her body.

She leaned against the back door. "I need to go back to California and take care of some personal business and get my things. I want to stop in Texas on the way. I'm sure my mother has my old manuscript hidden away somewhere. I want to try and find it. I think it will answer a lot of questions running through my mind right now."

Travis stopped hacking away at the overgrowth. He wiped the rain from his face with his forearm, and threw another handful of vines into the yard.

"When do you want to leave?"

"The sooner the better. But I have no way to get there, and Moonshine doesn't have car rentals."

He wiped the blade of the knife across his jeans, and placed it back into his boot. "You can take my truck."

He walked past her, entering back into the cottage. She followed him in, sensing a change in his behavior. Travis who usually appeared calm now seemed restless and unsettled. She picked up the leather bound book, along with the key, and headed into the living room.

"What's bothering you?"

He remained silent; staring out of the large picture window facing the front yard. This characteristic of Travis intrigued her. If he had no desire to answer a question, he never gave a reason as to why, he simply refused to respond. She knew it would be futile to ask it again. Instead, she turned her attention to the piano. She laid the book and key on top of the instrument and took a seat on the small bench. She raised the cover and gently ran her fingers over the ivory keys while watching him stare out of the picture window; wishing she could read his thoughts. Bringing her attention back to the piano, she walked her fingers down the keys, moving them with ease, gliding effortlessly, playing a melody that attempted to unlock a memory. She struggled to remember when she had played this particular piece before. There had to be an event, a location, maybe a musical she had performed in once. What is the name of the song, where had she heard it before, and why did it stir her so? The melody was beautiful unleashing a flood of emotion. Her spirit ached and her fingers trembled as she continued to play. The speed of her fingers increasing along with the beating of her heart.

Lost in the music she was unaware the song broke Travis gaze out of the window and brought his complete attention on her. He watched her as she played; her soul as lost in the music as she was here in Moonshine. He could see her mind struggling to remember, to hear the message the melody was trying to tell her.

She finished the piece and sat still, staring at the ivory keys through the tears welling up in her eyes and trickling down her cheeks. She quickly wiped them from her face not wanting Travis to see her crying. However, she realized it was too late, when she saw his dark eyes watching her. She stood quickly, collected the book and key from the top of the piano, and retreated to the big bay window. Curling up on the soft cushion, she turned her attention to the misty pane, watching the soft rain roll downward. A single tear followed suit as it escaped her eyes and trailed gently down her cheek.

"I don't know where that came from." She whispered softly. "Believe it or not, I've never played that song before."

Travis gave no response; he came over and sat near her on the window seat. Reaching forward he tenderly wiped the tear from her cheek. Her heart raced at his touch. She had been in this same situation before, alone with him in a secluded location, searching his eyes while the rain poured down outside. Just as before, she found herself deeply drawn to him. Their eyes locked on each other; neither one looked away. Bethany said the eyes were the window to the soul; that if you stare into someone's long enough you will connect with them. Yet, she felt at a disadvantage, she knew the longer Travis looked into hers, he could read her, connect with her, know what she was feeling. However, his eyes still held so many secrets, no matter how long she stared, she could never penetrate them.

Distracting herself with the miniature key, she held tightly in her fist, allowed her to pull her eyes away from his entrancing gaze. She wound and rewound the delicate chain around her index finger; all the while feeling his gaze upon her. She dare not look up again. If his heart truly belonged to another, why did he tempt her so? Was he oblivious of the affect he had on her when he sat so close? Did he not understand how painful it was for her to feel the slightest touch of his hand? She wondered about the mysterious woman of Eden who held his heart. Who was she? By what name did Travis call her? Why had she remained in Eden when so many others were forced to leave? Could Bronwyn ever compete with her for his love? She imagined some ethereal goddess of perfection locked in a tall watchtower, somewhat like Rapunzel awaiting her rescue by the remarkable Travis. She sighed lost in her thoughts, as she nervously wrapped the chain in and out of her fingers. His hand suddenly touched hers, catching her off guard. She looked up as he gently removed the chain from her fingers. He opened the clasp, holding it up as to place it around her neck. Feeling her face flush with color, she turned away and lifted her hair. His strong hands reached in front of her as he laid the key on her chest; then she felt his fingers gently touched her neck as he fastened the clasp.

She dropped her hair as he released the clasp; her face still colored with heat.

She fumbled with the key hanging between her breasts.

"Now I feel like Frodo Baggins." she laughed, trying to avert the awkwardness.

Travis smiled though his eyes were serious.

"The rain has stopped. You up for a little walk?"

They left the cottage with the book in tow. Travis led her into the trees and up the incline of a steep hill. Soon they stepped into a clearing overlooking the vast mountain range. The view from the ridge was more awe inspiring than any she had seen the entire week. The rolling hills and mountains became silhouetted against a deep lavender and rose sky, as the sun made its final decent in the cradle of the mountains; giving way to the evening stars glimmering through the violet, burgundy and pink hues of the evening.

She could hear the unseen orchestra once again. The melodious music of an invisible choir sang to her soul, a soothing tranquil song, and she wondered if she was at another doorway, another thin place. Travis led her to a bolder where they both could sit. It was like having front-row seats at the most amazing art exhibit she'd ever seen. The fresh painting of the Creator produced an exclusive masterpiece just for them. They sat in silence, watching the fiery sun burn out slowly, as it disappeared from view.

"I'm giving you the opportunity to turn back."

His words took her by surprise, removing her eyes off the sunset and upon him.

"What? Why?"

"Because you have no idea of the severity of the quest you are embarking on; and once you begin to write, there is no turning back."

His words angered her; so she held nothing back.

"Why would you offer me that? If you are a Prince of a world, and the people of that world are in exile and dying, why would you tell their one hope to turn tail and run? What kind of Prince are you?"

"The kind that believes everyone should have a choice. This is a war Bronwyn, and you could easily lose your life in the process, and then all would be lost anyway." His words softened. "You are not who we imagined the writer to be, and now; you being who you are, complicates things."

Again he spoke in riddles, upsetting her all the more. Tears of frustration stung in her eyes and she felt as if her heart would burst. She jumped from the bolder and walked to the edge of the cliff.

"Well I am sorry I am not some famous bestselling author, or some sage old scribe who translated the Bible in seven different languages. I'm sorry I came out of nowhere, and that I've never had a book published, and that all I have written is sappy love stories. But I am here, and according to you guys, I am supposed to do this. If it's my destiny, how can I live without at least trying?"

He approached her from behind, and turned her around to face him.

"That's not what I meant."

"Then please tell me what you mean. Unlike the rest of you, I can't read your thoughts."

He closed his eyes for a moment, as if he was contemplating the situation, and when he reopened them, she thought she caught a glimpse into this soul. Yes! It was there, a flash, the heat rose and her breathing became labored. She wanted to scream out as a memory tried to surface and then without realizing what she was doing, she impulsively reached up and stroked his face.

"What is it you're not telling me?"

He said nothing; he only placed his hand over hers then removed it from his cheek, holding it in his.

"There are some things I am not at liberty to tell. You must discover them on your own."

She calmed sensing he would tell her if he could, and if those were the rules of the game, then she would play by them.

"And discover them I will."

He smiled and kissed her hand tenderly before letting it go.

"I want you to leave tomorrow. You have two weeks to get your affairs in order, and then you must return to Moonshine. You unlocked the book of redemption. The enemy has been informed. Now it all begins."

THE BEGINNING.

ABOUT THE AUTHOR

Plucked from the hills of Tennessee, and deposited in sunny southern California, Denise Daisy has been described as one of the purest storytellers of all time. She has the knack for pulling of romance, suspense and a touch of fantasy, all in the same piece. Her descriptive passages are luscious, transporting the reader, as if they were walking alongside the characters.

Denise lives in San Diego with her daughter Journey. You can visit her at authordenisedaisy.wordpress.com/ and follow her on her facebook page, Author Denise Daisy.

The Secrets of Moonshine is the first book in The Moonshine Series. *The Second Secret, Haytham, The Secret in the Rubble* will be released November 2011

Denise's other novels include *The Haret*, the first book in The Haret series.

Made in the USA
Charleston, SC
03 February 2012